IRREFUTABLE EVIDENCE!

'Mary, the final test shows that you're pregnant.'

She shrugged and gave a little laugh. 'It's wrong, Dr Wade, just like that other one.'

'The frog test is nearly one hundred per cent accurate, Mary. And we ran it twice just to be certain. There's no doubt that you're pregnant.'

Dr Wade leaned back in his chair and clasped his hands over his flat abdomen. He studied the girl across from him once more. Her denials were not uncommon, even up to this point. However, few girls kept up the pretence in the face of irrefutable evidence and certainly they never made denials so calmly, so objectively. Or they flew out in anger. Or they became frightened and pleaded with him. But not this one. This one was perplexing.

'You know, Mary, you might as well tell me because it's going to start showing soon and then there'll be no way of denying it.'

'Dr Wade.' Mary spread out her hands, palms up. 'I'm not pregnant. I've never done anything to cause it. Your test is wrong.'

Childsong

BARBARA WOOD

SPHERE BOOKS LIMITED
30-32 Gray's Inn Road, London WC1X 8JL

First published in Great Britain by
Sphere Books Ltd 1982
Copyright © 1981 by Barbara Wood

TRADE
MARK

Set in Linotron Baskerville

Printed and bound in Great Britain by
Collins, Glasgow

This book is dedicated to
Dr Norman J. Rubaum

I wish to express my gratitude to
Dr Frederick Luthardt, of the
Department of Genetics at UCLA,
for taking time to help a total
stranger.

Author's Note

Parthenogenesis is a reality.

Childsong takes place in 1963. Since then, a new era in human sexuality and reproduction has come into being. In this age of cloning, artificial insemination, and genetic manipulation, the question of virgin birth (both spontaneous and laboratory-induced) is receiving more and more attention from the scientific community. The occurrence of this phenomenon in lower mammals (e.g., cats and rabbits) has been proven in the laboratory; in humans, however, the social, moral, and religious ramifications of virgin births make it a touchy and highly controversial issue.

The odds of the birth of fraternal quintuplets are one chance in fifty million; the odds of a woman conceiving virginally are one in one million, six hundred thousand. The Dionne quintuplets were accepted worldwide, a spontaneous virgin conception is not. Why?

All facts, magazine and book references, quotations and laboratory experiments cited in this novel are real; the research conducted by Dr Jonas Wade is a chronicle of the author's research for this book.

The characters and their story are fictitious.

Barbara Wood

CHAPTER 1

Mary loosened her robe and let it fall to the floor. As she felt the whisper of cool night air sweep her naked body, she drew up the corners of her mouth in a quizzical smile, tilting her head slightly to one side.

Before her stood Sebastian, the convolutions of his muscular body exaggerated in the pale moonlight. He was also nude, except for a cloth wrapped about his hips and gathered in a knot to hide his genitals.

Mary wanted to look down, to see how the knot might be unravelled, but did not want to lower her gaze; her eyes had been seized by Sebastian's, his stare across the room was as locking as an embrace.

Although the air was chill, she did not shiver. A warmth glowed inside her like wine, like a sunset, soft, compelling. Nor did Sebastian seem to mind the night air, his sinews stretching taut beneath perspiring, glistening skin. His hand, in a languid, unhurried gesture, reached down to the coil of cloth over his loins and in a graceful sweep disentangled the knot. Still Mary's eyes remained upon his face, fearful of seeing what the cloth had disclosed; yet she was anxious for it all the same.

When he suddenly took a step toward her, Mary's breath quickened. Reflexively her hand went to her breast, brushing a hard nipple.

He came toward her, his handsome face set grimly, austerely; his hair, long and wavy, lifted off his shoulders in the breeze, and as he drew nearer, emerging into the pool of moonlight, Mary saw the scars which spotted his perfect body: white welts where his flesh had been pierced.

He was incredibly, painfully handsome. Deep brooding eyes, a long straight nose, square chin rising from a strong,

1

sinewy neck. Swarthy, fluid, gleaming; powerful in the arms and hairless chest.

When he was inches from her and his eyes were penetrating, as if they could reach out and touch, Mary felt a movement deep in her abdomen; low in the pelvis, a surging that at first startled her, then overwhelmed her. Simply the nearness and nakedness and the forbidding gaze of Sebastian had caused this. She wondered what his touch might do, or his kiss.

She heaved a great sigh and reached for his hand. Taking it, she brought it first to her mouth, pressing her lips to the surprisingly hard and calloused palm, then she placed Sebastian's hand on her left breast. When she let go, the hand remained.

The heavy eyes continued to delve her, and when he bent his head and touched his lips to hers, and then his tongue to hers, Mary felt a peculiar constriction of her throat. For an instant, she could not breathe.

Then his other hand moved gently downward, barely caressing the intense flesh, until it settled upon a place that caused Mary to want to fill her lungs and cry out.

The hand searched and fondled while she stood stiffly, transfixed. There was ecstasy in her bewilderment. Sebastian's mouth continued to work on hers, the taste of him a marvel, and all the while those miraculous fingers exploring.

Then their bodies came together and pressed. His skin was warm and clammy. She felt his breath gasp in cadence with hers; they both gulped now, Mary trying to quell the growlings in her throat, Sebastian's hands becoming rougher, more insistent.

The hardness of his body amazed her, then excited her. Then there was something else. The lower hand was replaced by another probe; for now both hands were on her breasts. An unseen weapon, frightening and yet electrifying.

Mary opened her eyes, looked around the room in panic. While fear sprang from her ignorance of what was happening

2

to her, there arose a frenzy she had never known before and it overrode her instinct to defend herself.

With his arms now encircling her, Sebastian gently lowered Mary to the bed and then covered her with his body. He was heavy atop her, assailing and devouring, forcing the breath from her body. His mouth worked away from her lips, down her neck, until he found a nipple, and he sucked on it so violently that Mary whimpered.

Sebastian forced her legs apart. Mary stretched wide her eyes and her mouth; she opened herself to Sebastian, flung her arms out cruciform: a willing sacrifice.

A sweet, shooting, exalting pain suddenly filled her.

And then something else; a tide, following his thrusts like the wake of a boat. A melting of her body, starting at her feet and rising up, up along her legs, gathering momentum, swelling like an enormous wave until it rose above her in a climax that made her, for an instant, deaf and blind, then crashing, washing over her in ripples of delirium and satisfaction.

Mary snapped her eyes open.

She gaped up at the ceiling, panting. Holding her breath for a moment, she listened to the sleeping household and realised with relief that she had not cried out in her sleep.

Blinking uncertainly up at the night, Mary puzzled over the dream she had just had. She wondered why it had been with Sebastian and so awesomely sexual.

And how strange it had been...Sebastian entering her, filling her with that remarkable hardness, how strange that it should have felt so *real*, for Mary had, in reality, never even allowed Mike's hand down there. How could she have known what it would feel like?

She realised also as she lay motionless, staring, that her body had undergone a physical change.

What was different?

Her heart was pounding at an alarming rate, she was perspiring in the coolness of the night, her legs felt funny, as if she had run a great distance, and yet these were not what perplexed her now.

It lay between her legs, between her thighs; precisely, at

3

her groin. Unknown territory for devoutly Catholic Mary, the area had acutely altered in some mysterious way; something had happened down there.

Lying still and staring up into the infinity of the ceiling, Mary cautiously and anxiously moved her hand over the sharp crest of her right hip and hastily dropped her fingers into the delta between her thighs. Staying outside her clothing, Mary's fingertips did a hurried exploration of the tender area, and then sharply withdrew.

She touched her thumb to her forefinger. An unexplainable viscosity remained there.

Mary drew her hand all the way back and brough it to rest outside the covers. She closed her eyes and envisioned Sebastian once again, but she could not recapture the mystifying feelings he had sparked. She was emptied, no longer interested, and while she again considered the surprising notion that she should have dreamed about Sebastian instead of Mike, Mary Ann McFarland sank back into a deep and dreamless sleep.

By the light of morning Mary vigorously brushed her hair, wondering when the wave would finally be straightened out of it. She had only recently decided to change her hairstyle from a teased flip to the new 'surfer' look of straight down the back and parted in the middle, and rued the fact that she had had the flip permed in. She hoped very much that by summer, two months away, her hair would lie flat and straight between her shoulder blades and that she could sun-bleach it to a fashionable gold.

Mary's mother, however, conservative in all things, disapproved of the new loose look. Lucille McFarland wore her own short red hair in a teased bouffant which this morning would be crowned with a Jackie Kennedy pillbox hat worn to the back of her head. Mary's hat was similar, as was her wool two-piece suit, which she had gotten for Easter: a waist-length jacket and straight skirt to the knees. The effect was to eradicate curves and lines: the mannequin look of the First Lady.

From the problem of her hair Mary shifted her thoughts

to the memory of the unsettling predawn dream. More precisely, to the physical eruption which had been the end of the dream. Leaning close to the mirror to inspect a budding pimple on her chin, Mary felt a newer, more disturbing concern enter her mind; it was the problem of the impure nature of the dream. She was getting ready to take Holy Communion; last night she had gone to confession. Had the dream, because of its sexuality, nullified the sanctifying grace her penance had earned, or could the dream not be considered an impure thought since she had not had any control over it?

So intent upon the puzzle and upon inspecting her new pimple was Mary that she didn't notice her mother's entrance into the bedroom. She looked up. 'What?'

'I said, Mary Ann, that we'll be late for Mass if you stand in front of that mirror any longer.'

'I have a pimple.'

Lucille McFarland rolled back her eyes, threw out her hands and left the room. Mary hastily grabbed her hat, purse, and gloves, hurriedly slipped into her two-and-a-half-inch spike heels, and followed.

Ted McFarland and twelve-year-old Amy were already in the car when Mary and her mother came out of the house. As they climbed into the Lincoln Continental, Lucille said, 'Exposed to the danger of mortal sin because of a pimple.'

'Oh, Mother!'

Ted McFarland, backing the car down the steep drive, smiled and winked at his older daughter in the rear view mirror. Catching it, Mary grinned back.

Inside the church, amid the sprays of lilies, glittering votive candles, and beams of sunlight streaming through the stained-glass windows, the parishioners were solemn and quiet as they scuffled down the pews and knelt with bowed heads. Mary followed behind her mother and father, with Amy last. They dipped their fingers in the holy water, genuflected toward the massive crucifix dominating the far end of the church, filed into a pew, and knelt.

With a mother-of-pearl rosary working its way through

her fingers, Mary Ann McFarland tried hard to concentrate. She lifted her eyes slightly and scanned the crowd rapidly filling the church. She saw that Mike and his father and brothers had not yet arrived.

She let her eyes drift. Finally they settled upon Sebastian, who stood at the far side of the church, just next to the First Station of the Cross. Unable to look away, Mary let her gaze remain fixed upon him, marvelling again at the muscular body which had so ignited her in the dream.

A copy of Mantegna's *Sebastian* which hung in the Louvre, this painting of the holy martyr was embarrassingly lifelike. The blood was too real, the bulging muscles pierced by arrows, the sweat on his forehead, the incredible agony shining in his upturned face. It was like a photograph.

Mary had stared at the painting during many a boring sermon, but never, in all her years of attending St. Sebastian's Catholic church, had she even remotely entertained an indecent thought about the tortured saint. But now, because of that baffling dream, Mary could not ignore the eroticism of the picture. There was something about the sinews of his thighs she had never considered before, something daring, almost challenging, about the loincloth, something new in the way he writhed in his suffering that caused Mary to suck in her lower lip and chew on it.

Staring at him reminded her of the strange physical culmination of the dream and how pleasant it had been; she wondered if it would ever happen again. It also reminded her that she might no longer be in a state of grace.

When Father Crispin and the altar boys appeared from the sacristy, the congregation stood. Rising with them, Mary pressed the reassuring bead of an Our Father between her thumb and forefinger and asked God to forgive the dream and purify her so that she could, in clear conscience, take Holy Communion.

The spices of Apician dilled chicken clashed with the heady aroma of green chili soufflé.

Lucille McFarland attended gourmet cooking classes every Saturday morning at Pierce College with Shirley Thomas, and as a result every Sunday's table was dressed with exotic dishes giving off delectable steams. Today, although Easter, was no exception. Lucille and her two daughters had spent all afternoon preparing the feast: Amy had grated the two chunks of cheeses and diced the Ortega chilies; Mary had painstakingly separated egg yolks from whites, buttered the casserole dish, and chopped up fresh dill. The resulting effect was one of Christmas rather than Easter, each covered Dansk dish containing a surprise – a present to be unwrapped and savoured. Sunday dinners at the McFarland house were a time for communal experimentation and an exchange of opinions.

'Yuck!' said twelve-year-old Amy, pulling a face. 'I absolutely *hate* chicken.'

'Just be quiet and eat,' said Ted. 'It'll put hair on your chest.'

Amy swung her feet so that her body rocked back and forth. 'You know what? Sister Agatha's a vegetarian. Do you *believe* that? She actually goes to a health food store!'

Ted smiled across the table. 'At least she never has to worry about which day is Friday. Eat your chicken.'

Amy poked around in the sauce, picked out a chili and popped it into her mouth. 'Hey, Mary,' she said, 'have you heard the latest wind-up doll joke?'

Mary sighed. 'What is it?'

'It's the new President Kennedy doll. You wind it up and its brother walks fifty miles!' Amy threw back her head and laughed, receiving only a polite smile from her father and a raised eyebrow from her mother. Preoccupied, Mary continued to stare down at her food, one hand cradling her head.

'Then how about the new Helen Keller doll?' continued Amy.

'That's enough, young lady,' interjected Lucille. 'I don't know where you pick them up, but I find your latest jokes in poor taste.'

'Aw, Mom, all the kids in school are telling them!'

Shaking her head, Lucille muttered something about 'public schools' and reached for the soufflé.

'You wind it up and it walks into walls!'

7

'That's enough!' snapped Lucille, slamming a flat palm on the table. 'Why you find it so amusing to make fun of our President and a poor blind woman— '

'Lucille,' said Ted quietly. 'Twelve-year-olds have a different sense of humour. It has nothing to do with her school.'

'Hey, Mary,' said Amy, dropping her fork to her plate. 'How come you're so quiet? I'll bet it's because Mike didn't call today.'

Mary straightened up and rubbed the back of her neck. 'I wasn't expecting him to. He said he had relatives coming today, and besides, I have a term paper to finish.'

Ted ran a crust of bread around his plate. 'Is that the one you had to write in French? Need any help?'

'No, thanks, Daddy.'

'I'm going to take Spanish,' said Amy. 'Sister Agatha says you should learn a language that you can use. In Los Angeles, everyone should know Spanish.'

'I know,' Mary said. 'I was thinking of learning Swahili.'

Lucille's thin, precise eyebrows arched. 'Whatever for?'

'I've been thinking of joining the Peace Corps.'

'Well, that's certainly new. What happened to college?'

'I can go to college after I come back. It's only a two-year term and everybody's talking about doing it. I'd like to go to Tanganyika or somewhere like that.'

Lucille absently pushed a few straying auburn strands out of her face as she speared a shred of chicken with her fork. Mary made a new announcement every month, her entire future radically changed, plotted in detail, and spoken of with an energy and enthusiasm that would convince a stranger of her devotion. But her family knew different; next month it would be something else. 'Just graduate from high school first, and you still have a year of that ahead of you.'

'A year and eight weeks.'

Her mother raised her eyes to the celing. 'Eternity.'

Mary, turning to her father, said, 'Daddy, you understand, don't you?'

8

He smiled and pushed away from the table. 'I thought you wanted to go to art school and become a fashion designer.'

'Before that it was dancing,' came Amy.

Mary shrugged them off. 'This is different.'

With her two daughters taking care of the dishes, Lucille McFarland paused at the sliding glass door which led off the kitchen and onto the patio and shook her head disconsolately over the blackness outside.

The back yard was boundless and formidable, disappearing from the edge of the dining room light into a darkness that hid lawn, trees, cabanas, and birdbath. Only the swimming pool's nearest edge could be seen, white and dry. Beyond all this rose unseen the ivied hill upon which stood the next tier of houses, towering above Claridge Drive in the same way the McFarland house overlooked the street below them. This was Tarzana's finest residential section, south of Ventura Boulevard, with modern glass homes and palm trees and swimming pools and the wealthy parish of St. Sebastian's. Above, the Thomases' house glowed warmly against the spring night, and from far away Lucille could hear distant strains of back-yard laughter. She shook her head again and turned away.

'I certainly hope the pool man can make it tomorrow. I hate having it empty. It looks awful.'

'It's too cold to swim anyway, Mother.'

'That didn't stop you and Mike the other night. And darned near electrocuted yourself in the process.'

Mary watched her mother enshroud the remains of the chicken in cellophane and entomb it in the refrigerator and knew that tomorrow's supper was going to be one of Lucille McFarland's 'Tomato Surprises.' 'That wasn't my fault. I didn't cause the pool lights to short out.'

'It scared me to death, you screaming like that and Mike pulling you out of the pool.'

'I wasn't hurt, Mother, just startled.'

'Still, I don't like it. I read once of a woman who got killed in a hotel swimming pool when the night lights shorted out

9

because of an electrical leak. You could have been hurt very badly, Mary Ann.'

Exchanging glances with her sister, Mary hung up the damp dish cloth and announced she was going straight to her room.

'Aren't you going to watch Ed Sullivan with us? Judy Garland will be on and it's going to be in colour.'

'Can't, Mother, my report's due this week and I haven't typed it yet.'

As she started to leave the kitchen, Mary was stayed for a moment by her mother who placed a hand on her daughter's arm and said quietly, 'Do you feel all right, honey?'

Mary gave her mother a quick smile and a squeeze of the hand. 'Sure. Just got things on my mind. You know how it is.'

A moment later Mary paused on her way to her bedroom to look in the family den, and she watched for a few seconds as her father, with a glass of bourbon in one hand and the remote control in the other, flipped the channels of the large console TV set.

Ted McFarland was a handsome man. At forty-five he still had the lean, athletic body of his youth, which he maintained by swimming, vigorously every morning before going to work and then by exercising in a men's gym one night a week. His hair, short and slightly wavy, was dark brown with silver at the temples. His face was square and gentle with little lines at the corners of his eyes that gave him a look of easy humour.

Mary adored him. He earned good money, never raised his voice, and always seemed to be around when she needed him. The other night, after the frightening electrical shock in the pool, it had been her father, not Lucille or Mike, who had cradled her while she cried.

'I'm going to my room now, Daddy,' she said quietly.

As he looked up, his thumb automatically depressed the 'mute' button, causing the set to fall suddenly silent. 'No TV tonight? Is the paper that important?'

'Gotta type it if I want to get an A on it.'

10

He grinned and held out a hand. Mary went to the easy chair and sat on its arm as her father took hold of her by the waist. 'And besides,' she went on, watching the silent lips of a local news anchorman, 'I gotta keep up my grades if I want to stay in Ladies.'

'For a girl who always gets straight A's you certainly worry about your grades a lot.'

'I guess that's why I get straight A's.' Mary squinted at the newscaster and thought he looked a little green. 'Colour's off, Daddy.'

'I know. Someday they'll perfect the process. In the meantime, we suffer.'

'So what's news?'

'What's news? Well, the Negroes are still protesting in the South. Jackie's still expecting. And the market is still down. Same old thing. Oh, wait, I forgot. Sybil Burton finally left Richard today.'

Mary giggled. 'Oh, Daddy.' Wrapping her arms around his neck, she gave him a hug and a kiss. As she left the den, she heard the newscaster's voice suddenly come back on in midsentence: '. . .announced today that Father Hans Kung, one of the few official theologians of the Vatican Council, spoke out in favour of abolishing the Index of Forbidden Books . . .'

She sat at her desk and stared vacuously at the photograph of Richard Chamberlain, who, in the guise of Dr Kildare, dominated the bulletin board. Before her, on the desk top, were spread the various pictures she had cut out of magazines – Gothic spires, rose windows, naves and apses – all illustrating the text of her term paper, 'The Cathedrals of France.'

The typewriter remained covered as Mary continued to stare. On her record player was an album her best friend Germaine had lent her, the mournful folk singing of a new voice by the name of Joan Baez. Mary didn't care much for it and was playing it only because she had promised Germaine she would. The music did not reach Mary's consciousness; she was reflecting once again upon last night's dream.

Wishing on the one hand that she could shake the disturbing memory and yet finding pleasure in its recall, Mary wondered why her subconscious had chosen St. Sebastian for the role of lover instead of Mike.

It was odd, now that she thought about it, that in the seven months they had been going steady – ever since the beginning of the eleventh grade – Mary had never once dreamed about Mike Holland. And yet she had fantasised about him a great deal; although none of those daydreams ever intruded upon the sex act itself. Mary Ann McFarland never entertained sinful thoughts.

Sighing, she got up from the desk and languidly moved about the room. Posters and magazine pictures looked down at her: Vince Edwards as Dr Ben Casey; James Darren; a pensive profile of President Kennedy; and a new singing group called the Beach Boys. Strewn about the room were blue-and-white cheerleader pompoms, her Ladies sweater, cans of hair spray, Jan and Dean albums, and several snapshots of Mike Holland in his football uniform.

Mary stretched out on her bed and gazed up at the ceiling. The eroticism of St. Sebastian would not leave her; not merely the dream, but what it had ended in. Surely it had been wrong, to dream of sex with a saint. And surely, therefore, it would be wrong to hope for it to happen again, although that was what she secretly wished.

It was no use; to wish for its recurrence was a sin, to help it along by fantasising was a sin. Best to forget it, force it out of the mind. Mary fixed her eye on the blue plaster statue which stood on her dressing table, the Blessed Virgin with the supremely patient and suffering face, parted her lips slightly and whispered reluctantly, 'Hail, Mary, full of grace...'

CHAPTER 2

Mike Holland lived with his father and two brothers in a split-level ranch-style house not far from the McFarlands. Nathan Holland, a white-haired widower in his fifties, had raised his three boys without help from the time Mike was in St. Sebastian's grammar school and so had no trouble managing breakfast this morning for the four of them before going to his office. Today was Friday, the cleaning lady's day, so he would leave the dishes.

As Mike emerged sleepily into the sunny living room, squinting at the bright early-morning June sun, he heard his father's resonant bass voice call out, 'That you, Mike?'

'Yeah, Dad.'

'Come on, son, your brothers are way ahead of you.'

Stepping down into the dining room, Mike pulled out a chair and took his usual seat at the table. Timothy, fourteen years old, and Matthew, sixteen, were already wolfing plates of bacon and eggs. Mike wordlessly sipped his orange juice.

Nathan Holland, an insurance-company executive dressed in his usual three-piece suit minus the jacket, came out of the kitchen and placed a plate before his oldest son. 'Heard you coming in late last night, Mike.'

'CYO ran over.'

'Yeah,' said Timothy with a grin. 'You took Mary the long way home.'

'Can it, Tim.' Mike went sluggishly about his meal.

He hadn't slept well the night before; Mary had disturbed his dreams with nocturnal seduction. But the dreams had ended the same way his real dates with her always did, nowhere, so Mike had awakened frustrated and sullen.

'Sherry called you last night,' said Matthew who, although only a year younger, was smaller and slighter than Mike.

'Sherry's Rick's girl,' said Mike darkly.

'And besides,' piped Timothy, 'girls shouldn't call boys.'

'Just passing the message, Mike.'

'Yeah. Thanks, Matt.'

The three boys ate in silence, Timothy and Matthew with books spread out before them. The fourteen-year-old still attended St. Sebastian's parochial school and had twice as much homework as his two elder brothers, who went to Reseda High. But next year he'd be joining them and he was looking forward to it.

Nathan Holland came into the dining room again, drying his hands on a towel and rolling down his shirt-sleeves. 'Why so quiet, Mike?'

'Worrying about finals, Dad. I'll be glad when they're over.'

Feeling his father's heavy hand drop onto his shoulder and then lift off, Mike Holland choked down his anxiety. The anxiety that all the guys in the school envied him for something he didn't have. Who'd believe the truth anyway? That you go steady with the cutest girl in the school for nine months and you still haven't scored?

Mike stirred his cold scrambled eggs. Rick's really the lucky one, he thought unhappily. At least fat Sherry puts out.

'Mary Ann! Mary Ann McFarland, you get up this instant!'

She slowly opened her eyes and gazed lethargically at the ceiling. Staring at the pattern the June sun made as it poured through her curtains. Mary realised in irritation that this was going to be another one of those mornings. That made three in a row now, waking up nauseated.

The door opened and Lucille McFarland's head poked through. 'I won't call you again, young lady. If you want a ride to school, get up right now.'

With a heavy sigh, Mary struggled to sit up and blinked foggily as the door closed. The third morning in a row, too, when she didn't wake up with her usual drive and energy. Maybe it was because school was ending in two weeks. Maybe it was the Asian flu. Whatever, Mary heaved another sigh and swung her legs out of bed, she was going to have to overcome it by tomorrow. Cheerleader tryouts for next semester were being held and Mary was determined to be on the team again.

The late-spring sun was honey-warm and enticing, carrying with it, through the open classroom windows, the hot sweet breath of Santa Ana winds and the lure of golden days on blinding sun-washed shores. Watching the kids squirm and fidget in their seats, Mr. Slocum felt his bow tie rise up on his Adam's apple as he swallowed; he knew just how they felt, was not too old to recall the siren's call of summer and the youthful yearning to run free. Their attention span was waning; it was the same every year, from February to June: you could see their minds slip from their moorings and slowly drift away from you; young, firm bodies full of electricity and vitality, looking with increasing restlessness – as spring lapped the edge of summer – toward hot, dazzling days on the beach.

'Ladies and gentlemen,' he called tiredly for the fifth time, rapping his pointer on his desk. '*Please*.'

They snapped to attention, giving him bright round faces.

Mr. Slocum cleared his throat and continued with the lecture. For a few minutes his audience sat at silent attention, and, for these few minutes, Mr. Slocum knew he was getting through to them. Then, behind his back, as he chalked the chambers of the heart on the board, he lost them again.

Mary caught the subtle signal out of the corner of her eye. A few desks away, her best friend Germaine Massey was gesturing with her hand. Mary turned slightly and watched as Germaine furtively lifted up the cover of her three-ring binder, exposing the spine of a thick, dog-eared paperback book. Tilting her head, Mary read the title, *Fanny Hill*, and raised her eyebrows. Two copies of the forbidden novel were making the rounds of Reseda High; Germaine and Mary had been on the waiting list for a month.

'Miss McFarland!'

She whipped around. 'Yes, sir!'

'Can you name the arteries which supply the muscle of the heart?'

She flashed him a white smile. 'Yes, sir.'

Mr. Slocum waited a moment, then released a ragged sigh and said wearily, 'Then would you please share the knowledge with the rest of us?'

Soft, approving laughter rippled through the class. 'The coronary arteries, sir.'

Mr. Slocum fought back the impulse to smile at her and shook his head in resignation. He could never get angry with Mary Ann McFarland.

A breeze came up and swirled through the biology class, rattling the skeleton in the corner, and picking up on its way the pungency of formaldehyde; shafts of buttery sunlight pierced specimen jars which contained the sleeping bodies of frogs and human embryos and split into brilliant prisms on the other side. As he continued his lecture, Mr. Slocum kept his eyes on the eager faces before him, thinking what a pleasure it was to teach an honours class and regretting the approaching end of the school year.

From where he stood, Mr. Slocum could see under Mary's desk; her tight skirt had ridden up, exposing creamy thighs. The school had a rigid dress code; any girl suspected of wearing a skirt too short had to kneel down in the girls' vice-principal's office and if her hem didn't touch the floor she was sent home. And a good thing, too, else these coquettes would flaunt everything they had and then where would the educational system be?

Mr. Slocum looked away and concentrated on fat Sherry, who was trying to make eyes at Mike Holland. Teachers had to be supermen, had to keep thoughts like that out of their minds. Only last week a math teacher at Taft High had been dismissed for fondling a co-ed.

When Mr. Slocum returned to the diagram on the board,

Mary glanced over at Germaine and wrinkled her nose. Then she looked at Mike and grinned.

He had a hard time returning the smile; the corners of his mouth barely lifted. Mike was thinking again about last night, going over it and over it in his mind, trying to figure out where and how he blundered.

He and Mary had gone to CYO together, as they always did on Thursdays, and had spent two hours helping Father Crispin plan a summer carnival. But it was the hour following the meeting that Mike now thought about with his chin resting on his fists and his eyes fixed unseeingly on Mr. Slocum's chalkboard heart. He was once again driving his Corvair up into the hills of Tarzana.

'You've passed my street, Mike,' Mary had said.

He grinned. 'I know.' The car sped up a little, squealing around a curve.

'Oh come on, Mike, you know my mother'll be mad if I don't get right home.'

'Tell her the meeting ran late.'

'Mike— '

As the crest of the hill neared and Tarzana dropped away from them, Mary had stopped protesting. It wasn't often they could be totally alone like this, and Mike knew she was as anxious for such opportunities as he was; she just needed a little coaxing...

He pulled the Corvair off the road and onto a dirt turnout. This stretch of Mulholland Drive was dark, and trees protected the shallow turnout from oncoming headlights. Before them, scattered like Christmas lights on black velvet, was the San Fernando Valley.

'Mary,' he said quietly, killing the engine and turning to face her. 'We have to talk.'

'I don't want to, Mike, not now.'

'We have to. It's something we can't just ignore. If my father decides to take me and my brothers back to Boston, then I have to have your promise.'

Mary stared out the window at the twinkling sea of lights. 'It makes me sad to talk about it, Mike. To even think about it. You being gone for the whole summer. I'll be lonely.'

17

'That's exactly what we have to talk about and why I need your promise.'

He dropped his hand gently on her shoulder. Then his fingers toyed with the ends of her hair. 'Mary,' he said softly, 'you have to promise me there won't be another guy.'

'Oh, Mike.' She shifted around to regard him. 'How can you even think of such a thing?'

'Promise me, Mary.'

'All right, Mike,' she said demurely. 'I promise. I won't even look at another guy.'

'Make it a real promise, Mary.'

'I mean it, Mike. I swear by St. Theresa that I'll be true.'

He relaxed a little. 'If we go, and my dad seems pretty sure that we will, we'll be leaving the day after school lets out. That's only two weeks away.'

Mary returned to staring out the windshield. 'I know.'

'Two weeks, Mary, and then three long months before we see each other again.'

She nodded slowly, not speaking.

'Hey, Mary...' He shifted his great weight along the seat until his massive arm fell around her shoulders. When his left hand crept over her arm and slipped down her breast, she said, 'No, Mike, don't,' and gently pushed his hand away.

'Why not?' he whispered, his forehead pressed against her hair. 'You always like it. You always let me do it. And besides, we've been going steady long enough. Two semesters now. Come on, Mary, everyone does it.'

She shook her head weakly. 'Not everyone, Mike, and I don't want to do what you want. We've talked about it before. It's not right, not until after we're married.'

He stiffened slightly, then melted against her again. 'That's not what I was talking about, Mary.' His voice was soft and persuasive, his lips brushing her ear as he spoke. 'I meant; you know, just the usual stuff.'

Placing a hand under her chin and drawing her face around, Mike kissed her, delicately at first, then more passionately. When he tried with his tongue to pry her mouth open, she drew back. 'No...Mike, don't do that...'

18

'Okay...' he breathed. Then his hand came up again, this time under her blouse. Mary closed her eyes and felt her breath catch in her throat.

But when his fingers explored under the elastic of her bra, she pushed his hand away again. 'Not now, Mike, please...'

'Why not? You always like it.'

'They're sensitive, Mike, they're sore. Please,' her eyes searched his face imploringly. 'Not now...'

Mike was anguished, almost angry for a moment, then his eyes flickered and he softened once more. 'Mary,' he said smoothly, drawing her against him, 'I want you badly. You know I do. And in two weeks I'm gonna be gone. Who knows, my dad might even decide to *stay* in Boston and then I'll never come back.'

She brought her head about sharply. 'Mike!'

He caught her mouth in a violent kiss, catching her lips apart, and thrust his tongue between her teeth. For the briefest moment Mary responded; a groan escaped her throat, then she snapped her head back.

'I want to go all the way with you,' he said huskily. 'Right here. Right now.'

'No, Mike—'

'You'll like it, I know you will. I won't hurt you. We'll do it any way you want.'

'No—'

'You won't even have to take your clothes off.'

When she suddenly burst into tears, covering her face with her hands, Mike released a long, impatient sigh and lifted his arm slightly off her shoulders.

Mary cried for some minutes, and when the sobbing abated, Mike said, 'Hey, I'm sorry.'

She gulped and dried her eyes with her knuckles. 'I want it, too, but we *can't*. Not until we're married.'

He regarded her for a moment, then said unhappily, 'We might never see each other again. I love you, Mary. Do you love me?'

When she said, 'Yes,' she started crying again, so Mike

had started the engine and they had driven home in icy silence.

'Mr. Holland, if you don't mind!' The pointer came down with a loud crack on Mr. Slocum's desk.

Mike swivelled around, startled.

'I don't blame you, Mr. Holland, for preferring to gaze at young ladies instead of me, but I expect you to at least keep your ears aimed in my direction. Now will you kindly answer the question?'

As a murmur of amusement rumbled through the class, Mike scowled down at his hands. 'I'm sorry, I didn't hear it.'

Mr. Slocum sighed again; he couldn't get mad at Mike Holland either. With short trim blond hair, a handsome rugged face, and broad shoulders straining against the fabric of his Ivy League shirt, Mike Holland was not only the class president and captain of the football team, he was also a straight-A honour student.

'Can you tell us the difference between veins and arteries?'

Casting a quick, unconscious glance at Mary, Mike recited a perfect textbook answer, and as he did so, Mr. Slocum let his eyes slide back to the McFarland girl, who instantly shot him a disarming smile.

The biology teacher knew her type: a natural leader, the queen bee. Look how all attention in the class seemed to radiate from her, like spokes from the hub of a wagon wheel; the kids looked to Mary, subconsciously, for the right thing to do, their eyes flitting to her, then away. There was one in nearly every class; sometimes they were a nuisance, the class clown, other times they were simply the trend-setters, the examples by which the rest of the herd set their standards and tempos. They travelled in packs, teen-agers, the herding instinct was strong, and whether they realised it or not, they held unspoken elections and chose untitled leaders to give them direction through the confusion of adolescence. Unwittingly, they chose the prettiest, the handsomest, equating excellence in appearance with excellence in mind. In this case, Mary Ann McFarland had both. Slocum wondered, as

20

he reached up to draw down the anatomical chart, how aware of her influence on the other kids Mary was. He was also suddenly, acutely conscious of the moon of sweat under his armpit.

'Who can give me the names of the largest artery and largest vein in the body?'

As the chart came down and several hands shot up, Mr. Slocum thought sadly: it's such a shame. He was teaching them every system in the body – today they were on the circulatory system – except for one: forbidden, illegal even, to bring such a topic into the classroom. They could talk about genes and chromosomes, white mice and black mice, the whole business of generation and pairing and offspring, as long as he skirted the central point of *how* those genes got passed along. He settled his gaze on Mary – titillating, the prospect of lecturing her and her kind on the reproductive system – then he withdrew his eyes and gave his throat a professional clearing. 'Arteries *from* the heart, veins *to* the heart...'

As the rest of the class scribbled in their notebooks, Mike Holland returned to thinking about last night's debacle in the Corvair. He looked again at Mary, her pretty face held rapt by Slocum's lecture, and knew she had forgotten the incident. Why were girls like that? How could they sob and cry one minute like the world was going to end and the next be laughing and giggling and making eyes at short fat biology teachers?

The last period of the day was PE and although today was only a lecture on feminine hygiene, the girls still had to change into gym clothes. In the heat of the afternoon, two hundred girls sat cross-legged on the gymnasium floor, switching from one aching buttock to another as they watched in boredom a Walt Disney cartoon on menstruation. They had seen the film, since the fifth grade, at least ten times.

Later, in the locker room and changing back into street clothes, Mary heard the usual chatter around her. The girls were talking about a movie currently showing in the West Valley.

'Can you imagine doing it with Warren Beatty?' came the shrill voice of a girl named Sheila. One of the few who did not stand behind her open locker door for a bit of privacy, she was wriggling out of her black gym shorts and into a tight skirt. 'I've seen that movie three times and I could see it again!'

Mary was sitting on the narrow bench that ran the length of the lockers, absently removing her spotless gym shoes.

'Natalie Wood was right to hold out,' said a girl in a beehive hairdo.

'I wouldn't have,' said Sheila. 'Who could resist him! And besides, look where holding out got her. In a mental hospital!'

Mary glanced up at Germaine, who was hurriedly getting changed, and smiled. Mary's best friend occupied the next locker and rarely took part in the usual locker-room dialogue. A quiet, introspective girl with radical views. Germaine Massey as a rule voiced her opinions only to Mary.

Slowly undressing and folding her blouse and shorts into neat little squares and depositing them in her gym bag, Mary said quietly, 'They're talking about *Splendour in the Grass*.'

'I know,' said Germaine, hurriedly stuffing her dirty gym clothes haphazardly into her three-ring notebook. 'It's positively decadent. They talk about sex as if it's something special.' Germaine slammed her locker shut and proceeded to draw a comb through her long black hair, which streamed over her shoulders and down to her hips.

Mary felt herself smile as she pulled her dress over her head, saying as she did so, 'All I can think about right now is that lousy B I got on my French report. Just because, as that witch put it, I didn't make enough use of the subjunctive! How the heck am I supposed to use the subjunctive in a report on Cathedrals?'

Germaine shrugged. 'You'll make it up in the final. You always do.'

While Mary set about assiduously applying a fresh layer

of black eyeliner to her lids, using the mirror inside her locker door, Germaine sat down to wait.

The locker-room crowd started to thin out as more and more metal doors clanged shut and girls hurried off for the weekend. But since it was the last period of the day, many stayed behind to tease repairs into bouffants or to apply drops of clear nail polish to nylon runs. Most of the chatter was about the coming evening and the various Friday-night plans everyone had.

'Just listen to them, Mare,' said Germaine, dropping her comb into her beaded leather shoulder bag. 'They're all talking about necking at the drive-in like it's a big thing. I'll bet not one of them has gone all the way. They're too scared. I'll bet every one of them is still a virgin.'

Mary cast a quick glance at her friend and returned to her makeup. Germaine Massey was a Progressive, a beatnik, and, with her boy friend, a student of political science at UCLA, went to basement coffeehouses to listen to poetry that didn't rhyme, attended political rallies, and experimented in something called free love.

Right now, sitting on the bench in her bulky knit sweater and pleated skirt and black tights, Germaine flipped through the thick copy of *Fanny Hill*. 'This won't take me long, Mare,' she murmured, her long black hair falling forward and obscuring her face. 'God, do you believe this? She calls it a pistol, of all things!'

Finishing with her eyes, Mary recapped the bottle of liquid eyeliner and replaced it in the small makeup box she kept at the back of her locker. As she did so, her hand brushed against a small bundle modestly hidden in the dark recess and she wondered for an instant what it was. Then, remembering the napkin she always kept for emergencies, she frowned slightly and tried to recall something.

But Germaine's voice intervened and stole the thought.

At three o'clock Mary and Germaine went to their coat lockers and bumped into Mike and his friend Rick, both in their Lettermen sweaters.

'Hi, Mary. Can't give you a ride home today, sorry. Lettermen meeting.'

'That's okay, Mike, I'll call my mother. What time will you be by tonight?'

'It'll have to be after seven. I promised my dad I'd get the pool cleaned before the weekend. 'Bye.'

Mary stood wistfully by her locker as she watched the two broad-shouldered young men disappear into the hallway crowd.

Before leaving the building, Mike and Rick ducked into the boys' room, which was cloudy with cigarette smoke, and, plopping their books on the shoulder-high tile wall by the door, went straight to the sinks. They both pulled out combs, ran them under faucets, and started combing their hair.

Mike glanced at Rick in the mirror. 'D'you make out last night?'

'Naw. Sherry's mom wouldn't let her go out, and besides, I had to study. How 'bout you? D'you score?'

Mike flashed a knowing grin. 'We found a great new spot up on Mulholland Drive.' He knocked his comb against the sink and slipped it into his hip pocket. 'Can't lose.'

Rick shook his head and whistled enviously.

As Lucille McFarland pulled the Continental onto Claridge Drive and manoeuvered it around the many parked trucks of Mexican gardeners, she said, 'Must be the flu. Good thing it's Friday.'

'But I have tryouts tomorrow!'

'Were you able to eat lunch?'

'Yes, but not much, and then afterward I felt nauseated again. It comes and goes. Mostly I feel really tired, like drained, you know?'

Lucille nodded and snapped the car radio on. Searching up and down the dial for a minute for a news broadcast, she switched it off and said, 'No new Pope yet, I guess.'

Lucille steered the bulky Continental up the steep driveway and brought it to a halt before the front door. 'Well!' She sat for a moment with an eye fixed on the miniature cypress trees which lined the front of the house.

'Maybe I'd better take you to see someone. Unfortunately Dr Chandler died of a heart attack a couple of months ago, so I'm going to have to find someone else. Let's go into the house, I'll give Shirley a call. Maybe she can recommend someone.'

Dr Jonas Wade's office was in a glassy new building on the corner of Reseda and Ventura with a fifth-floor view of the roof of Gelson's Supermarket. The waiting room was pleasant and subdued, done in gentle shades of blue and green, with plush carpeting, many plants, and an enormous aquarium full of exotic fish. Lucille McFarland was at once impressed. Dr. Jonas Wade had come very highly recommended, not only by Shirley Thomas but by two of Lucille's other friends. She had then called his office and had been told that Dr Wade's last appointment for the day had been cancelled and that Mary could come in then. It was five o'clock.

The wait seemed interminable. Mary desperately hoped Dr Wade would be a very old man, that the visit would be quick and impersonal, and that he would send her home with a box of pills that would make her feel better for tryouts in the morning.

When the nurse called her name, Mary wiped her moist palms down her skirt and followed the woman inside. Lucille remained in the waiting room, idly flipping through a copy of *Glamour*.

Old Dr Chandler's office had been in an adobe building which he had occupied the entire thirty-three years of his practice and had never in all that time been modernised. It had been the only doctor's office Mary ever knew. She missed it now as she was led into a cold, pristine exam room that had glaring modern wallpaper and abstract paintings and white, glacial lights. And when the nurse asked her to remove all her clothes, Mary's heart sank.

Putting on the paper gown and trying to cover as much of herself as possible with it, she sat on the edge of the exam table and swung her legs nervously.

The nurse came back a minute later and surprised Mary

even further. With a practiced smile and a little rubber tourniquet, she stuck a needle into Mary's arm and withdrew a syringeful of blood. Then she gave the girl a plastic cup, a cotton alcohol swab, and instructions on how to catch the urine 'midstream.' This was awkwardly accomplished in the tiny bathroom adjoining the exam room.

Mary resumed her seat on the edge of the table. She was devastated when Dr Wade entered the room.

He was a tall man in his early forties who seemed even taller because of his slenderness and long white lab coat. His hair was black with a few strands of silver. His smile was smooth, as if, Mary thought fleetingly, he had stood in front of a mirror practicing it before coming in. His eyes, almost black, were bright and unsettling, as though they could see through the paper gown. There wasn't, as far as Mary was concerned, enough age on him; he wasn't *old* enough.

'Hi,' he said, glancing down at the chart in his hands. 'Which do you prefer, Mary or Mary Ann?'

She spoke in a small voice. 'Mary, I guess.'

'Okay, Mary, I'm Dr Wade. Now I see here' – he opened the chart – 'on this form your mother filled out for us that you have the flu.' His smile stretched into a grin. 'Shall we see if her diagnosis is correct?'

Mary nodded.

He set the chart down and proceeded to wash his hands in the sink. 'Where do you go to school, Mary?'

'Reseda High.'

'Eleventh grade?'

'Yes.'

'School's almost out, isn't it?'

'Yes.'

Drying his hands on a paper towel, Dr Wade turned and smiled and leaned against the sink. 'I'll bet you're excited. Got any special plans for the summer? Going on any trips?'

She shook her head.

Still smiling and talking in a tone that sounded as if he had known her for years, Dr Wade proceeded to ask a series of questions. Mary came out with a short, barely audible 'yes'

26

or 'no' for each, trying earnestly to remember if she had ever had whooping cough or measles or severe illness or recurring headaches or dizziness and a few things she didn't even understand. Dr Wade seemed satisfied with each answer, making little notes in the chart and looking up at her now and then.

Finally he said, 'Okay, Mary, now about your problem. Can you tell me what it feels like?'

She haltingly described the lethargy and nausea of the last three days, and said 'no' to his questions about sore throat, vomiting, diarrhoea, headaches, chills or fever. All the while his silver pen, glinting in the bright overhead lights, scratched across the chart.

When he clicked the pen and slid it into his pocket, there was a soft knock at the door and the nurse entered, coming all the way in and closing the door behind her. She wordlessly handed him some coloured papers.

The silence was loud and uncomfortable for Mary as she sat in her flimsy paper gown, one hand clutching the back flaps together. She stared at Dr Wade's face as he read each report: first the yellow, then the red, then the blue, finally the white. His impassive expression never changed.

When at last he placed the papers in the chart and brought his head up with a smile, Mary's heart jumped. This was the part she had been dreading.

Jonas Wade's fingers were surprisingly cool as they gently probed her neck, pulled down her lower eyelids, drew back her hair for him to look in her ears, and touched her chin as he placed a stick on her tongue. All the while his voice was deep and relaxed.

'What do you plan to do after high school, Mary?'

The cold stethoscope was on her back. 'I don't know. I guess I'll apply to Berkeley.'

'My old alma mater. Breathe in, please. Hold it. Now release it slowly.'

'But I was thinking I might join the Peace Corps.'

'Again, please. In, hold it, out slowly.' The cold disc moved. 'The Peace Corps, really! I've often thought that would be a great adventure.'

He moved to the front and the silent nurse seemed to Mary to lean closer. Dr Wade's fingers drew down the front of the gown and he slid the stethoscope under her left breast. Mary closed her eyes.

'I thought of somewhere like East Africa,' he said quietly, 'but I guess the San Fernando Valley's a wild enough place for me.'

Mary tried to smile, and breathed a sigh of relief when he took the stethoscope away. Then he banged a little hammer on her knees and ran his pen up the bottoms of her feet.

'Would you please lie down?'

Mary's mouth went dry. She stretched out, fists clenched at her sides, and stared at the acoustic ceiling as Dr Wade probed her abdomen. When he brought the tissue gown up to her shoulders and exposed her chest to the cold air, she drew in her breath and held it.

'Would you put your right arm over your head, please?'

She closed her eyes again. His fingers massaged her breast and armpit. She winced.

'Is that tender?'

'Yes,' she whispered.

He did it again. 'And here?'

'Yes.'

'And here?'

'Yes...'

Then he did the same thing to the other breast, saying, 'Tell me, Mary, which is worse, going to the doctor or going to the dentist?'

Her eyes flew open. Dr Wade was smiling down at her. 'Well,—'

'For me, the dentist is the worst. You know, Mary, I'm embarrassed to say this, but when I have to go to the dentist for even a filling, I have to take a tranquiliser because I get so scared that my knees knock.'

Her eyes widened.

'Is this tender?'

The word 'yes' came out in a breath.

When he finally pulled the gown down and stepped away,

Mary sat up before he could tell her to do so. She glanced at the nurse, who was still smiling in a fixed way.

Dr Wade was back at the sink and writing in the chart again. 'Tell me, Mary,' he said without looking up at her, 'when did you first start your period? How old were you?'

Mary's ears became instantly inflamed. 'Oh...uh...when I was twelve.'

'Are you regular?'

She licked her lips with a dry tongue. 'Well, yes. Well, I mean, no. Sometimes it's only twenty-five days and sometimes it's over thirty.'

'When was your last one?'

'Uh...' She swallowed hard and tried to think. Then it came to her, the elusive thought in the locker room. Her forehead wrinkled in a frown. 'I guess I don't remember.'

He nodded, continued writing. 'Can you try? Was it less than a month ago?'

She glanced at the nurse, wondering why the woman wasn't embarrassed. 'Well, no. Let me think.' Mary's eyebrows came together as she thought back. She didn't keep track of her cycle on a calendar as some girls did; she had never seen the need for it. But now that she looked back through May and into April, it did seem like a long time. 'I guess before Easter.'

Dr Wade nodded and made another entry in the chart. Then he slid the pen back in his pocket and turned a charming smile to Mary. 'We're almost through. You've been an angel. I have to step out for a minute, but I'll be right back.'

Dr Wade did not come back. Instead, the nurse returned a few minutes later and helped Mary back into her clothes, after which she led the girl into a pleasant, comfortably furnished office.

The walls were panelled with dark wood and supported shelves of impressive-looking books. There were various etchings and water colours covering the panelling, and a series of framed diplomas and certificates. On the heavy wooden desk was a stack of medical journals that looked as if it might topple, a wire sculpture of a nut-and-bolt man on skis, an antelope-foot pencil holder, an early-American reading lamp, and a photograph of a woman with her arms around two teen-agers.

When Dr Wade came in and quietly closed the door behind him, Mary sank into the leather chair and tried to appear at ease. She wished now she had her purse with her so that her fingers could twist something other than themselves.

He sat behind the desk, spread the chart before him and gave Mary a warm smile. 'You know, I wish all my patients were as nice and cooperative as you.'

She cleared her throat and whispered, 'Thank you.'

'You're a very pretty girl, Mary. I'll bet you have lots of friends.'

She shrugged.

Dr Wade laughed warmly, leaning casually on his elbows. 'Going steady?'

'Yes.'

'He's a lucky guy. Now then.' Jonas Wade cleared his voice and let the smile fade into seriousness. 'While I was examining you, Mary, I had the lab in this building run tests on your blood and urine samples. It's something I do routinely with almost all my new patients when they come in for the first time. Especially when they come in with a complaint like yours. Now, so far, Mary, you appear quite healthy.'

Her eyebrows arched.

'But that's not to say there isn't something, ah, *wrong* with you. It's just that your preliminary lab tests show us that your haemoglobin is normal. Your white cell count is normal; red cell count.' His fingers brushed over the pastel sheets in the chart. 'These indicate that, as far as we can tell, there is no infection or anaemia involved.' His hand rested on the last report, the lavender one, the one that gave him the result of the test he had run himself while Mary was getting dressed.

He faced her squarely, his eyes holding hers. 'I need to know just a couple more things.' Dr Wade's voice adjusted

30

slightly. 'Tell me, Mary, have you ever had sexual intercourse?'

Her eyebrows shot even higher. 'I beg your pardon?'

'Have you ever gone all the way with a boy?'

Mary's eyes were wide, startled. 'Why, no, Dr Wade.'

'You're sure.'

'Of course I'm sure. Never.'

He studied her face for a moment, then said in a quieter tone, 'Mary, let me assure you that whatever goes on between us in here will be held in the strictest confidence. My nurse won't know. I won't even put it in your chart.' To emphasise this point, he closed the folder and pushed it away. 'This is just between you and me. Think of it only as a medical question, like when I asked you if you had had your tonsils out.'

She dropped her eyes to the manila chart and frowned. Then she looked again at Dr Wade, her eyes innocent and questioning. 'Well,' she gave a little shrug, 'I'm telling the truth. I've never been to bed with a boy.'

'Mhmmmm.' Jonas Wade brought his hands up and made a steeple of his long, slender fingers. He considered the lavender report at his elbow and carefully watched the girl's face.

'You know, Mary, it's possible you've gone all the way and don't know it.'

She forced a weak laugh and wished her cheeks weren't burning. 'I would know, Dr Wade. I have never even been *undressed* with Mike. Well' – she suddenly looked down and studied her hands – 'at least not below the waist. You know...I've never let him him put his hand...down there...'

She heard Dr Wade stir in his chair, and when she looked up he was gathering up her chart. 'I guess that's everything, Mary.' He flashed a disarming grin and spoke in a louder voice. 'Some disorders don't show up on blood and urine tests right away. They have to incubate. We'll run cultures and we'll see if they tell us what's wrong with you. We won't know the final results until all the tests are in. In the meantime, I want you to take it easy for a while, drink lots of fluids, eat well, and get lots of sleep. Okay?'

'Okay.'

'And when I get the final results, I'll give you a call.'

CHAPTER 3

Mary threw up the next morning, but despite protestations from her mother she was able to talk her father into driving her to the school auditorium, where cheerleader tryouts were being held. Though tired, Mary persevered, and at the end, knowing her performance had not been her best, she was relieved and elated to be told she was on the team again.

That afternoon she started studying for finals which would be the week after next; after supper she watched a TV special with her family explaining the conclave currently being held at the Vatican; and before her usual Saturday night date with Mike, went to confession.

She felt a wave of nausea sweep over her as she knelt in the little box whispering to Father Crispin and apologised to him, explaining that she had the flu. Her penance for her weekly sins was a light five Hail Marys.

After church on Sunday Mary spent the day by the pool reading the latest bestseller, *Ship of Fools*, while her father watched the Dodgers play the Giants on TV, her mother spent the afternoon chauffeuring three of St. Sebastian's nuns on errands, and Amy religiously studied her Baltimore Catechism in preparation for her coming confirmation.

The next morning, Monday, Mary felt no better and was kept home from school by her mother. That afternoon, Dr Wade's office nurse called and asked if Mary could come into the office first thing the next morning on her way to school to give one more urine sample. Mary was instructed not to drink anything after seven o'clock that evening, to be sure to urinate before going to bed that night, and to try to hold it until she came into the office the next morning.

Monday evening the McFarlands gathered in their den to watch news films of black smoke rising up from the Sistine Chapel.

Tuesday, feeling a little better, Mary went to school, and on her way stopped to give a sample to Dr Wade's nurse.

It was late Wednesday afternoon when Mary, coming out of her bedroom, ran into her father, who was just stepping into the hall and buttoning a fresh shirt.

'Hi, Daddy! When did you get home?'

They gave each other a kiss and then walked down the hall together, arms about each other's waists. 'About fifteen minutes ago. Your radio was playing so loud you didn't hear me. Say, who the heck *is* Tom Dooley anyway?'

'Oh, Daddy!' She gave him a playful squeeze. His waist was firm and hard beneath his shirt, and Mary liked the feel of it. She was glad he had made a habit of going to the gym every Wednesday night for a workout. Not like so many other fathers Ted's age who had let themselves get flabby.

'Feeling better, kitten?'

'*Much* better! I guess I'm over whatever it was I had.'

'How was school today?'

'Great! I got an A on my government speech. *And*...' She grinned up at him, her eyes sparkling.

'And what?'

'And the best news of all! Mike's dad has decided to turn down that promotion in Boston! They're all going to stay in Tarzana for the summer!'

Ted McFarland laughed softly. 'I don't know if that's such a blessing, kitten.'

'Now Mike and I can go to Malibu every day with the other kids!'

Mary and her father entered the dining room, where Amy was already seated and Lucille was putting the last of the plates on the table. Ted released his daughter, saying, 'I suppose now you'll be badgering me for a new bathing suit.'

33

Her eyes flashed at him as she went around the table. 'You read my mind, Daddy.'

'But not one of those indecent ones,' murmured Lucille, pulling out her chair and sitting down.

'Oh, Mother.'

Amy chanted: 'It was an itsy-bitsy, teeny-weeny yellow polka dot—' Mary, passing behind her, gave her little sister a yank on the hair.

After everyone was seated, Ted said Grace and then proceeded to carve the roast.

'Just think,' said Mary excitedly. 'Twelve whole weeks in the sun with Mike! God, I'm excited!'

Dropping large spoonfuls of broccoli on each girl's plate, Lucille said, 'I hope you'll manage to squeeze in some time for me. All that crepe Shirley Thomas gave me is screaming to be made into dresses.'

'Oh, sure!' said Mary. 'I haven't forgotten.' They had made plans to do some sewing together during the summer, there was enough yardage for a look-alike set.

Lucille McFarland brushed an orange strand of hair off her forehead. 'It's a scorcher today. In the nineties, they said. Guess we're in for a hot summer.'

Mary looked across the table at her mother's flushed cheeks. Long ago she had envied her mom the natural rosiness which caused her not to need rouge as other women did, until one day, when she was fourteen, Mary had discovered that her mother's lovely red cheeks were the result of an occasional afternoon cocktail.

Dinners on Wednesdays were always eaten at five-thirty because Ted had to get to his gym and Lucille had a meeting of the Altar and Rosary Society. It was also, conveniently, the night for Amy's weekly class with Sister Agatha for confirmation.

'Going out with Mike tonight?' asked Ted as he ate.

Mary nodded vigorously. 'A new movie at the Corbin. *Mondo Cane*. Everyone's seeing it.'

'How're the catechism classes going, Amy? Need any help?'

'Uh-uh.' The twelve-year-old shook her head, fluffing her

chestnut Buster Brown haircut. 'Sister Agatha answers all my questions. It's just like before Communion. Same old thing.'

Ted smiled and nodded, thinking for the moment of his own days of catechism back in Chicago when he had been planning to become a priest. But that had been before the war had broken out. In 1941 Ted McFarland had left the seminary to join the armed services, and after three years in the South Pacific, he had no longer felt a religious vocation. He had gone on to become a stockbroker instead and sometimes, when his memory was triggered as it was now, he wondered what things would be like today if he hadn't made that decision.

'But I still don't think it's fair about babies.'

He blinked at Amy, who was again swinging her legs so that her body rocked as she ate. 'What was that?' he said.

'I said I don't think it's fair about babies.'

'What about them?'

'Daddy, you weren't listening! Sister Agatha told us last week about Limbo and about all the unbaptised babies there. And I don't think it's fair for God to do that to them because they can't help it.'

'Well, Amy,' said Ted slowly. 'If they're not baptised then they still have original sin on their souls, and you know that no one can go to heaven with original sin. That's why we get baptised.'

'And that's why,' came Mary quietly, 'the doctors saved Mrs. Franchimoni's baby and let Mrs. Franchimoni die.'

Lucille jerked her head up. 'Mary Ann McFarland, who told you that!'

'Father Crispin did. But first I heard it from Germaine, who overheard her mother talking to a neighbour about it.'

'Germaine Massey, that beatnik. Her parents are socialists, you know.'

'So?'

'So that's the same as communists as far as I'm concerned, and I say if they want communism, let them go and live under Khrushchev and see how much they like it then.'

35

'What about Mrs. Franchimoni's baby?' said Amy, eyes eager.

'Germaine says that the doctors told *Mr.* Franchimoni that his wife was in grave danger and that they should sacrifice the baby to save her life. But Mr. Franchimoni talked to Father Crispin about it and Father Crispin told him the baby should be saved at all costs. So he told the doctors to save the baby, and because of it, Mrs. Franchimoni died.'

'That's awful!' cried Amy.

'Mary,' said Ted quietly, putting his fork down and clasping his hands before him on the table. 'It's not quite as simple as you tell it. There's a lot more involved here.'

'Oh, I know, Daddy. After I heard about it from Germaine, I asked Father Crispin about it and he explained.'

'What did he say?'

'He said that there's a difference between mortal life and spiritual life and that it's the spiritual life we want to save. He said that since the mother is baptised, then she will go to heaven when she dies, but the baby has to be given a chance to be baptised too so that he can also go to heaven. Father Crispin said that the mother can receive last rites and die in sanctifying grace and be guaranteed of going to heaven, and then that way when she dies and the baby is born, the baby can be baptised and will also get to go to heaven.'

Ted nodded thoughtfully. Then he looked at Amy, whose head was tilted to one side. 'Do you understand?'

'Sorta, Daddy.'

'What it means is, if you save the mother and let the baby die, then only one soul has a chance of going to heaven. But if you let the mother die and bring the baby into the world and baptise him, then two souls can go to heaven. That's the important difference, Amy, *souls* instead of earthly lives. Father Crispin is right. Okay, Amy?'

'I guess. I wouldn't want a baby to go to Limbo.'

The dinner table fell silent after this, filled only with the sounds of knives and forks against plates. Amy stared into

36

her broccoli, wondering why someone as all-powerful and loving as God would keep babies out of heaven; Lucille McFarland thought about Rosemary Franchimoni and their last conversation together; Ted reflected on Arthur Franchimoni's subsequent withdrawal from the Church; and Mary wondered, as she distastefully picked at the broccoli, when Mike was going to be picking her up.

The silence was broken by the sound of the phone ringing. Amy, always competitive to be the first to answer it, jumped up, dashed from the dining room, and could be faintly heard talking.

A moment later she was back at the table. 'It's Dr Wade.'

'Oh? What does he want?'

'Dunno. He's on the phone.'

Lucille got up and went into the next room. After a few seconds of subliminal conversation, she came back to her chair and said, 'He wants me to bring Mary in after supper.'

'Tonight? What for?'

'He has the final test results and wants to tell us in person.'

'Oh, Mother. I'm all over that now. I'm fine, didn't you tell him that? Gosh, Mike's going to be here soon—'

'We paid for it so we might as well hear what he has found. He probably wants to give you some vitamins or something. It can't hurt to go in.'

Mary was infinitely more relaxed this time, sitting in the leather chair and slowly looking around the elegant office; no embarrassing physical exam this time, just a verbal report on her tests. When Dr Wade suddenly came in, softly closing the door behind him, Mary noticed a few more details about the man. He was perhaps not quite as tall as he had seemed before, nor as young. His face tonight showed creases around the eyes and mouth; a few more strands of grey streaked his black hair. But the smile was the same, radiating confidence and genuine friendship so that Mary decided Dr Jonas Wade was a nice replacement for old Dr Chandler.

'Hi, Mary,' he said quietly, extending a hand. She timidly shook hands with him – his grasp was firm and heavy – and said, 'Hi, Dr Wade.'

'Well, now.' He went around his desk and cleared away a few papers before sitting down. Flashing a grin at her, he said to the girl, 'When I was a kid I thought a doctor's life was the easiest one in the world. All you had to do was place sticks on people's tongues and drive Cadillacs! Boy, was I wrong.'

Mary laughed.

'Okay, Mary, all your tests are in.' He reached for her folder and opened it. 'Blood and urine remain just about the same. No high white count, differential normal, hematocrit' – Dr Wade looked up – 'well, that's just medical mumbo jumbo for the things inside you that make you tick. You took biology, didn't you?'

'And human physiology.'

'Good. Then you will have an understanding of what I want to talk to you about. I mean, you certainly must understand how infections show up in the blood and about how modern science has come up with fancy ways of diagnosing conditions simply from a drop of urine.'

'Oh, sure,' she said.

Dr Wade took a moment to glance down at the reports in the chart, seemed to mull over his next words, and then raised his eyes once again to Mary. She was surprised to see that the smile had disappeared and that his eyes had taken on a look of seriousness. 'Mary, I have to ask you something. And I want you to understand that I'm not trying to be nosy or trying to pass judgement or anything like that. After all, you are seventeen years old, an adult really, and you appreciate the fact that all I'm here for is to see to your best interests.'

Her blue eyes were round, waiting.

'Mary, I know I asked you this last Friday, but I'm going to ask you again. And I want you to think about it before you answer me. Have you ever gone all the way with a boy?'

She stared at him for a moment, her eyebrows furrowed, then her face cleared and she said simply, 'No, Dr Wade.'

'You're sure.'

'Of course I am. I'd tell you, honest.'

Jonas Wade studied the girl's face again the same way he had during their last session and was puzzled. Finally he said, 'Mary, the last time you were here, the lab downstairs ran routine blood and urine tests on you, and they found absolutely nothing wrong with you. Then, when I examined you physically, you told me your breasts were tender and that you had missed your last two periods. So, while you were getting dressed, I ran a test on you myself, right here in the office.' He withdrew the lavender slip from her chart and held it up. 'Mary, have you ever heard of the Gravindex?'

She shook her head.

'It's a test that was developed about two years ago and is now in common use in most doctors' offices. Gravindex, Mary,' he paused, watching her face, 'is a pregnancy test.'

She gazed back at him, her face expressionless.

'I ran the test while you were here in my office and the result was positive.' He continued to hold the lavender slip up for her to see. 'So that was why I asked you if you had gone to bed with a boy.'

Mary's eyes flickered to the paper in his hand then back to his face.

'By positive, Mary,' he went on, still puzzled by her behaviour, 'I mean that the test told me you were pregnant.'

She shrugged. 'The test was wrong.'

'That was my conclusion when you answered no to my question. Sometimes the Gravindex throws a false positive, so I decided to run a more reliable test, just to be sure. Have you ever heard of a frog test?'

'No.'

'We take a drop of urine from a woman and inject it into a male frog. A few hours later we examine the frog's urine under a microscope and if there are spermatozoa present, that means the woman is pregnant.'

Mary continued to stare at him, her hands resting idly in her lap.

'That's why my nurse asked you to come in Tuesday

morning with another specimen. It has to be done with the first urine of the day. We injected it into the frog, Mary, and he produced spermatozoa.'

Dr Wade fell silent and considered the girl's expression. She showed only mild interest in what he had to say.

'Mary, the final test shows that you're pregnant.'

She shrugged again and gave a little laugh. 'It's wrong, Dr Wade, just like that other one.'

'The frog test is nearly one hundred per cent accurate, Mary. And we ran it twice just to be certain. There's no doubt that you're pregnant.'

Mary smiled. 'Doubt to the frog maybe, but there's no way I can be pregnant.'

Dr Wade leaned back in his chair and clasped his hands over his flat abdomen. He studied the girl across from him once more.

Her denials were not uncommon, even up to this point. However, few girls kept up the pretense in the face of irrefutable evidence, and certainly they never made denials so calmly, so objectively. This was the point where they broke down and cried and confessed. Or they flew out in anger. Or they became frightened and pleaded with him. But not this one. This one was perplexing.

'You know, Mary, you might as well tell me because it's going to start showing soon and then there'll be no way of denying it.'

'Dr Wade.' Mary spread out her hands, palms up. 'I'm not pregnant. I've never done anything to cause it. Your test is wrong.'

'There's the other evidence as well. You've missed two periods. Your breasts are tender. You've had morning sickness.'

She smiled helplessly. 'What can I tell you? I obviously have something else wrong with me.'

Dr Wade frowned and leaned forward, placing his hands flat on the desk. 'You know, Mary, it is possible, it has been known in some rare instances, for a woman to become pregnant simply by having a man's penis between her thighs. He doesn't necessarily have to enter her.'

40

Mary dropped her gaze to her hands. She felt her face burn. 'I've never done that, Dr Wade,' she said quietly. 'I told you that. I've only ever let Mike touch me here,' she brushed a hand across her chest. 'And I've *never* let him take his...thing out.'

'And yet you're pregnant.'

She brought her head up, her eyes filled with bafflement. 'All I can say is that I'm not and that you'll see how wrong you are when nothing happens.'

'Mary, something *is* going to happen. Your abdomen is going to start to swell and then you'll have to admit it.'

Mary laughed and looked up at the ceiling. It was like arguing with Amy.

'Mary,' said Dr Wade slowly. 'Do you believe me when I tell you I'm your friend and that I have only your best interest at heart?'

'Sure.'

He kept his eyes on her face and pursed his lips for an instant before saying, 'I'm going to have to tell your parents.'

'Okay.'

'How would you like me to handle it?'

Mary waved a hand. 'Call my mother in right now. She's in the waiting room.'

Dr Wade stared at the girl, trying to mask his surprise. Even the most stubborn girls broke down when it came time to tell the parents.

'What will your mother say when I tell her you're pregnant?'

'She won't believe you. She knows I would never do anything like that.'

'Are you sure?'

Mary tilted her head to the side, her eyes wide and innocent. 'Of course. Mother knows I wouldn't lie to her.'

'What about your father?'

'Daddy? He's the same as Mother.'

Dr Wade nodded slowly and considered his next step. When there seemed no other choice, he pressed a button on his intercom and asked the nurse to bring Mrs. McFarland in.

When Lucille was seated opposite him, he took a moment before speaking to appraise her.

She was not a bad-looking woman; slender and tanned. Not much makeup, although the red might not be the natural colour of her hair. Sharp blue eyes, much like her daughter's, similar nose and chin. The family resemblance was strong; Lucille must have been as pretty as Mary when she was young. Now she was in her early forties and Dr Wade could see in the lines on her face that Lucille McFarland spent too much time in the sun. Her clothes were expensive and conservative, but Dr Wade had already been able to deduce from the address on the chart Mary's social and economic status. The mother radiated self-confidence and appeared quite intelligent. He had the disquieting feeling that this was not going to be an easy meeting.

Clearing his throat, Jonas Wade briefly summarised the routine tests he had run, the physical examination he had done on Mary, and cautiously approached the crucial subject.

'Because of certain physical aspects of your daughter's condition, Mrs. McFarland, I felt the need to run further tests, special tests, and that was why I had Mary give us another urine specimen yesterday morning. Those tests are now in and their findings are conclusive.'

Sitting on the edge of the chair, with her hands folded in her lap, Lucille said, 'What's wrong with my daughter, Dr Wade?'

'All the evidence, Mrs. McFarland, points to pregnancy. I have to tell you that your daughter is pregnant.'

There was a moment of stunned silence, then Lucille let out a 'what!' and turned to Mary.

'It's not true, Mother. I told him the tests were wrong. I've never done anything...'

Jonas Wade kept a careful eye on Mary as she spoke and was again baffled by her behaviour. It was starting to occur to him that the girl might actually believe what she said.

'Very well then,' said Lucille crisply, recovering at once.

42

'Your test must have been in error, Doctor, since my daughter says it can't be possible.'

Jonas Wade sighed and took a moment to examine his fingernails. He wondered, as he did so, what insanity had made him think that keeping his office open late on Wednesdays would be a good idea. He wished now he was at the Country Club with his colleagues.

'Mrs. McFarland, our lab ran two frog tests and both showed definite traces of pregnancy hormones in Mary's urine. She has missed two periods. Her breasts are swelling and tender. She has had morning sickness. I don't think I am in error.'

There was another silence, and then Lucille, narrowing her eyes, turned to Mary again. 'Tell me the truth, young lady, have you ever done anything—'

'No, Mother, honestly! He's wrong. I haven't even come *close* to doing anything like that.'

Lucille held her cold gaze on her daughter's face and she spoke. 'Dr Wade, did you examine my daughter for virginity?'

Jonas's mind whispered, 'Uh oh,' as he said patiently, 'No, I didn't do a pelvic exam. It's not something I routinely do on seventeen-year-old patients.'

Lucille turned her hard blue eyes to him and said, 'Then it would seem in order. That would clear this whole thing up.'

'I'm afraid not, Mrs. McFarland. The intact hymen is no proof of virginity. That's just a myth. There is a natural opening in the hymen so a girl can still have sexual intercourse without there being any break or stretching.'

Mary sank deep into the chair, crushed with embarrassment.

'It *is* a good idea, however,' he went on, 'to do a pelvic exam. If your daughter is pregnant, I should be able to see the obvious physical changes.'

Mary felt her mouth go dry. Please, God, she thought frantically, make all this go away.

'If you're asking my permission, Doctor,' she heard her mother's voice say, 'then you have it.'

43

Full of dread, Mary saw out of the corner of her eye Dr Wade's hand depress the intercom button, then she heard his voice ask the nurse to please come in.

Ten minutes later Mary was staring unhappily at the white ceiling of the exam room as she lay on her back. She clutched the cold metal sides of the table with sweating hands, and when she heard the exam room door open, she gulped.

The nurse had helped her undress, lie down and put her feet up in stirrups. The impersonal woman now stood by as Dr Wade situated himself between Mary's legs.

'This will only take a minute,' came his deep, reassuring voice. 'It won't hurt at all. You'll feel my hands pressing on your abdomen, nothing more.'

She sucked in her breath and, bracing herself, closed her eyes. When Dr Wade's gloved fingers slid into her vagina, Mary snapped her eyes open and forgot, for an instant, where she was and what was happening. It reminded her of something, of a dream she had had...

But when his other hand pressed down onto her pelvis, the elusive memory vanished and Mary was snatched back to the devastating humility of the moment.

She came into his office and sank into the chair beside her mother. 'Well?' said Lucille.

'It was awful.'

Lucille reached over and wordlessly patted her daughter's arm.

Mary's lower lip was quivering when the doctor came back to his desk; she lowered her head so she wouldn't have to look at him.

'Mrs. McFarland, the pelvic exam has corroborated the rest of the evidence. Now there is no doubt that Mary is pregnant.'

The girl jerked her head up, her mouth hanging open.

He looked at her and said, 'Visualisation shows the classic purple discolouration of the area. And palpation revealed that the uterus is soft and about the size of an orange. Definitely a pregnant uterus.'

'It can't be. . .' she whispered.

Lucille said, 'Dr Wade, what about the maidenhead?'

He shrugged. 'For what it's worth, Mrs. McFarland, it is intact. But that doesn't necessarily mean— '

'Nor does the size of the womb mean anything. I know about these things, Dr Wade. I had a hysterectomy because my womb was getting large. And frog tests aren't infallible either. You could have mixed up the specimens. Used someone else's by mistake. These things happen all the time.'

'Mrs. McFarland— '

'Dr Wade, my daughter would never do such a thing.' The woman rose, signalling to Mary to also stand. 'Frogs aren't infallible and neither are doctors. We'll go to someone else. Good evening.'

CHAPTER 4

Lucille buried her face in her hands and murmured, 'Oh dear God, dear God. . .'

Mary, slumped on the edge of her bed, searched the clutter of her room for words to say; her lips opened and closed experimentally on embryonic thoughts, but nothing would come. She was as stunned by the news as was her mother, whose thin shoulders started now to rise and fall in silent tears.

Far off in the coldly air-conditioned house came the sound of the front door opening and closing; Ted's voice calling out, his heavy footfall approaching the bedroom. Then he stood in the doorway, shirt collar unbuttoned, tie wrenched askew, jacket slung over one shoulder and hooked on a finger.

'What's up?'

Mary stared up at her father and, for an instant, felt sorry for him, but when her mouth opened to reply, it was Lucille's voice, coming from between her hands, that said shakily, 'Dr Evans just called. He said Mary's pregnant.'

Ted appeared at first not to have heard; he stood unmoving in the doorway, staring down at his wife and daughter. Then, like an actor trying out a new line, he said slowly, 'Mary's pregnant?'

'It's not true, Daddy,' she whispered. 'They're wrong.'

'Will you stop saying that!' Lucille drew her hands away from her face and straightened up, sniffing back the sobs. 'Where did I go wrong, Mary Ann? Why did you do this to me?'

Mary stared at her mother's swollen face. 'I don't know what to say.'

'You can start by telling us who the boy is. Mike Holland?'

'No!' Mary's voice came out a whine. 'Why can't you believe me! Mike and I never did anything!'

'What kind of fool do you take me for? Mary Ann!' Lucille's voice rose. 'I'm so ashamed!'

Mary looked pleadingly at her father. Ted tried to make an instant appraisal of the moment, figure out how to handle it and take command, but it was beyond his ken. This was something that only happened to other men's daughters.

'You've humiliated us,' came Lucille's thready voice. Her slender body trembled, her eyes welled again with tears.

Mary opened her mouth and spread out her hands, trying to make an offering.

'I believed you the first time,' continued Lucille, slowly coming to her feet. 'I made a fool of myself in front of Dr Wade. But Dr Evans is a gynaecologist. He says there's no doubt at all that you're pregnant. And I suppose, Mary Ann, what hurts me the most is that you lied to me.'

Ted finally stepped forward. 'We have to talk about this.'

Lucille dropped back a step. 'Not now, I'm too upset. I. . .I have to think. . .' She walked stiffly to the door. Pausing, she stood with her back to her husband and daughter and said, 'You have mortally wounded me, Mary Ann.'

The door closed softly behind her as she left; her footsteps could be heard fading down the hall.

Mary gazed up expectantly at her father. After a long moment passed, she timidly opened her mouth and whispered, 'Daddy...'

Visibly shaken, Ted McFarland sat on the edge of the bed and looked questioningly at his daughter. He didn't know what to say, how to start it, how to make his mouth form the words. He suddenly felt as if the world had been yanked out from under him and he was tumbling slowly in space.

'What happened?' he finally heard himself say.

'I don't know, Daddy. Both doctors say I'm going to have a baby.'

He nodded slowly. Somewhere at the periphery of his mind was the vague memory of Lucille's voice coming on during 'Perry Mason' about some fancy doctor in a flashy office who couldn't diagnose a simple case of the flu when he saw one, something about tests and the affrontery to accuse their daughter of being pregnant. And then Saturday afternoon as they sat sipping pina coladas by the pool while steaks simmered on the barbecue, Lucille had been smearing her thin brown body with suntan butter and saying that she was going to take Mary, who continued to be nauseated in the mornings, to a woman's doctor, a Dr Evans recommended by one of her friends who had had a hysterectomy recently.

Staring down now at Mary, Ted wondered: Where was I all this time?

'It's not true...' he heard a small voice say. 'I don't know what *is* wrong with me, Daddy, but I'm not what the doctors say I am.'

Ted cleared his throat, hoping that would get the words started; but still nothing came out.

'I know they did tests on me, Daddy, and I know they're doctors, but it just isn't possible.'

Ted was finally able to release a long sigh and shift his weight on the bed. 'Mary,' he said quietly. 'I can't help but feel this is all my fault.'

'Why?'

47

'I guess I wasn't a good enough parent. I didn't teach you properly— '

'Daddy! It has nothing to do with you. I have something wrong with me, an illness or something, that the doctors can't figure out. What does that have to do with your being a good father or not?'

'Kitten.' Ted brought his hand up and rested it alongside her face. 'Maybe your mother was right. Maybe I should have left you and Amy in Catholic school. Maybe this wouldn't have— '

'But, Daddy— '

'Listen to me, kitten. I don't think you've done anything bad, okay? Do you believe me?'

She nodded uncertainly.

'You probably didn't know what you were doing. Even now you probably don't realise what it is you've done. I always thought your mother taught you the facts of life— '

'Daddy,' she said beseechingly. 'I *know* how it's done, and I've never done anything like that. Like I told the doctors, I've never even come *close*.'

Ted frowned and searched his daughter's face. 'Mary, I don't think two doctors would tell you you're pregnant when you aren't.'

'But I'm not!' she cried. 'Daddy!' Tears suddenly filled her eyes and tumbled down her cheeks. 'You have to believe me! I'm innocent!'

'Hey...' he whispered, putting his arm around her and drawing her against him. Mary went limp and rested her head on his chest.She wept for another minute and then gradually grew silent and still. Ted held her tightly as he stared in wonder around the room.

'Mary,' he said quietly. 'I want you to trust me, okay?'

Her head went up and down against his shirt.

'I don't condemn you. I'm not angry or anything like that. I'm on your side, Mary, because you're my little girl. So I want to help you. Do you believe me?'

She nodded again.

'Kitten...I want you to tell me something.'

'Yes, Daddy?' came her muffled voice.

He drew in a breath. 'Who is the boy?'

There was a long silence in which neither father nor daughter moved; they appeared not even to breathe. Then Mary slowly and mechanically drew back from her father and stared at him. 'You believe them,' she whispered.

'I have to, kitten.'

'Why? Why do you have to believe them but you don't have to believe me?'

'Just tell me who it is, Mary. Is it Mike?'

She recoiled as if she had been struck. 'Daddy!' she wailed, her face twisted in horror. 'Oh, Daddy! Oh, God!'

When she leaped off the bed, Ted shot up and seized her arm. 'Don't run from me, kitten.'

'You're just like Mother! You really think I did it.'

'Mary—'

'*I can't believe this is happening to me—*'

In a sudden, swift move Mary wrested her arm free and ran to the door. 'Wait, Mary!' called Ted, going after her. But his own eyes were so blinded by tears that he couldn't see which way she ran.

Dr Jonas Wade was finishing up the last of his paperwork. The late-afternoon sun streamed through the large windows of his office, bringing in a summer heat that was offset by the building's refrigeration system. After sending his nurse home a short while before, he had set himself to the task of finishing charts, dictating correspondence, and making a start in the pile of medical journals.

It had been a slow afternoon. With the temperature over ninety and a haze of smog filling the valley basin, several patients had cancelled their appointments. Who could blame them? Even Gelson's Supermarket, he could see from where he sat, was like a ghost town. The sun wouldn't be setting for two hours yet; this was the hottest part of the day.

Dr Wade lifted his head when he thought he heard a sound coming from beyond the outer office. Someone was rattling the doorknob. When there came a quiet knocking, he rose and went out to the waiting room. Beyond the door he could hear footsteps walking away down the hall.

Jonas Wade opened the door and looked out. He was surprised to see Mary Ann McFarland standing by the elevators.

'Mary?' he called.

She turned around. For a moment she simply stared, then her mouth stretched into an apologetic smile and she walked toward him. 'Hi, Dr Wade. I thought you had gone home. Your door was locked.'

'Well, the office is closed. Did you want to see me?'

She gazed at him across the space and wondered why she had come here.

'You can come in if you like,' he said, stepping back and holding the door open.

When she walked hesitantly through, Jonas Wade saw the swelling of her eyes. He also noticed she was not as neat and prim as he had seen her last: her hair was messy, as if she had just gotten out of bed, and half her blouse had come untucked from her skirt. Mary followed him into the office and continued to stand after he had sat behind his desk. Then she absently fingered the nut-and-bolt skier as she tried to think of what to say.

After an awkward silence, Dr Wade said, 'How did you get here, Mary?'

'Bicycle...'

'In this heat?'

She raised her eyes to the large plate-glass windows and squinted at the yellow smoggy sun. 'Yes, I guess it is hot...'

'Mary, please sit down.'

She did so, but only at the edge of the chair, as if she might at any moment run.

'Would you like a cold drink?' he asked, watching her fingers twist and wring. 'I think we have a Pepsi in the fridge.'

'No, thank you.' Her head was bowed.

'What can I do for you, Mary?'

Her fingers plucked at her skirt, digging into the fabric and smoothing it out again. She considered Dr. Wade's voice. It was quiet and reassuring. 'I want to talk.'

'Okay.'

She slowly drew her head up and gazed at him. Dr. Wade's face was serious, but there was something about his eyes that was comforting. 'I don't really know why I came here. I just had to go somewhere. I just had to get *away*.'

'From what?'

'Home.'

'Why?'

She bowed her head again. 'I guess maybe I should have gone to Father Crispin instead, but sometimes he's not at the church. He goes places, you know, to hospitals and things. But I knew you would be here, Dr Wade, because it's Wednesday and, well, last Wednesday...'

'Yes, I remember last Wednesday.'

Mary brought her eyes up to him again. 'Dr Wade, please tell me it isn't true! Tell me I'm not what they say I am!'

'Who are *they*, Mary?'

'Dr Evans and my parents. My mother took me to see him after we left you and he said I'm going to have a baby.'

'I see...'

'And my mother was so upset!' The words came out in a rush now. Tears streamed down Mary's cheeks as she spoke rapidly. 'I've never seen her so upset! And Daddy's no better because he thinks I did it with Mike. But I've never done it, Dr Wade, because I've been taught it's wrong and that you shouldn't do it until you're married and that it's a sin but I don't know why they won't believe me because *I am telling the truth!*'

Dr Wade leaned back in his chair, his manner patient and attentive. 'I know Dr Evans personally. He's an excellent doctor, Mary.'

'But he's wrong.'

'Mary.' Jonas Wade abruptly rose and strode around his desk. The girl kept her eyes on him as he took a seat in the chair next to her. He leaned forward, resting his elbows on his knees. 'Mary, you're an intelligent girl. I'll bet you get good grades.'

51

'I'm an honour student.'

'I'm impressed. You also told me you took human physiology, so you must realise that what you're claiming isn't possible.'

She shook her head. 'It's because of what I learned in school that I know what you and Dr Evans say isn't possible.'

Dr Wade considered this for a moment. 'Mary, do you know anything about contraception?'

'I know that it's wrong.'

'I see.' He drew back from her. He weighed his next words before saying, 'You go to St. Sebastian's, don't you?'

'Yes.'

'I thought so. And you belong to CYO?'

'Yes.'

Jonas Wade nodded slowly. Keeping his eyes on her face, he tried to see beyond the youthful features, now twisted in confusion and pain, tried to delve the wintry blue eyes to see if some small shred, some fleeting shadow of her thoughts could be glimpsed there. But all Jonas Wade found was the guileless honesty of the innocent, the frank bewilderment of the wrongly accused. And then a thought struck him, and for the moment, gave him pause. It occurred to Jonas Wade that the girl was telling the truth.

And as if this instrusive idea had found a switch in his brain, pressed it, and triggered off a dusty memory, Dr Jonas Wade, staring at the unabashed innocence of the face before him, found himself remembering something he had read, not long ago, about an unmarried mother in England who had caused a stir by claiming to have been a virgin...

'Mary,' said Dr Wade finally. 'Do your parents know you're here?'

'No. Even *I* didn't know I was coming here. I just ran out of the house and grabbed my bike and rode as far as I could. I don't know what made me come here. I guess I just had to talk to someone and there didn't seem to be anyone else...'

'I'll have to call them, Mary.'

She sighed. 'I know.' Shifting her gaze back to the window

and the flat yellow sky, Mary heard Dr Wade dial the telephone.

He lived in a split-level ranch-style home in the better part of Woodland Hills, north of Chalk Hill, on a eucalyptus-lined street where wagon wheels supported mailboxes and the houses were set far back from the road behind leaf-strewn lawns and circular drives. The Wade house sat on a full acre; a strung-out, haphazard connection of rooms built in the peculiarly Southern California architectural style pictur-esquely called 'rancho'. Large picture windows gave out onto a neat front yard and corral-style fencing, and in the rear, upon a rambling back yard congested with orange and avocado trees, a Spanish-tile swimming pool, and down at the far end, unused horse stables.

Jonas Wade now leaned against the cool glass of this window, sipping a tequila sunrise and watching a group of young people expend their energies in the pool. From the kitchen came aromas of Penny Wade's indoor barbecue dinner, and occasionally, through the glass, Jonas could hear the squeals of Cortney and her friends as they tossed one another into the water.

But he wasn't thinking about what he saw, smelled or heard; Jonas Wade, since delivering Mary Ann McFarland into the care of her distraught parents, had been unable to get the girl out of his mind.

He had been part of that scene several times in his career: frenzied teen-ager, anguished parents. Only this time it had been slightly different – the girl not so frenzied, and that un-nerving continued protestation of her innocence.

As Jonas Wade absently watched the playful flirting of the swimmers, he felt another thought wrestle for his attention; it had come to him during his brief visit with the McFarland girl: the sliver of a memory about a magazine article – where? when? – about a similar situation. An article he had glanced over and then immediately put out of his mind, remembered now for the familiarity of the circumstances. In England. A doctor researching the case, believing the woman to be telling the truth. Some tests. Some interesting evidence. But the findings...what?

Penny whisked through the living room, her wedgies clacking on the polished parquet floor; Jonas caught a glimpse of her as she sped behind him – petite, agile, wearing tennis shorts and a halter, her black hair still in big plastic rollers. As she passed through, Penny called over her shoulder, 'Dinner'll be ready in ten minutes. Call the kids in, will you?'

Jonas pushed away from the window, drank down the last of the sunrise, and walked to the back door. Opening it, he felt the oppressive afternoon sweep over him, carrying with its hot breath the scents of new eucalyptus leaves, rotting fruit, dead grass and dust, and pool chlorine. He hated, for the moment, to pull the teen-agers out of their revelling and into the cold air-conditioned house. He stared at their slender brown bodies glistening and dripping; two girls and two guys, laughing and shrieking.

'Hey, kids!' he called.

They paused and turned to look at him: eighteen-year-old Cortney on the diving board poised to jump; her best friend Sarah Long sitting on the steps; nineteen-year-old Brad and his fraternity brother Tom suspended in the deep end waiting to catch Cortney.

'Supper's on, get dried off!'

Jonas turned back into the house, hearing Cortney's final splash, then the slapping of wet feet on the pavement, gasps, and laughter. He closed the door on them.

Going back to the bar for a refill, Jonas nodded and smiled at Carmelita as she bustled past; not a bad housekeeper, even if she didn't speak English. Sometimes they made the best ones; living in fear of discovery by the immigration authorities, they worked hard and were always cheerful. And once a week, the Wades were treated to enchiladas and tostadas that could only be found south of the border.

From the bar he went to his study and hesitated in the doorway, uncertain of why he had come in here.

His eyes settled on the new certificate which lay on his desk waiting to be framed and hung up; an honour, to be reelected president of the Society of Galen for yet another year. When he had received it last Saturday night, at the June meeting of the secret and elitist club which had a total membership of twenty, Jonas had been proud and momentarily speechless. Only a day later, the glory had faded, as these brief honours always did. After all, he had been one of the founders of the Society of Galen, had been the one to limit membership to twenty, and had seen to it that, over the years, only the most select and patrician physicians were granted the coveted admission. So they had elected him president again, to sit at the head of the table when they met each month at Lawry's to engage in some stimulating medical talk. A Pyrrhic victory, really.

He brought his eyes away and scanned the shelves of books and magazines lining one wall. Something nagged at him; it had been in these somewhere, in all of this, that he had read about that case in England.

Only barely hearing the teen-age cries that suddenly filled the house, Jonas went to the wall of shelves and trailed his eyes first over the book spines, then over the stacks of magazines. Reading the titles – JAMA, *Scientific American, California Physicians' Medical Journal* – he felt his mind slowly open up and admit, bit by bit, a few more recollections of the elusive article.

In London. An unmarried woman gave birth to a daughter. She insisted she had never been with a man. Her doctors scoffed. But a geneticist – what was her name? – had taken up the cause. Performed tests on the child. Skin grafts. Some primitive and unreliable chromosomatic tests. And the result had been—

Jonas closed his eyes. What had the findings been!

'Honey?'

He spun around.

Penny, her hair combed out and teased into a perfect bouffant, was smiling in the doorway. 'Beans are on!' Then she was gone, wedgies clop-clopping down the hall.

Jonas paused another moment, then went to the phone on his desk. Wednesday night. No telling if Bernie would be home or not.

Bernie had been home and had said he would come over after dinner. Through the T-bone steaks and Brussels sprouts and avocado-and-grapefruit salad Jonas continued to dwell on the McFarland problem. After calling his best friend, a geneticist at UCLA, Jonas Wade had spent a few more minutes trying to remember where he had read the article, then had come to the table in refracted thought.

Cortney and Brad, with their guests for the evening, dominated the dinner conversation with a serious debate on which drive-in to go to. The choice was between *Lawrence of Arabia* and a 'beach-blanket' movie; the foursome was firmly divided.

When Carmelita served the sugared strawberries, Wade shook himself out of his distraction and tried to pay attention to his company. He looked fondly upon Cortney, an unblemished youthful image of Penny. He compared himself to Ted McFarland, who had sat grey-faced and impotent in his office a few hours earlier, and thanked God that he had never had any serious trouble with Cortney. There had been that brief phase three years ago, when she was fifteen, when she had gotten in with a bad crowd. Leather jackets, cars with front ends lowered, Cortney blasting the house with 'Red River Rock,' spit curls and ugly pins in her hair, cracking gum and sassing back at Penny. But Jonas had pulled Cortney out of Birmingham High and had used his influence to get her into the newly opened Taft High. Now she was studying drama at San Fernando Valley State College and getting straight A's. It wouldn't be long before she found a young man to marry – like Brad's Alpha Phi brother Tom, an energetic economics student who was clearly going to make his way in the world and who clearly had his eye on Cortney. And then Brad would go from UCLA to Stanford Law School like his grandfather, fulfill his ambition to become a trial attorney, marry someone like Cortney, and settle down here in the valley. Then Jonas and Penny would have the house to themselves at last and life would move comfortably on.

56

Jonas Wade looked down at his strawberries. And boringly on, whispered a voice at the back of his mind.

Bernie showed up while Carmelita was doing the dishes and Penny was in her sewing room fixing new canvas to her rug-hooking frame. The kids streamed out through the front door; they had settled on miniature golfing, so Jonas and his friend had peace and privacy.

After fixing a couple of drinks, the two men settled into the dark, leathery comfort of Jonas Wade's study and talked a bit about the rising tide of unrest in the South, voicing particular concern over the action of Governor Wallace when the federalised national guard troops had taken over the University of Alabama. Then, relaxing, they moved onto more local news: would the new proposed freeway take the pressure off Sepulveda Pass? Finally, Jonas worked the conversation around to what was on his mind.

Bernie Schwartz, a forty-four-year-old geneticist who did his work at UCLA, was a short, plump, balding man who listened to his best friend's story with keen interest. They shared more than just the Avenida Hacienda in Woodland Hills and Saturday mornings golfing at the Country Club; Jonas and Bernie were of like minds – intellectually thirsty and always ready for a good debate. A few years before, Jonas had tried his best to get Bernie into the Society of Galen, but his own founding law of medical doctors only had foiled that plan. So they held private meetings, once a week over drinks and rare steaks, away from the company of women and kids, agreeing or arguing, depending on the issue.

Now Bernie sipped his scotch and listened intently, and when Jonas came to the end of Mary McFarland's short tale and asked, 'So what do you think?' Bernie Schwartz said, 'Me? You want my opinion? You're the doctor, Jonas, I'm just a humble country geneticist.'

'Give me your opinion, Bernie.'

'Okay, she's either lying to protect the boy, or she really has forgotten the sexual encounter. I say send her to a psychiatrist.'

Jonas gave a few moments to thought, staring into his

drink, then said, 'Bernie, what are you doing in the lab these days?'

The silvery, bushy eyebrows arched. 'We're working with nucleotide components and DNA synthesis. Specifically, catalysing ATP into amino acids. Why?'

'What can you tell me about parthenogenesis?'

'Parthenogenesis? Well, by definition, it's the development of an ovum into an embryo without benefit of sperm. Literally, virgin birth. Why?'

'I know what the word means, Bernie, what I want you to do is enlighten me on the phenomenon as it occurs in nature.'

'I assume you mean animals as opposed to plants. Okay...' He hoisted his chunky shoulders. 'From what I recall, it occurs naturally in some species of lower animals, guppies for instance, and there's a lizard species that is all female and self-reproducing. Some frogs, maybe— '

'Higher up the scale than that.'

'Okay, let me see, some farmers are causing parthenogenesis to occur in a strain of turkeys, to improve the breed I think— '

'I'm not interested in manmade parthenogenesis, Bernie, I'm talking *spontaneous* parthenogenesis.'

Bernie fixed his sharp little eyes on his friend. 'Spontaneous parthenogenesis occurs only in lower animals, Jonas.'

'Not in mammals?'

'Mammals? I've never heard of it occurring naturally in mammals.' The tiny eyes stretched. 'Wait a minute, you don't think this girl— '

'I heard or read somewhere about experimentation on fatherless mice. What do you know about that?'

'Fatherless mice...' Bernie's Semitic face darkened. 'That was some time ago, Jonas, but it wasn't spontaneous, it was laboratory-induced.' He scratched his chin thoughtfully. 'Mammalian parthenogenesis is a subject that's touched upon now and then, but not given much serious notice. God, where did I read about it lately? One of my throwaway periodicals – they're studying that breed of turkeys...'

'Tell me about the turkeys then.'

'Okay, let me think now. It was in Maryland, a place called Beltsville. Some turkey farmer noticed that embryonic growth started on its own in a large number of unfertilised eggs. Although most of them stopped developing before the embryo was fully formed, I think something like one in six actually reached maturity and were hatched. Experiments were then performed by mating those parthenogenic turkeys, the ones that came out of the "fatherless" eggs, with cocks whose daughters had produced parthenogenic eggs. Soon, farmers had poults that were laying eggs that had never had sperm.'

'I don't see how that's possible.'

Bernie shrugged again. 'As far as I remember, all of the parthenogenic birds had the diploid number of chromosomes that was the normal number in their body cells.'

'How can that be?'

'Evidently the chromosomes of the unfertilised egg simply doubled.'

Jonas stared at his drink as he swirled it around his glass. 'Do they know what caused the embryos to start to grow without being fertilised?'

Bernie thought a moment. 'I don't recall exactly. But I don't think they found out why.' He downed the rest of his scotch and gave another characteristic shrug. 'There just isn't much data in that field, Jonas. Ask the man in the street and he won't know what parthenogenesis means. A lot of furor was raised a few years back by that Spurway business and for a few months every geneticist in the world was watching London, but since then it's died down.'

Jonas slapped a fist into his palm. 'That's it! Spurway! Dr Helen Spurway!' He bolted to his feet and marched over to the bookshelves. 'She's the one I read about somewhere...'

'It was eight years ago, Jonas, in nineteen fifty-five.'

'Damn.' Dr Wade fingered the stack of recent scientific journals. Then he did a quick mental check of his schedule for tomorrow: surgery in the morning, no patients in the afternoon; he could go to the UCLA Medical Library.

'Jonas,' came Bernie's quiet voice. 'You still want my opinion?'

'Of course.'

'Send her to a psychiatrist.'

Jonas Wade heaved a sigh and turned away from the magazines. 'I suppose I agree with you. I recommended psychiatric help to her parents this afternoon and they didn't exactly jump at it. According to the girl's mother, their priest is all they need.'

'Oy vay.'

'They have a point, Bernie. Anyway, if they ask my opinion again, I'll push for psychiatric counselling. In the meantime, I'm going to see if I can't find out what makes those turkeys tick.'

CHAPTER 5

He should have been there by now. He wished he were.

Sitting in the den with a double scotch and staring at the dead TV screen, Ted McFarland wished fervently this could have been a normal Wednesday night. His gym night. He hated not going; if ever he needed the release, it was now.

But of course he couldn't leave. Not now. Someone had to hold things together; someone had to be a ballast, at least *act* strong. With the house dark and quiet, filled with the sultry heat of June, someone had to sit and watch.

But for what?

Amy was at her catechism class, Mary was locked in her room not speaking to anyone, and Lucille...

Ted heard from the next room the occasional clink of the scotch bottle against her glass.

Lucille's initial anger with Mary had melted into sorrow and then into disappointment; now she was struggling to find a way to communicate with her daughter, to find out from

Mary what should be done, to ask her why she had done this, let the family down, tainted them all. But Ted knew what Lucille was really contending with: sudden, unhappy reminders of her past.

He continued to stare at the lifeless TV set. He had vetoed a rush visit to Father Crispin, which was what Lucille had wanted to do after leaving Dr Wade's office. Ted knew such a meeting with the priest was right premature and would come to nothing. For one thing, Lucille had been drinking. And Mary was sullen and uncommunicative. But certainly tomorrow; Father Crispin would know what to do.

Ted McFarland loved his older daughter so much it created a blinding ache in his chest. The reason was no mystery: having never known his own mother and having been brought up in a home for boys, Ted had grown up with fantasy notions of sisters and daughters. When Lucille had been in labour, Ted had spent the night lighting candles and praying in the church for a baby girl.

Amy had been a delight to him, too, but she had come five years later, and then there had been that unpleasantness about her birth that had tarnished her specialness.

Mary was his total pride, his trophy, his reason for breathing. She delighted his eyes with her young and slender beauty, made him laugh with her wit and innocent charm. Mary had a heart-shaped face and stunning blue eyes and long, tanned legs. Watching her emerge into womanhood was like watching the opening of a rose, and Ted, unlike many men, had not lamented the loss of his daughter's childhood.

But now – he stared darkly ahead – she was emerging too far. He could not bear to picture her in a pregnant state with a large belly hidden under maternity clothes. He could not face the thought of seeing her gradually stretch and distort, puff up and balloon out until nothing of the lithe beauty remained. It was like the desecration of a temple, graffiti on a church wall; she would get varicose veins like purple ropes, stretch marks, sagging breasts—

Ted suddenly dropped his glass and doubled over, clutching his stomach as if he had been kicked.

Mary, Mary, cried his tormented mind. My beautiful Mary. Where did I go wrong?

She stood in front of the full-length mirror that hung on the inside of her closet door and gazed at her naked body.

In the golden light of her desk lamp, which she had directed upon herself, with the rest of the room in darkness, Mary stared hypnotically.

It was the first time she had ever really seen her nude body. In the bathroom whenever she bathed she only caught glimpses of bare shoulders and back in the steamy glass; and whenever she dressed and undressed here in the bedroom she always unconsciously turned her back to the mirror. In the shower during PE all the girls clutched their small towels to the front in nervous modesty; Mary had seen few naked females. Her mother had her own bathroom and dressing room off the master bedroom, and whenever Amy used the bathroom she shared with her sister, she always locked it, entering and leaving in a thick bathrobe. Even in the summer, they got in and out of their swimsuits separately, respecting one another's privacy.

It was fascinating now to stand boldly before the mirror and brazenly inspect her naked form. There was embarrassment, a feeling of doing something shameful; Mary felt uneasy beneath the scrutiny of her own eyes.

And yet she had to see, she had to know.

Was there anything different?

The shoulders were the same, angular and straight, like a swimmer's; the arms long and gently muscular; the hips softly swelling out from a narrow waist; thighs not too fleshy – firm and tight; the legs long and smooth. Her skin was the colour of an early sunrise. Mary's usual deep summer tan had only barely begun. Not a blemish anywhere; soft, satiny, rising and falling in shadow and light.

Her eyes came to rest on her breasts. She stared at the nipples. They seemed darker somehow, slightly larger than they had been before. And the breasts themselves, was it her imagination that they appeared larger? That they tingled?

Mary hesitantly brought up a hand, softly cupped one breast and pressed lightly. She winced.

With her other hand, she crossed over and covered the other breast, gingerly embracing it and feeling the soreness.

The reflection in the mirror of the golden body with arms crossed and hands cradling the breasts caused Mary to think, for a fleeting moment, of herself as Venus rising out of a shell.

She let her arms drop and continued to stare transfixed at herself. Mary felt as if she were gazing at another female, trespassing upon this woman's modesty with her exploring eyes. She felt detached, impersonal, as if she inspected a statue.

Muffled footsteps approaching from down the hall caused Mary to suck in her breath and listen. The footsteps paused before her bedroom door, then continued to the left and eventually faded into her parents' bedroom.

Mary released a sigh; her eyes continued their search. When they came to her abdomen, she brought up her hands and rested them on the cool skin below her navel. They lay flat, trying to sense through the wall of flesh and muscle what lay beneath. Mary had a tight, flat belly. But what had Dr Wade said? 'It's going to start showing soon...'

She frowned. *What* was going to start showing? There was a mystery here, beneath her hands, and whatever it was, Mary did not like it. Dr Wade had to be wrong; nothing was growing under there.

When her fingertips accidentally brushed the edge of her pubic hair, she drew her hands away. She returned to staring at her face.

What was happening to her? What had caused the morning sickness and the unexplainable swelling of her breasts? Two doctors said it was pregnancy, and yet Mary knew that was impossible.

She frowned again, trying to put together what little she knew about such things. Maybe she should talk to Germaine. Germaine was so worldly and educated; her UCLA boyfriend was twenty and he had introduced Germaine to the

63

liberal life. They belonged to CORE and were always talking about revolution and free love. But it was not a subject Mary could comfortably discuss. As close as they were and as many secrets as they shared, the sex thing had always been something unspoken, understood.

So Mary tried to search her own limited knowledge on the subject to learn what might really be wrong with her.

Then she remembered something. Her period. When was the last time she had had to report it in PE so she didn't have to shower? It had been a long time ago. . .

Mary was distracted by the sound of more footsteps down the hall, heavier ones, and then the soft murmuring of voices.

'Psychiatric counselling,' said Lucille softly, sitting at her dressing table with her chin resting on her hands. 'I don't know, Ted, I don't care for the idea.'

'I think it's for her own good,' came Ted's tired voice.

Lucille stared at herself in the mirror, seeing a stranger there. 'Do you know what this reminds me of, Ted?' she said in a near whisper. Lucille was speaking more to herself than to her husband. 'Rosemary Franchimoni.'

'Not now, Lucille— '

She continued in a subdued voice, 'I had a long talk with Rosemary Franchimoni just before she died – you know, at the hospital – and she told me, just before she died, that she hadn't wanted that baby in the first place. Ted, she didn't even want that baby. She told me she was frightened because the doctor had warned her not to get pregnant again.'

Lucille watched her lips as they moved. Behind her, Ted stood in the centre of the bedroom, unmoving.

'It wasn't fair, Ted. Nobody asked Rosemary Franchimoni what *she* wanted. . .' Lucille swallowed with difficulty. 'It's not Mary's fault, Ted, it's that boy's fault. I know how men will force themselves, saying it's their *right*. And women have to. . .' She shook her head and tried to focus on the image of the woman before her. 'I mean, it's all right for me now, I'm one of the lucky ones. I'm safe, ever since I had it all taken out— '

'Lucille, for God's sake— '

64

'But what if I hadn't had that operation? What if we weren't safe, had that thing always hanging over us? What if I could get pregnant and die from it?'

The unspoken answer hung in the air. In the mirror, Lucille met Ted's gaze and clung to it. 'You know what you have to do,' she said distantly.

He stared at her quizzically.

Lucille got to her feet and turned around. 'You have to find someone, Ted. You have to spare your daughter this shame.'

It took a few seconds for her meaning to sink in, and when it did, Ted gaped at his wife in disbelief. 'What did you say?' he whispered.

'You know what I mean. I want you to find someone who'll take care of Mary. Get rid of that thing...'

'No,' he whispered. 'I won't do that.'

'You have to. You can't let her go through life with it. It will ruin her, you have to protect our daughter, Ted. Take her to someone.'

'But I can't. I mean...' He turned away from her and searched the room for an exit. 'I don't know about these things. I've never heard of anyone. I wouldn't even know where to begin.'

'Then let Nathan Holland take care of it. We both know it was his son that did it to her.'

'Nathan...' Ted rubbed his forehead.

'I want you to talk to him, tell him it's his responsibility. Tell him how his boy has ruined our daughter. Ted!' Lucille raised her voice. 'I don't want her to go through life with it! I want that thing gotten rid of!'

'Dear Jesus—'

'Ted, you have to do this for me. For us!' She reached out for his arm but he stepped away. 'I won't let her suffer the shame, the agony of it. I want her spared. Ted, you're her father, *do something*'.

He turned slowly around and looked at his wife with heavy, sad eyes. Then he nodded. 'Nathan. Yes... He has to be told...' Then he could think of nothing more to say.

With her naked back flat against her bedroom door, Mary gaped in wide-eyed shock into the darkness before her.

From the moment Ted had first entered the master bedroom, she had heard every word of the conversation.

Moving blindly, Mary pushed away from the door, rushed to her desk and pulled open a drawer. Her hand fell upon the diary, a plastic-bound little book with a gold lock, and brought it out to the light. Mary had written in this diary during two of her junior high school years and then had discarded it as childish and immature.

Driven now by an impulse she could not define, Mary sat down at the desk, flipped through pages full of gossip, teacher crushes, movies and fads, and thirteen-year-old dreams until she came to the last written page.

On the blank page next to it she wrote:

I'm a virgin and no one believes me. I want to die.

CHAPTER 6

'Mrs Kennedy's condition this morning is reported as continued normal and healthy. On the foreign scene, black smoke continues to rise from the Sistine Chapel as no successor has yet been found to Pope John the Twenty-third. A spokesman for the College of Cardinals said early this morning that an agreement should be reached— '

Ted clicked off the radio.

The Holland house appeared around the curve; it sat on the crest of Taylor Road amid sycamore and palm trees. Ted slowly eased his Continental up the steep drive and killed the engine before the car had rolled to a complete stop.

It was a nice home, the Hollands', one of the nicest in the neighbourhood. Nathan Holland, in his position as an insurance-company executive, could afford gardeners, cleaning ladies, and year-round maintenance on the house. Ted had always admired the environment Nat Holland raised his boys in.

He also liked Nat Holland. They had known each other for just over a year, ever since Mary had first started bringing Mike home last summer. He and Lucille had come here twice for dinner, and in December for a Christmas party. It was phenomenal how Nathan Holland managed three boys, kept the house always in order, and paid full-time attention to his demanding job.

Ted reached over, turned the ignition key to 'battery' and flicked the air conditioner on. Eleven o'clock in the morning and already the air was hot and heavy. Ted stared ahead at the neatly sculpted hedge skirting the house.

Lucille had not uttered a word this morning. She had groaned awake to the clanging alarm, scuffled into the bath-room, and gulped down four Bayer aspirins and a packet of Fizrin. She had later wordlessly brewed a pot of strong coffee and made a plate of toast and bacon which no one touched. She had looked awful, worse than Ted could ever remember. Lucille's face had been haggard and drawn, the eyes supported on two purple half moons, the whites mapped with red lines. Her hair had been a poor facsimile of her usual bouffant; there were holes in it and places where the teasing stuck out. She had said nothing to Ted when he had announced his intention of going to visit Nathan Holland.

Ted felt no better than his wife. There was a peculiar pounding in his head that he hadn't felt since the morning after his bachelor party nineteen years before. He felt deflated and purposeless.

As Ted rested his head on the steering wheel he was immediately stabbed with the pain of a guilty memory. The night before, after Lucille had drifted off into a deep sleep, Ted had been jangled to awareness by the ringing of the phone. It had been Amy. Calling to see where everyone was. Catechism had been over for half an hour and she was still waiting for Mom to pick her up.

Ted now raised his head and screwed his eyes tightly. Amy, we forgot all about you...

The twelve-year-old had been disappointed to come home to find no lights on in the house and both her mother and sister already asleep; she had had some important news to tell them, but now it seemed it would have to wait.

The whole evening had been so twisted, like a bad dream, that Ted wished he could forget it; but he knew that in remembering there was emotion, and emotion fired him with enough will to keep moving. He had to talk to Nathan Holland. That was the only next logical step. Maybe between the two of them they could figure out what to do.

When the front door suddenly opened, Ted snapped back to life. He turned off the air conditioner, grabbed the car keys, and jumped out of the car.

'Hi, Nat,' he called, giving a small wave.

Holland grinned. 'I thought I heard you pull up. Come on in. Getting hot out here!'

Shortly after getting up that morning, Ted had given Nathan Holland a call, telling him there was something important they had to discuss. When Nat had suggested Ted drop by his office, Ted had said he preferred that they be totally alone. So they had agreed to meet here at eleven.

'I really appreciate your taking time off like this for me,' he said as they shook hands.

'Not at all, Ted.' Nathan closed the front door and led the way into the cool interior. 'I've already been to the office. Told my secretary I was going to take a long lunch. Care for some coffee?'

Ted hesitated. 'Yes. Please. The boys around?'

Nathan spoke over his shoulder as he headed toward the kitchen. 'Mike and Matt are at school, but it's only a half-day session so I expect they'll be home before long. Last day of school tomorrow, you know.'

'Yes...' Ted rubbed his temples as he looked around the living room. 'I know...' He walked over to the couch and stared down at it. 'Where's young Timothy?' he called out.

'Down the street in a neighbour's pool. School's been out

for him for a week now. I'll be there in a minute, Ted, make yourself comfortable.'

That was easy to do in the Holland living room. Decorated in the currently popular Spanish style with thick shag carpeting, deep leather furniture, black wrought iron, Spanish wood and potted ferns, the room was restful, conducive to sitting back and relaxing. But Ted couldn't relax. His mind would not let go of the memory of Lucille's voice the night before. The appalling intimation of her words. 'You're her father. Get rid of that thing.'

Of course Ted had no intention of following such a course. Last night, in his haze of scotch, it had almost sounded like a godsend; quick, secretive, nip it in the bud before it can blossom. Clear the dirt away before anyone knows it's there. But in the light of morning Ted was sickened by the mere hint of abortion, and he was certain Lucille had also seen the monstrousness of her words.

When Nathan returned with a tray bearing two cups of coffee, bowls of cream and sugar, and a few slices of pound cake, Ted sat down.

'It's nice to see you again,' said Nathan. 'How're Lucille and the girls?'

'Oh. . .fine. You and the boys?'

'Couldn't be better.'

The men sat opposite one another, Ted on the bronze-green velvet couch and Nathan in a black-leather captain's chair. The tray was placed between them on a low Spanish wood coffe table.

The idea of putting anything into his stomach revolted Ted, but he managed to force a bit of hot black coffee between his lips. Then he cradled the cup in both hands.

He eyed the man across from him. Nathan Holland was a large robust man in his fifties with a head of thick white leonine hair. His voice was bass, making Ted think of an actor or a singer. His grey eyes seemed always amused. 'How's the insurance business, Nat?'

'Can't complain. And the market?'

Ted frowned into his steaming coffee. How long was he going to keep this up?

Finally, putting his cup down and facing Nathan squarely, Ted said, 'I didn't come here to talk any kind of business, Nat. I'm afraid it's something serious.'

Nathan Holland nodded slowly, eyeing his visitor over the rim of his cup as he drank.

'Nat, I've got a problem. And I want you to know this isn't easy for me.'

Nathan put down his cup and gazed earnestly at his friend. 'What's up?'

Ted ran a dry tongue over his lips and tried to think of a way to say the words. There was only one way: 'Nat, my daughter is pregnant.'

The grey eyes remained unblinking for a moment, the ruddy face expressionless. Finally, after what seemed to Ted too long, Nathan Holland said, 'What?'

'I said my daughter is pregnant.'

'Which one?'

Ted frowned. Which one? 'Mary. Mary is pregnant.'

'Oh, for— ' Nathan Holland slapped his palms on his knees and sat back in the chair. 'I can't believe it.'

Ted stared down at his hands, wishing they had something to do, and murmured, 'I know. I can't either. It's like...' He shook his head.

'Ted.' Nathan's voice was low. 'When did you find out?'

'Yesterday afternoon.'

'Can there be any doubt? Another doctor maybe— '

'No, Lucille took Mary to two doctors. They both agreed.'

There was another long silence, then Nathan said, 'What does Mary say?'

Ted felt a sudden rage boil up within him; the fury of frustration, of being so impotent. He shot to his feet and strode to the enormous flagstone fireplace, leaned one elbow on the mantel, and glowered darkly into the black pit. 'She denies it,' he said in a tight voice. 'That's half the misery of it, Nat: Mary insists it isn't possible, that she isn't pregnant.'

Nathan nodded gravely, his eyes full of sympathy. 'I guess

maybe they usually do. Poor thing, she must be frightened to death.'

Ted brought up his other arm and rested it also on the Spanish wood mantel. Then he bent his head until his forehead rested on his fists.

Somewhere in the house a clock ticked softly. From the kitchen came the click and hum of the refrigerator regulating itself. Outside, the swimming-pool filter gurgled; a trio of starlings trilled to one another in the marble birdbath.

Hours and weeks and days went by as the two men remained motionless, their coffee growing cold, the house growing increasingly silent around them. When, in the distance, an unseen clock chimed the half hour, Ted heard Nathan's heavy voice say softly, 'I know why you've come here, Ted. You think it's Mike.'

He took in a deep breath and let it out slowly. 'Yes.'

'Okay. Let's talk about it.'

Ted turned around and looked at the man in the chair. Their eyes met for an instant, and then they both averted their faces. 'Listen, Nat, I'm not accusing him, okay? Mary never said anything. She even denies being pregnant. If she's doing it to protect someone, I want to know who it is and bring it out in the open so she won't have to lie anymore. And Mike, well, he seemed like the likely one.'

Nathan Holland felt a great weight descend upon his shoulders. He rose to his feet like a tired old man. 'Okay, Ted, we'll talk to Mike. Then what?'

Ted returned to staring into the cold fireplace. Then what? He had no idea. What did fathers of pregnant girls do? What do you do with a girl not yet in the twelfth grade that has a baby growing inside her, getting bigger every day? What do you say to her? How do you act around her? What about the neighbours? The church congregation? What do you do about the rest of her high school education? How do you hide her? And what about at the end? What do you do with a baby no one wants?

Hearing Lucille's voice echo again in his head, Ted pushed away from the fireplace and strode around the couch.

71

Slamming his fist into his palm, he said, 'Nat, I don't know what to do! I just don't know what to do!'

'We'll think of something, Ted, don't worry. We'll take care of Mary.'

Yes, thought Ted bleakly, but who'll take care of the rest of us?

When the back door of the house slammed, both men whipped around. They stared unmoving in the direction of the kitchen and heard sounds of cupboards opening and closing, the refrigerator door opening and closing, the rattling of a cookie box. Presently Mike emerged with a glass of milk in one hand and a plate of ginger snaps in the other.

Looking up, he started. 'Hey! Wow, you startled me. Hi, Mr. McFarland. What are you doing home, Dad?'

'Son, we want to talk to you. Can you join us for a minute?'

Mike shrugged. 'Sure.' But when he neared them and saw their faces, he stopped where he was with the glass halfway to his lips. 'Hey, what's up? You look like you're going to a funeral.'

'Mike, please sit down.'

He looked from his father to Ted McFarland and back to his father. 'All right. . .'

When all three were seated, with Mike on the couch next to Ted and his snack on the table with the cold coffee, Nathan cleared his bass voice and said, 'Son, Mr McFarland is here because of a serious matter. And we think it concerns you.'

'Okay, Dad.'

'Mike, Mary McFarland is pregnant.'

The same stunned silence that had followed Ted's first announcement to Nathan once again filled the living room. Seventeen-year-old Mike Holland, a youthful replica of his ruddy father, stared with the same grey eyes. He also, after a long moment, said, 'What?'

'Mary McFarland is pregnant.'

'Aw— ' His hands curled into fists. 'Aw, no, Dad! I don't believe it!'

'It's true,' came Ted quietly, studying the boy's face.

'Oh, wow! Oh, man!' Mike got to his feet and walked away from the two men. 'Oh, Jesus—'

'Mike,' said Nathan Holland. 'Are you responsible?'

The boy whirled around. 'Am I *what*?'

'Come clean, Mike. Tell me the truth.'

Staring at the sombre faces of the two seated men, Mike Holland felt his bowels suddenly crawl. 'Hey, look—' He spread out his hands. 'It can't be me, honest! I mean, Mary and me, we never—'

'Mike!' Nathan rose to his feet and regarded his son with mounting anger. 'Did you get Mary McFarland pregnant?'

'Aw, Dad, I—' He searched frantically around the room. 'No, it's not possible. I mean, Jesus, she and I never did anything.'

'Don't give me that!' shouted Nathan, his face turning red. 'I've heard you on the phone bragging to your friends about your conquests! I've heard you tell Rick on the phone about Mulholland Drive. Come on, Mike, *what do you take me for!*'

As the boy slowly backed away, jerking his head from side to side, Ted McFarland stared at father and son in horror. A new thought was beginning to come together in his brain, an idea that had not, until this moment, occurred to him. But now that it had, he felt his blood start to race.

Mary had been spoiled.

And Mike Holland had bragged to his friends about having done it!

'Mike,' he said with choked control, 'Mike, it's only natural you'd deny it. I wouldn't expect otherwise. But for the love of God, Mary's trying to protect you and she's going through hell for it.'

'Hey,' the youth's face was stricken. 'Mr McFarland, honest, I've never done anything with Mary—'

'What about boasting to your friends?'

'She would never let me touch her!'

Ted flew to his feet, his pulse thumping in his ears. 'Why don't you be a man and admit it!'

Nathan turned around. 'Come on, Ted, let's try to be calm about this. We're adults, we have control of the situation.'

Ted brought his fists up to his eyes. In his mind he saw

Mike's big rough hands all over Mary's soft skin; climbing on top of her, rutting with her like a sweating beast. Ted was strangled with rage, confusion, and jealousy.

'Now listen,' came Nathan's steady voice. 'We've got to get to the truth here. Mike, tell me straight, have you ever had sex with Mary?'

'No, Dad.' Mike gulped and fell back a step. 'Honest, she would never let me— '

'Mike, you've bragged about it to your friends, and now you're denying it?'

'Jesus, Dad, I had to say something to the guys. I couldn't tell them Mary wouldn't put out— '

Something snapped inside Ted McFarland. He lunged at Mike, his hands curled into fists. As the boy fell back, Nathan jumped forward and threw his arms around Ted, nearly knocking the two of them off their feet.

'You bastard!' cried Ted. 'You *had to say something to the guys*? Mary wouldn't *put out*?'

'Ted!' boomed Nathan Holland, wrestling with him. 'Come on now, calm down!'

Ted fell abruptly still. He glowered at Mike, his breathing laboured. Nathan stepped uncertainly away but kept a staying hand on Ted's arm. 'Shouting and threats aren't going to get us anywhere,' he said evenly.

Ted's breathing slowed, his forehead folded into creases.

'Okay now,' said Nathan more quietly. 'Let's sit down.'

'Admit what you did to my daughter,' said Ted, glaring at Mike. 'You thought you were man enough to screw her, now be man enough to own up to it.'

'Honest, Mr McFarland, I— '

'Mike,' came Nathan firmly. 'Mike, sit down. Come on, son, we have to talk about this.'

The teenager kept a wary eye on Ted McFarland as he took a seat on the edge of the sofa. Then slowly, as if they were very old, the two men also sat.

Nathan's resonant bass came out calm and steady. 'Mary's pregnant, Mike, and you've been going with her for a year and you've told all your friends that you went to bed with her. No, don't interrupt me, son. I'm not saying I don't

74

believe you, Mike, but that's not the issue here. The issue is responsibility. You made the decision that you were adult enough to brag about having sex with Mary, now you have to be adult enough to take the responsibility for the consequences.'

'But it's not my baby, Dad.'

'I've told you, son, that's beside the point. You shouldn't have spouted off to your friends like you did. So the baby is as good as yours.' Nathan drew in a heavy breath and let it out slowly. He turned to Ted. 'Are you all right? Do you want a drink?'

'No...' Ted's voice was thick. 'No, Nat, I'm all right. I'm sorry...I don't know what got into me.'

'It's okay, I understand. Now, what are we going to do?'

'Do? You mean action? Make a decision? I don't know, Nat. I haven't had time— '

'Have you talked to Father Crispin about it?'

'Not yet.'

Nathan leaned forward and dropped a heavy hand on his friend's arm. 'We'll work it out, Ted. We have to decide what's to be done with Mary, with the baby. I don't know yet, they're so young to get married, but if that's what— '

'No shotgun weddings, Nat.'

'Maybe Father Crispin can help. We'll go together, you and I.'

Ted tried to focus on the robust face, saw the sympathy and worry in the grey eyes. He swallowed hard and straightened up. 'I'll have to give it some thought before I talk to Father Crispin. Lucille and I, we have to get ourselves together. It all happened so fast.'

'What does the doctor say?'

'About what?'

'The baby, Ted. When is it due?'

'Oh...yes.' When were they in Wade's office collecting Mary after she had run off? Only last night? 'He said she's due in January.'

The words seemed to continue to ring in the air as the three occupants of the Holland living room found something to settle their gazes upon. Soon, the weight of the words, the crunching significance of them, would penetrate.

Ted felt himself come stiffly to his feet. He looked down at Mike, his anger dissipated along with his potency; the youth looked as old as his two companions.

Nathan walked Ted to the door. 'I'm sorry, Ted, I really am. I feel responsible. And Mike' – the bass voice broke – 'well, I don't know what I'm going to do about Mike. But we'll work it out, Ted. Call me. Keep me informed.'

Ted, unable to meet his friend's gaze, said quietly, 'I'll let you know what Father Crispin says.'

Dr Jonas Wade removed his glasses and placed them on the table; taking hold of the bridge of his nose between his thumb and index finger, he gently massaged away the indentations created by the glasses. Then he stared thoughtfully at the magazines spread out before him, his attractive face moulded into a scowl.

He had found it. The elusive article, the item he had read a few years back. And he had found more, one article leading to another, sending him back to the periodical desk eight times so that now he sat in the cool and quiet of the UCLA Medical Library before a table strewn with opened-out journals.

And what, in the end, after two hours of reading, had they told him?

He had looked first into the turkeys: *Scientific American*, February, 1961. That article had said essentially what Bernie had told him. Then: *Science News Letter*, November 1957. Those same fatherless turkeys in Maryland were now posing an even more interesting situation: an increase of parthenogenesis – defined here as the 'spontaneous development of embryonic tissue in an unfertilized egg' – was occurring in turkeys and chickens that had been inoculated with a new fowl pox vaccine. Poultry scientists at the USDA Research Centre had observed that *unmated* birds vaccinated with the serum were giving birth to healthy normal offspring without having come in contact with sperm. However, the factor involved in the actual 'trigger' action had not been determined. There was debate as to whether it was the vaccine itself or an unknown contaminant in the serum that was the 'activating agent.' Whatever, Dr. Marlow Olson's Small White turkeys were opening new questions in the field of cell growth and development.

Life magazine, April 16, 1956, went even further. Considering that scientists had not known parthenongenesis to be possible in higher animals (it was, as Bernie had said, found in nature in some amphibians and plants), the fact that turkeys had been discovered to exhibit the 'virgin birth' ability made it possible for one to extrapolate out the odds of the phenomenon occurring in humans. Although, *Life* stated cautiously, 'that would be extremely rare.'

So Jonas Wade had found Bernie's fatherless turkeys and had also found the answer to the question Bernie had not been able to answer two nights before: No, scientists did not know what caused the unfertilized eggs to start to grow.

Jonas had gone on to ferret out the article he had originally come here to find. He had found it – and more.

In 1955 in England, a thirty-year-old woman had come forward to claim that her daughter had been produced without the aid of a father; conception, she had said, had occurred during a bombing raid in the war. Her cause had been taken up by Dr Stanley Balfour-Lynn of Queen Charlotte's Maternity Hospital and by Dr Helen Spurway, a lecturer on eugenics at London's University College. The challenge was met by geneticists and embryologists the world over, and by *Lancet*, the notoriously conservative British medical journal.

The only means of proving or disproving the woman's claim was by scrupulous blood and serum tests of the daughter and a long-term skin graft. Skin grafts were impossible between any humans other than identical twins; even a normal child's cells differed slightly from its mother's because they contained some of the father's antigens: the graft would be rejected.

After the chromosomatic studies were done, the results showed mother and daughter to have *identical* genetic constitutions. However, the skin graft failed. This last was not conclusive, argued the advocates of parthenogenesis, for any of a number of complications could have been the cause of the graft rejection; the failure could not be conclusively attributed to the presence of male antigens.

Jonas Wade retrieved the controversial issue of *Lancet*, November 5, 1955, and read again the reluctant concession that 'we may have to re-examine... our belief that spontaneous parthenogenesis is... absent in mammals.' Dr Wade held his eyes on the crucial sentence. 'Possibly some of the unmarried mothers whose obstinacy is condemned in old books ...may have been telling the truth.'

Sounds of the library filtered in and out of Jonas Wade's consciousness: a telephone ringing, someone pulling out the chair next to him and sitting down, a group of white-jacketed medical students murmuring in the stacks.

Lancet, which had initially scoffed Dr. Spurway's claims, had ultimately said it *may* be possible...

Jonas dropped the journal and stared vacantly. This was more frustrating than he could bear; he had found more than he had expected and yet, paradoxically, crushingly less than he had hoped for. After a few months of publicity and uproar – there before him were *Time* magazine, *Newsweek*, and even a clipping from *The Manchester Guardian* – the sensation had died down and eventually had been forgotten.

It still was not proof, the stodgy old scientific community had said; all you have is *negative* evidence – the child's cells *don't* have this or that – and to make a theory stick you need positive evidence. And where are you going to get that?

Jonas studied the fine hairs on his knuckles. That was eight years ago. Science and research had made strides since then. Surely there was someone, somewhere...

'Fascinating,' said Bernie without much conviction.

They were sitting at an outdoor café in Westwood Village eating ham-on-pumpernickel sandwiches and washing them down with bottles of Heineken's. An hour earlier, Jonas had called the Genetics Department and had asked Bernie to join him for lunch, then he had Thermofaxed the magazine articles and left the library.

'That's all you can say? Fascinating?'

'What do you want me to do, Jonas?'

Jonas Wade shook his head. He had shown Bernie the articles, told him his ideas. 'It's maddening, Bernie. The more I read, the more ignorant I am.'

'I have an inverse-proportion theory about research; want to hear it?'

'I've heard it a hundred times, Bernie; you're stalling.'

'Yes, I suppose I am. You think I'm the expert with the answers to this one, but I'm not. Okay' – he wiped his mouth with his napkin – 'the Spurway case aside, because that wasn't proven in the lofty eyes of science, were you able to find anything at all on parthenogenesis in mammals?'

'Nothing. Just minnows and sea urchins and lizards and birds. Vultures sometimes reproduce parthenogenically in nature. I learned that much. But I found nothing in the higher life forms.'

Bernie frowned and bit into his pickle. He chewed thoughtfully, then said, 'I always wondered why this place serves kosher pickles with their ham sandwiches.'

'Bernie.'

'Says so right on the menu.'

'I need your help, Bernie.'

'Why? You're so certain the girl is telling the truth? All right, the critical factor, Jonas, is whether or not parthenogenesis is possible in mammals. Am I right? From turkeys you cannot logically extrapolate out to humans. *However*' – he raised a fat finger – 'From let's say mice, definitely yes. And I think I know where you can find out that much.'

Bernie Schwartz put down his sandwich, wiped his hands on his napkin, and withdrew a leather-bound note pad from inside his tweed jacket. As he jotted something in it, he said, 'This is the person you want to talk to. Right here at UCLA.' He ripped off the sheet and handed it across.

Jonas read the name. 'Henderson, embryologist. Is he good?'

'She. And, yes, she's the best in her field. You can catch her in the lab almost anytime. Third floor. You don't have to call first, she loves visitors and she loves to talk. And if *she* says mammalian parthenogenesis isn't possible, my friend, then you can be assured it isn't. And put your meshugana idea to rest.'

The day had been unbearably hot. Mary lay on her bed gazing up at the light fixture in the centre of the ceiling, wishing her room didn't have a western exposure; that always made it the hottest room of the house in the summer, and the central air conditioner did little to bring relief.

Mary had not gone to school this morning. After a sleepless night of crying through the long dark hours she had awakened with a throbbing headache and the now-familiar morning sickness. When she retched in the bathroom and nothing came up, she remembered she had not eaten anything since noon the day before.

After that she had smelled bacon and coffee coming from the kitchen and, nauseated by the aromas, had stayed locked in her room. It was a marvel to her that, after yesterday, her mother could still carry on the normal routine.

No one had come to her door. No one had bothered to check on her. She had heard her father leave around eleven, and then Amy had gone out at noon, her bathing suit and towel rolled under an arm. Mary had heard her mother move about the house, closing all the windows and drapes and turning on the air conditioner. Then she had gone into the master bedroom and had closed the door.

Now it was dusk and Mary had still not left her room. She had also not heard her mother come out. Amy had not come home and, worse, neither had her father.

This last worried Mary the most as she lay on the unmade bed staring at the ceiling. She had spent the entire day waiting for his return, to find out what he was going to do next.

Last night her mother had told him to 'get rid of that thing.' Now Mary lay suspended, waiting and wondering.

The phone rang.

She tensed, listened.

There was no sound in the house. No movement in the master bedroom.

When it rang a third time, Mary jumped up and ran out of her room. Of the three phones in the house, Mary chose the one in the kitchen, the one farthest away from the bedrooms, and picked it up on the fifth ring with a breathless: 'Hello?'

'Mare?' came Germaine's voice. 'You all right?'

Mary fell against the cold wall. 'Hi, Germaine.'

'Why weren't you in school today? We all missed you.'

'I didn't feel well again.'

'Didn't that doctor ever find out what's wrong with you?'

Mary sighed. It seemed so long ago, that first visit. Germaine knew about Dr Wade, but not about his findings or Dr Evans. 'No. I guess I have something mysterious.'

'Hey, we got grades today. Guess what! I'm getting a B in French! Can you beat that! She actually liked my report on existentialism! Mare? Did you hear me?'

'Yes.'

'Will you be coming tomorrow?'

'I don't know.'

'Last day, Mare, big deal, you know.' There was a moment of silence. 'Well, I'll let you go then. Meet you by the flagpole at the usual time?'

'Yes.'

'And if you need anything, hey, you know, give a call.'

'Yes. Thanks.'

Mary stood with the receiver to her ear, listening to the dial tone until it turned into an off-the-hook siren. She gazed around the kitchen, at the half-opened drawers, the drops of coffee congealing on the formica, the melted butter, the plate of cold greasy bacon. Then she stared at the phone on the wall.

Depressing the button to get the dial tone again, she mechanically dialled Mike's number.

Timothy answered. 'White House, John-John speaking.'

'Hi, Tim, it's me, is Mike there?'

'Yeah, Mary, hold on.'

She heard the fourteen-year-old scream out, his voice breaking, and listened for a response. There was a distant reply, then Timothy shouted, 'It's Mary!' Another distant response, and then Timothy putting his hand over the mouthpiece.

Listening to the rapid, muffled dialogue, Mary felt herself slide down the wall until she was crouched on the floor, the coiled phone cord stretched straight. Finally, after Timothy impatiently dropped the phone with a sharp thud, Mike's voice came on. 'Hello.'

'Mike?' Mary's hand grasped the earpiece until her fingers were white. 'Mike, can you come over right away?'

His voice came from far away. 'Mary... I was just going to call you.'

Something in his tone alarmed her. 'Mike,' she said just above a whisper, 'was my dad there today?'

A pause, then: 'Yes.'

She swallowed with difficulty. 'Then... you know?'

'Yes.'

She closed her eyes. 'Mike, I have to talk to you.'

'Yeah, Mary, I have to talk to you, too. Mary...' His voice sounded thick, cottony. 'God, Mary, I was so shocked. It really knocked me off my gourd. All day I've been thinking about it. I mean, it's like it's not real, you know? Mary, I've gotta know something.'

'What?'

'Who'd you do it with?'

Her eyes snapped open. They raced around the jumbled kitchen; the mess her mother had left — so unlike the meticulous Lucille. God, what was happening?

'Mike,' she said in a tight voice, her knees drawn up to her chest. 'Mike, I didn't...I swear to you I never did anything with anybody. It's not true what the doctors say, they're wrong. But, God, I'm scared and my folks don't believe me and I don't know who to turn to.' Mary saw tears fill her eyes; they washed away the kitchen. 'Mike, you have to come over, I need you.'

'I can't, Mary, not right now— '

'Then I'll come to you. Or we'll meet somewhere. I have to explain this to you. We have to talk about it, figure out what's wrong.'

Mary listened to the silence at the other end and, misunderstanding it, whispered, 'Oh, Mike, don't do this to me...'

His voice came out through a choke. 'God, Mary, I'm sorry. I'm so fucking sorry. I... I love you so goddamn much. Mary!' he blurted. 'I don't care, honest! I'll stand by you, I swear it. I'll even marry you, but I have to know. I have to know, Mary' – Mike squeezed the words out – 'why someone else and not me?'

'Mike, oh Mike... you don't understand. And I don't know how to make you.'

'Mary, if you love me' – his voice wrestled for control – 'if you love me, you'll be honest with me. We have to be truthful with one another, we always have. No secrets, Mary, that's what love is all about. We'll get through this together, I promise, but don't shut me out, don't lie to me.'

'I'm not lying—'

'You can tell your dad what you want, but you have to trust *me*, Mary. And this hurts, you know? It hurts loving you and knowing you did it with some other guy and you don't respect me enough to come clean with me—'

'But I didn't—'

'The worst part is that you won't tell me the truth! Trust me, for God's sake!'

Mary closed her eyes, tasted the tears as they tumbled onto her lips. For a moment, the temptation was there – tell him anything, make up a story, invent a guy, maybe a friend of Germaine's, a friend of her boy friend Rudy, and you had some wine and you didn't really want to do it and you didn't really like it, but you made the mistake and now you're sorry and then everything will be all right with Mike and he'll come over and hold you and comfort you— 'Mike,' her voice grave, 'I'm telling you the truth. I've never let anyone touch me. Say that you believe me.'

His voice came out twisted. 'God, Mary... I can't talk anymore. I've gotta think. I've gotta figure what to do. Everyone – my dad and my brothers – they think the baby's mine. I've gotta think this out, Mary...'

She stared in horror at the half-open kitchen cupboard

before her. Mary's lips formed the words: There is no baby. But no voice came out.

Mike continued haltingly, dwindling. 'I can't see you right now, Mary. Not until I know what to do. I have to get myself together, you know? You and I, Mary, we have to work this out together, but you're fighting me and I...I...'

Her voice came out dull, lifeless. 'You haven't listened to a word I've said.' She hung up the receiver.

Mary sat this way, dazed, for some minutes, neither moving nor making a sound; the telephone rang twelve times but she left it alone. Then she burst into tears and brought her hands up to her face. Sobbing, huddled between the kitchen table and the wall, Mary cried, 'Daddy...'

Ted was not surprised to find the house in darkness. He stood for a moment to adjust his eyes, then, flicking on the hall light, wearily made his way to the den.

His first concern was the scotch. After that, he would look in on the rest of the family, and then maybe his life. It was while he was pouring that he heard a crash, and then the shattering of glass.

Dropping his tumbler and bottle, he dashed from the den and into the hall. He looked right and left and saw a light coming from under the girls' bathroom door.

Running to it, Ted listened for a second, then said, 'Mary?' There was no answer. 'Amy?' Still nothing.

He tried the knob. It was locked.

'Hey! Who's in there! Answer me! Mary? Amy?'

He banged on the door with two fists.

The door to the master bedroom opened and a sleepy Lucille looked out. 'What's the noise— '

'Mary!' Ted thumped the door harder. 'Mary! Open up!'

Lucille, holding onto the wall for support, made her way to Ted's side. 'What is it?'

Ignoring her, he took a few steps back, lifted his right leg and slammed his foot against the door. He did it again, leaving black prints on the paint.

'Ted!' cried Lucille.

The sixth blow caused the door to burst open, and Ted flew inside.

They found Mary crumpled on the bathroom floor in a pool of blood. In the sink lay a Gillette Super Blue Blade.

CHAPTER 7

What she hated most was the look on her father's face.

At least her mother had the consideration to stand at the window and look down at the street, but Ted had to sit on the edge of the bed, his eyes never leaving his daughter's face. He reminded her of a cocker spaniel.

Mary lay with her arms outside the covers. Both wrists and both hands were bandaged; the blade had done as much damage to her fingertips as to her wrists. She ignored the fresh morning sunlight that spilled past Lucille and into the room. For Mary the world was sunless.

She had come to the evening before in the emergency room, lying on her back with one arm extended out on a small table. Dr Wade had been in the process of sewing up her wrist. When the glaring lights overhead blinded her, causing her to roll her head away, she heard a familiar voice say quietly, 'You're all right, Mary. You didn't lose much blood. You fainted from the emotional strain, not from blood loss.'

She had rolled her head back to look at him and had noticed how the overhead lights glinted off the few silver strands in his black hair. Then she had closed her eyes and gone back to sleep.

She had awakened again during the night, alone in a private room with a plastic tube coming down from a suspended bottle and running into her arm. She had lain awake a long time, searching the darkness for a memory, but had finally drifted off again.

When she had awakened this morning, the tube was out of her arm and a cheery nurse's aide was setting a bowl of warm water before her. With gentle hands she had soaped Mary's face, helped her brush her teeth, and then combed out her hair. During the whole time Mary had said nothing.

The same nurse's aide had returned later with a breakfast of juice and runny eggs and toast, which she had patiently fed to the girl, all the while chatting about what a nice day it was outside.

Finally, her parents had come.

And now Ted sat while Lucille stood, his eyes so full of pain and bewilderment that Mary couldn't bear to look at him.

'We told Amy you had appendicitis,' he said, looking sorrowfully at her white lobster-claw hands. 'Your mother called the school and told them the same thing. They'll mail your report card.'

She kept her eyes fixed on the metal bar bolted into the ceiling from which hung a curtain that could be drawn around the bed. She wished she could do that now. Block her parents out.

'Mary...'

'Yes Daddy.'

'Mary, can't you look at me?'

She gave it a moment's thought, then turned to face him. He looked a lot older since two days ago.

'I'm sorry, kitten,' he said simply.

'I am too, Daddy.'

'Mary.' Ted shifted self-consciously on the bed. 'Mary, I—'

She gazed steadily at him. 'Daddy, I don't know why I did it. I just...did it.'

'You gave us such a scare!' He wished desperately he could hold her hand. Talking without touching seemed like no communication at all. 'Mary...kitten, why didn't you come to us? We're your parents. You can always turn to us.'

Her eyes were dull, faraway.

'Anyway,' he whispered, 'I just thank God I got home when I did.'

She rolled her head away.

The silence in the room was filled with a background of hospital sounds: footsteps beyond the closed door; carts rattling by; the operator's voice paging a doctor for surgery.

Then there was a quiet knock.

Mary felt her heart jump. If it's Mike, I'll—

Germaine's head poked through. 'Mare?'

Ted was at once on his feet. 'Dr Wade left instructions that there were to be no visitors.'

'Yeah, I know, Mr. McFarland.' Germaine came all the way in and closed the door behind her. 'I told them I was her sister. Mare? Want me to leave?'

'I'm afraid Mary is in no condition to see anyone right now.'

'It's all right, Daddy, I'm glad she's here.'

The girl slowly approached the bed, her eyes quickly taking in the bandaged hands, then, swinging her shoulder bag onto a chair, Germaine sat on the bed with one leg tucked under her. 'You weren't at the flagpole this morning.'

Mary smiled weakly. 'I was busy.'

'Yeah, so I see. I called the house and Amy said you'd had an attack of appendicitis and your dad rushed you to Encino Hospital.' Germaine smiled until dimples engraved her cheeks. 'I see you had your appendix removed.'

Mary lifted her arms. 'Both of them.'

'Oh, wow, Mare...'

Ted stood away from the bed and watched in amazement as his daughter came to life in the presence of her friend.

'It must have been just after I called, huh, Mare?'

Mary bit her lower lip. 'About that time.'

'Oh, man, why didn't you say something! I thought you sounded weird. Why didn't you talk to me, Mare? I'm your best friend!'

'I guess I just couldn't...I mean, it isn't as simple as that.

It's *why* I did it. You don't know what— ' Tears filled her eyes and tumbled onto the pillow.

When Germaine fell impulsively forward and rested her cheek against Mary's, with her silky black hair running all over the pillow and blankets, Ted checked the impulse to intervene. He held back, fascinated, watching Mary's poor lobster-claw arms come up and around her friend's back and embrace her. He heard them murmuring intimately, with Germaine gently stroking Mary's forehead and kissing her cheek.

When Germaine drew back, straightening up and tossing her long hair off her shoulders, she brushed tears off her face. 'You could've told me, Mare. You know you can tell me anything. I would've talked you out of it. Nothing's worth checking out.'

'I know . . . of all people, I guess I should have been able to tell you. But by then, I don't know, I guess I felt like the whole world was against me.'

Ted swallowed down his pain.

'They don't believe me,' continued Mary. 'So I guess I thought you wouldn't either. After all, it's my word against two doctors.'

The girl in the baggy sweatshirt and patched pedal pushers seemed to consider this. Then she said, 'I'm not saying I can dig it either, Mare, but after all, who am I to say? If you believe in what you say, then I guess that's all there is to it. So I have to believe it too.'

Mary smiled in loving gratitude for a moment, bringing the tip of one bandaged hand up to Germaine's cheek, then the silence was disturbed by another knock at the door.

'Oh, for God's sake,' muttered Ted, going to open it.

When he saw Father Crispin, he immediately fell back, holding the door.

'Good morning Ted.'

'Good morning, Father.'

The door swung closed as Father Crispin walked around the bed, Ted right behind him. 'Good morning, Mary.'

She seemed to shrink into the covers. 'Good morning, Father.'

'Thank you for coming,' murmured Ted. He glanced over his shoulder at Lucille and saw that she did not seem aware of the priest's arrival.

Father Lionel Crispin drew up a chair and sat down with his hands clasped. Portly and fifty years old with grey hair and a balding patch on the top, like a monk's tonsure, the man in the black clerical suit and white collar regarded Mary sternly.

After a moment he said, 'How do you feel this morning?'

'All right, I guess, Father.'

He looked across at Germaine and pursed his lips. 'Your father has told me everything, Mary. I can only say that I wish you had come to me in the first place. I've known you since you were a baby, Mary, I baptized you. You know you can trust me. You can always come to me in an hour of need.'

'Yes, Father.'

Lionel Crispin regarded the girl with a reassuring smile on his round face, but in his heart he was disturbed. Mary Ann McFarland had been one of the best pupils at St. Sebastian's grammar school. The nuns adored her. She was the brightest and most energetic member of his CYO group. And always, every Saturday, her confessed sins were paltry compared with those of most of the teen-agers.

He was troubled for three reasons: she had not confessed her sin of sexual intercourse; she had attempted suicide; and, the most horrifying, as a pregnant female, she had attempted murder.

'I've brought you something,' he said, reaching into his coat pocket and withdrawing a long black rosary, the silver crucifix glinting in the overhead light. He dangled it before her, then draped it over her right hand.

'Blessed by His Holiness himself.'

'Thank you, Father.'

'Would you like to take Communion this evening?'

'No. . .Father.'

Of course not, he thought in grave concern. Communion means confession, and you're not ready to tell me.

He looked up at Ted, his eyebrows raised. A mute

F

communication passed between the two men, then the priest turned again to the girl, this time smiling confidently at her.

Father Crispin opened his mouth to say something more, but was interrupted by a brief rap on the door and then the sudden appearance of Dr Wade.

'Good morning,' he said to everyone in the room.

Seeing him, Mary brightened a little and tried without success to push herself farther up in bed.

As Father Crispin rose, Ted said, 'Dr Wade, this is Father Crispin, our family priest.'

They shook hands.

Jonas Wade came around the bed and gave his best smile to Mary. 'How's my prettiest patient today?'

'All right, I guess.'

'You guess? Well, we'll see about that.'

He turned around and nodded to the two men. At once Ted went to Lucille's side, and lightly touched her elbow. She turned as if in a dream and allowed herself to be led from the room. Also on cue, Germaine jumped up, grabbed her purse, and said, 'I gotta run, Mare. But I'll be back this afternoon.'

Dr Wade closed the door behind them all, with a quiet word to the McFarlands and Father Crispin. Then he turned back to Mary and approached the bed.

She smiled up at him. While Dr Wade was not what she would call handsome, there was something about his face, his manner, his expression, that Mary found appealing. And this morning, tall and erect in his tailored suit, she thought him very striking.

'Well, Mary Ann McFarland. We meet again.' He took a seat in the chair Father Crispin had vacated and leaned forward with his elbows on his knees. 'How are they treating you here?'

'All right.'

'And how are the hands feeling?' Lifting the rosary and laying it aside, he took hold of her left wrist, turned it over and inspected the bandage. He did the same with the right. 'I'd say you were pretty nervous when you did this, Mary.

Those double-edged razors are tricky if you don't handle them right. Be glad you didn't cut any tendons.'

He sat back in the chair and regarded his patient. For some reason, she looked a lot smaller than he remembered. 'Do you want to tell me about it?' he said quietly.

Mary shrugged against the pillow. 'I don't know.'

'Do you know why you did it?'

She averted her eyes. 'I guess.'

'Let's talk about it.'

She rolled her head back and beheld Dr Wade with sapphire eyes. 'Daddy wasn't there. And Mike— '

'He's your boy friend?'

'We're going steady. We were going to get married. He didn't believe me. Just like everyone else.'

'What do you mean, your father wasn't there?'

Mary brought her right hand up before her eyes and studied the white wrapping. 'I guess I wanted him to be there and he just wasn't.'

'Your mother said she was there.'

'Yes. . .'

'But you preferred to talk to your father.'

'Yes.'

'Didn't you know he was at work? I mean, why should you have expected him to be at home?'

She dropped her hand. 'Because he wasn't at work yesterday. He was out. . .looking for a. . .'

Jonas Wade frowned. 'Looking for what, Mary?'

'Someone to do an abortion,' she whispered.

'Oh.' Dr Wade looked at his fingernails. 'I see.'

'That's why I did it.'

'Did you try calling anyone for help?'

'I didn't want help. Ever since you told my mother I was expecting, everyone has been unhappy. Absolutely everyone is upset. Even Father Crispin. He hasn't said so, but I can tell he is. Everyone is unhappy because of me, or because of this thing inside me. So I decided that everyone would be happy if I killed myself and this thing with me.'

'Mary, suicide is never a solution to anything You are

sensible enough to know that your parents would be grief-stricken if you were to kill yourself.'

'Oh, I don't know—'

'Of course you know that. Maybe you were trying to punish them. Did you ever think of that?'

Her eyes flared with anger, the pupils dilating. 'They deserve it, don't they? Not believing me when I tell the truth, calling me a liar, accusing Mike, talking about abortions and things! That's monstrous! How come all of a sudden they believe in abortions?'

'I'd say you're pretty angry about this whole thing.'

'I haven't done anything wrong, Dr Wade, but everyone is treating me like a criminal. Well, if they don't want me around, fine! I can easily take care of that!'

'Mary,' Dr Wade's voice was gently compelling. 'Have you told your parents any of this? Do they know how you feel?'

Again she rolled her head away. 'No.'

'Why?'

'Because.'

'That's not an answer.'

'Because they don't care.'

'You seem to think *I* do.'

She snapped her head around, her eyes illuminated. 'Yes, that's right! You *do* care, and you understand too. Night before last, when my parents came to your office to get me, you said you didn't think I was lying.'

'Yes, but, Mary,' he frowned and examined his manicure again. 'That didn't mean I believe you either. There *is* a difference. I only said that I thought you believed what you were saying, not that it was necessarily the truth.'

'It doesn't matter, Dr Wade. What's important is that you don't think I'm lying when I say I'm a virgin. You don't think I've done anything wrong.'

Dr Wade had difficulty masking his disquiet. His dark eyes narrowed a little, the creases in his forehead deepened as he studied her face, seeing once again the youthful evidence of something that was, in a few years, going to blossom into real beauty. She was so small and helpless, staring hopefully at him with incredibly blue eyes. Jonas thought about his frustrating afternoon the day before in the Medical Library and the lunch afterward with Bernie; he considered, for a brief moment, telling the girl about it, then quickly abandoned the idea as reckless. He would wait, at least until he had had a chance to talk to the embryologist Bernie had recommended.

'Dr Wade,' said Mary softly. 'If you think I believe myself when I say I've never been to bed with a boy, do *you* believe I haven't?'

'The mind can do funny things, Mary. Maybe you did something and simply don't remember.'

She shook her head firmly. 'Dr Wade, I'm a virgin.'

Father Crispin and the McFarlands were sitting at the end of the corridor on plastic chairs and holding styrofoam cups of bitter coffee.

'Thank you for waiting,' said Dr Wade. 'This won't take long. Father Crispin, I appreciate your help in this.'

He led them around the corner, past the nurses' station, and to a door marked 'Doctors Only.' Inside, both Ted and the priest guided Lucille to a Naugahyde chair, and when they were all seated in the tiny lounge, Dr Wade said, 'Mr. McFarland, you and your wife are going to have to make an important decision. Father Crispin and I will advise you, but ultimately it is up to you.

Ted, holding Lucille's hand, nodded in grey-faced misery.

Jonas Wade went on: 'In cases of suicide attempt, particularly if the victim is a minor, I have an obligation to report the incident to the police. The reason for this is not prosecution but to provide some sort of protection for the victim. In the instances of minors, they become wards of the court and are removed from the circumstances that led them to the suicide attempt.'

Ted leaned forward to speak, but Dr Wade held up a hand. 'Please hear me out first. Now, each case is different. The circumstances, the living environment of the child, varies from case to case. Very often, the victim is benefited by action on the part of the authorities. Such as taking the child out of an intolerable home situation.'

Ted felt Lucille's fingers stir beneath his hand. He looked at her face; her eyes were focused earnestly on the doctor.

'However,' continued Jonas Wade, 'I'm not so sure that authoritative intervention would be in Mary's best interest. That is, considering what I know of her home life and her activities with the Church. I don't feel bound to report this case if the four of us can come up with a workable solution.'

The little lounge, smelling of stale cigarette smoke, was filled with silence for a moment, while the four occupants chose something to stare at while thinking. Finally Ted asked softly, 'Did Mary talk to you, Dr Wade?'

'Yes, she did, but I can't disclose what she said. She has as much right to doctor-patient confidentiality as an adult. What I will say, however, is that we must act quickly.'

'Doctor.' The voice was flat, without inflection. It came from Lucille, who had a peculiar pallor about her. Without makeup and the habitual care to her hairdo, Lucille McFarland looked war-torn. 'Why did she do it?'

He spread out his hands. 'Why don't you ask her that?'

Lucille shook her head, unable to say more.

Now Ted spoke. 'Dr Wade, I don't understand why Mary opens up to strangers, people who aren't family, and yet she shuts *us* out. Doesn't she trust us?'

'Mr. McFarland, your daughter is looking for anyone right now who will believe her. Apparently you and your wife demonstrated enough lack of credulity in her claim, so she spurns you.'

'But surely she can't be telling the truth!'

Dr Wade rubbed the side of his nose. 'Certain aspects of this case are most unusual. This peculiar defence of her virginity...' He considered for an instant telling them of his suspicions and his research, then decided to wait until he had talked to Dr Dorothy Henderson. 'Anyway, it's not whether she is in fact telling the truth or not, it's how she regards her culpability and your refusal to believe her.'

'Is this sort of thing common?' asked Father Crispin.

94

'It's extremely rare, Father. Many girls will claim rape if they don't want to admit to having willingly had sexual relations. But the claim of virginity in the face of obvious pregnancy is truly rare, although there have been some instances, written up in psychiatric journals, women who have claimed right up to the moment of delivery, and even afterward, that they've never been with a man. By and large, they are psychological cases.'

'No!' whispered Lucille. 'My daughter is not psychotic.'

'I didn't say she was, Mrs. McFarland. Besides, that's not what should concern us most at this point. The reality is, Mr. and Mrs. McFarland, you have a pregnant teen-ager on your hands, one who is emotionally unstable and who needs supervision, and you have to decide what is to be done with her. Since abortion is illegal and I assume marriage is out of the question'—he paused, watched their faces— 'that leaves you with only two options. Either to keep Mary at home or to send her away until the baby is born.'

Again they all fell silent, so Jonas Wade chanced a quick look at his watch. He was going to telephone Dr. Henderson as soon as he was through here.

'What do you mean,' came Ted's weary voice, 'send her away?'

'I believe it's in Mary's best interest, Mr. McFarland, for her to be placed under protective supervision. Let us say, custodial care.'

He scanned the three faces before him and rested longest on that of Father Crispin. Jonas Wade could see in the beefy jowls and bristly eyebrows, and in the small alert eyes of the priest, that the man was greatly agitated. And he could guess why. Mary Ann McFarland, from what Dr Wade could see, was the model Catholic girl. Dutifully confessing her most shameful and private sins to her family priest. And yet, to the priest's chagrin, Mary had blithely left this one out of the confessional.

'Dr Wade,' came Lionel Crispin's voice. 'I don't want to presume to know how you will advise Mr. and Mrs. McFarland, and I also don't wish to trespass upon your authority here, but let me say that I have some strong feelings regarding this case and would appreciate the opportunity to put my suggestion to the test.'

'On the contrary, Father, I welcome your involvement.'

'Very well, then,' said Father Crispin, slapping his hands together. 'This is what I propose we do with Mary.'

CHAPTER 8

'Good afternoon, Dr Wade. I'm Dorothy Henderson, how do you do?'

Jonas took the firm handshake. 'I appreciate your taking the time to see me, Dr Henderson.'

'No trouble at all! Please, step into my domain.'

Jonas Wade's initial thought was: handsome. Dr. Dorothy Henderson, embryologist, was a handsome woman. Then, as he followed her into the laboratory, he altered his impression to: faded elegance, royalty in exile. She walked before him like a princess, her square broad shoulders supporting her immaculate white lab coat as if she carried the burdens of state. Her walk was fluid and graceful; her body slender and still in its first youth, even though the UCLA researcher was clearly not a day younger than fifty. Auburn hair that was obviously very long and thick was parted at the top and drawn back to the nape of the neck in an abundant knot; streaks of pure white marbled the perfect hairdo; she was a prima ballerina past her glory. When she turned, Dorothy Henderson smiled with excellent teeth and sparkling green eyes, her skin smooth and glowing, but furrowed and lined with years of smiling and frowning – an actress who had known the pinnacle of her career and who has graciously acceded to the newcomers. When she spoke, her voice came out surprisingly, almost embarrassingly strong; this woman had never had to whisper – an opera star, a stateswoman, the hostess, perhaps, of Capitol Hill. Whatever, what

Dorothy Henderson did not look like, Jonas decided as she proceeded to give him a rudimentary tour of her lab, was a scientist.

'Did Bernie tell you what we are doing here, Dr.Wade?'

'No, I haven't a clue.'

'Are you familiar with cloning?'

He looked around the small laboratory, noted the two assistants who worked quietly at their benches, scanned the equipment, picked up pungent, undefinable odours, and heard, just behind the gurgling of liquids and the hum of an incubator, the soft, regular tick of a spectrometer.

'I've heard the word. Something to do with creating test-tube life?'

'I'll give you the literal translation first, Dr Wade. It's Greek for crowd or throng; a clone is a large group of one thing. Our own translation, however, is a little distorted to suit our purpose; in science clones are the populations of particular or individual organisms which have been derived from a single parent. And by that, of course, we mean asexually.'

Jonas let his eyes travel to the centre of the pristine, twenty-by-thirty room and settled upon a bank of glass cages – aquaria – in the centre. Covered with mesh lids and containing a couple of inches of murky water, the aquaria housed colonies of staring, glistening frogs.

'What we are doing here, Dr Wade, is, basically, asexually reproducing generations of frogs from a single, donor parent, and we achieve this by transplanting the nucleus of a differentiated cell taken from the body of a frog into the cytoplasm of a frog ovum, and then nurturing it into growth, presumably with the result being a mature duplicate of the first frog.'

She walked slowly in front of him, speaking like an art-museum guide, pointing out apparatus and explaining technique.

'First we take a frog egg and destroy the nucleus by using a tiny beam of ultraviolet light. These are South African clawed frogs and their fragile ova cannot withstand mechanical manipulation. After we have placed the enucleated egg or eggs in a specially treated culture dish, we then take a donor cell – Dorothy Henderson paused behind a young oriental woman seated upon a high stool, working intently over a dissecting microscope – 'taken from the intestines of a tadpole, draw it up into a sterile micropipette, and inject its nucleus into the enucleated egg. The eggs are then incubated in the special medium and the results are examined.'

She led him to the large metal 'oven' whose glass-window door revealed shelves of Petri dishes. 'Once they reach the blastula stage, they are transplanted into an environment that will enable them to mature into tadpoles.'

They next came to stand before a small, algae-coated tank where the second lab assistant sat over a microscope, holding a syringe in one hand and a pen in the other; she made notations on a clipboard as she kept her eye over the lens.

'All members of a particular clone, Dr Wade, will either cease developing because of genetic defects all at the same exact time, or they will all mature normally and emerge identical in appearance and constitution.'

Dorothy Henderson flashed him a warm, charming smile, then led Jonas Wade to the row of tanks in the centre of the lab. Each was labelled *'Xenopus laevis'* with a successive Roman numeral after it, and each contained a clone of frogs. The first aquarium, however, was labelled *'Xenopus laevis; Primus,'* and housed only one frog.

'This is Primus,' said Dr Henderson, tapping the grimy glass with her finger. 'He was the original parent. All of these, Dr Wade' – she swept her arm down the bank of six aquaria – 'are successive generations, each cloned from the preceeding one. They are all, virtually, carbon copies of Primus.'

Jonas Wade bent down, examined the frog, then straightened and said, shaking his head, 'He has quite a family.'

'Oh no, Dr Wade, please keep in mind that these frogs are not offspring of Primus. They *are* Primus.'

He stared down into the cold, lifeless eyes of the frog; occasionally, Primus blinked, his only sign of life. 'Fascinating...'

'This is not a new idea, Dr Wade. Scientists have been seriously experimenting with cloning ever since Gottlieb Haberlandt in 1902.' Dr Henderson gently touched Jonas's arm. 'But I'm afraid we must stop here, Dr Wade, with the amphibians. Science would love dearly to move ahead to higher animals, but we haven't the technology. The mammalian egg is one twelfth the size of a frog egg – about one hundredth of an inch in diameter – whereas the frog's egg is one eighth of an inch. In this laboratory we operate under the normal magnification of a standard dissecting microscope, but for the minute human egg we would require very special equipment not yet perfected. Someday, however, Dr Wade, science will be able to enucleate a human egg, transplant into it a body cell taken from a living person, and produce an identical twin of that person. However,' she hoisted her shoulders, 'when that event will take place, your guess is as good as mine.'

He shook his head a second time and gave another slow look around the lab. He had heard occasional reports about this sort of experimentation but he had had no idea it had advanced so far. There, before him, sat Primus, duplicated over and over again, *ad infinitum*.

Dorothy Henderson, reading his face – a look she had seen so many times and was now used to – said softly, 'Please don't be disturbed by what we're doing here, Dr Wade. We are not genetic manipulators; we are not Nazis. Cloning is only a small part of the exciting new era that is opening up in the field of sexual reproduction. Frozen sperm and artificial insemination were the science fiction of yesterday but are today's reality. Tomorrow we will see conception in a test tube, embryo transplants from one woman to another, artificial wombs, gender predetermination of a foetus and, of course, human cloning.' She smiled patiently at him, her hands thrust into the pockets of her lab coat. 'But you didn't come here for a quick course in cloning, did you, Dr Wade?'

He tore his eyes away from Primus and smiled at the embryologist. Dorothy Henderson was very much, after all, the scientist. 'No, I didn't, although I wouldn't mind coming back sometime for a more in-depth lesson.'

'You're more than welcome, Dr Wade; I so seldom get visitors. Shall we go into my excuse for an office?'

He followed her into a cramped, glassed-in cubicle at one end of the lab which, suprisingly, was very quiet when the door was shut. Dorothy Henderson took a seat behind her cluttered desk and said as Jonas sat opposite her, 'I'm sorry I haven't any coffee to offer you. The percolator broke down and we can't afford to replace it.'

He sat back in the metal-and-vinyl chair, folded his hands in his lap, and said with a smile, 'I'll try not to take up too much of your time, Dr Henderson. Did Bernie tell you why I came here?'

'Only that you had some questions he thought I might be able to answer for you.'

Jonas Wade opened his mouth to speak, then found himself at a maddening loss for words; he had thought he would know how to begin, now he wasn't so sure.

All morning, during office hours seeing patients and during one appendectomy at Encino Hospital, he had been preparing himself for this interview. So much hinged upon what this woman could tell him; Dr Henderson was pivotal to his research. She would decide for him one way or another: to continue with his line of thinking, or drop it altogether.

For, as Bernie said, it all hinged upon one factor: could parthenogenesis occur spontaneously in mammals, and if so, how?

He decided to move cautiously. 'Dr Henderson, what can you tell me about parthenogenesis?'

The elegant woman, appearing so out of place amid the sterility and scientific atmosphere of her lab, raised her eyebrows slightly and said, 'Parthenogenesis is the development of an ovum into an embryo without the stimulation of a male sperm.'

'What I meant was, does it happen in fact or is that merely an abstract concept?'

'Oh, by no means is it merely a concept, Dr Wade; science has known for a long time that ova can develop parthenogenically into an embryo when influenced by some kind of stimulus that is either chemical, physiological, or mechanical. The process has been proven many times in the laboratory. Once researchers were able to trigger parthenogenesis in the batrachians – that is, toads and frogs – then there was no longer any doubt that the same might be accomplished with all vertebrates. In a way, parthenogenesis is what we are proving here in this lab.'

Jonas Wade looked down at his hands. He noticed that his heart was starting to race. This was the crucial moment, the question Bernie had not been able to answer, the one that decided it all for him...

'Dr Henderson, what about in mammals? Is parthenogenesis possible in mammals?'

To his immense shock, Dr Henderson returned with a matter-of-fact 'Yes.'

Jonas stared at her. 'Are you sure?'

'I'm very sure, Dr Wade. It has been done in the laboratory. With mice and rabbits especially. The ova receive a stimulus and start natural development.'

'Actually, Dr Henderson, it's not laboratory-induced parthenogenesis I'm interested in. Do you know of any instances of mammalian parthenogenesis occuring in nature?'

'In nature?'

'Spontaneously.'

'Spontaneously...' A fine-boned, slender hand rose up to rub her forehead absently. Then Dorothy Henderson said, 'The ova of cats and ferrets have been known to start dividing without male fertilization. Although, in nature, Dr Wade, you are talking about an uncontrolled environment. There is no way we can check it. Outside of the laboratory, all is conjecture.'

'Then perhaps you can elucidate me on exactly *how* parthenogenesis works. How does it come about?'

'By *how*, I presume you mean what gets the egg started. We don't know, Dr Wade, other than that a stimulus is required that imitates the action of the sperm. Remember, Doctor, all a sperm does is invade the egg and trigger cell division. If another agent can act the same way, cell division will commence. Let me give you an example or two of laboratory activating agents. First' – she held up a tapered finger – 'there is the example of the sea urchin. In the lab, you take some unfertilized sea urchin eggs, put them in sea water, add a little chloroform or strychnine, and the eggs will start developing on their own and the result will be mature, normal sea urchins. Or, in another experiment' – a second narrow finger shot up – 'the eggs are subjected to the physiological shock of a hypertonic action of the solution, normal cleavage takes place, and the result is, again, normal healthy *fatherless* sea urchins. Exact replicas of the donor. The first of these is an example of chemical stimulation, the second, of physiological stimulation. With frogs, partheno-genesis is achieved by introducing foreign protein directly into the egg by the prick of a needle. This is a combination of both.'

'But, Dr Henderson, an ovum has only half the chromo-somal complement of an adult cell. In order to develop embryonically, the egg would need the normal number of diploid chromosomes. I was always under the impression the sperm supplied the other set.'

A brief smile passed over her lips. 'And you're right, Dr Wade. In normal conception the chromosomes of the sperm link up with those of the ovum, each one containing twenty-three. You recall that during the maturation phase of the ovum, before fertilization by a sperm, the ovum divides and releases the second polar body, which contains half of the egg chromosomes. In parthenogenesis, the maturing egg, for some unknown reason, does not expulse the polar body but keeps it; the chromosomes contained within it come back and link up with those in the first polar body. The nonexpulsed polar body becomes, in effect, the male pronucleus and fuses with the female pronucleus to form the zygote. When the egg is then exposed to a stimulus of some sort, chemical or otherwise, segmentation begins, and since the egg contains the necessary forty-six chromosomes, embryonic maturation takes place.'

'What has been done in the lab with mammals?'

'It's a simple procedure. The ova of, say, rabbits are placed in a culture dish in a medium of blood plasma and embryo extract, they are exposed to a cold temperature shock, and they are thereby activated. Those that go beyond the polar-body extrusion and start cleaving are placed in the Fallopian tubes of rabbits that have been injected with pregnancy hormones so the body will not reject the transplanted zygotes. Those which develop beyond the blastocyst stage and don't have to be surgically removed usually make it to full term. It is even possible, Dr Wade, to trigger embryonic development of an ovum in a rabbit by applying a cold compress directly to the Fallopian tubes of an ovulating rabbit. The success rate is extremely rare, of course, but a few normal healthy rabbits have been produced without sperm.'

'Dr Henderson,' Jonas Wade was having a hard time controlling himself. Already she had told him more than he had hoped for. 'Can we talk about humans?'

Her expression did not change. 'Certainly. Spontaneous or artificially induced?'

'Spontaneous.'

'A titillating notion, Doctor, but not a new one. Hundreds of studies have been made on human ova and some of those studies have found that a few eggs removed from the follicles had already begun to cleave before they left the ovary; that is, without any possible contact with a sperm. I believe the rate was something like six out of four hundred. In some studies, particularly in Philadelphia about two decades ago, the findings were that about three fourths of one per cent of all human ova begin developing parthenogenically on their own before they even start their trip down the Fallopian tube. Taking that statistic out to its farthest extrapolation, you would have virgin births as frequently as fraternal twins. However, most of those maturing eggs are discharged during ovulation or menstruation, or they grow into dermoid cysts and tumors and are removed surgically. But some researchers contend that *a few* continue to develop normally. One scientist went so far as to estimate one case in a thousand births.'

'Surely you can't mean that!'

Dr Henderson laughed softly. 'No, Dr Wade, I was merely quoting a colleague. As in every field of research, there are lunatic fringes, both at the conservative and liberal edges. Some scientists stamp their feet and scream that human parthenogenesis is in no way possible.'

'Where do you stand, Doctor?'

Her eyes seemed to twinkle. 'I certainly don't discount the possibility.'

'And the probability?'

'The majority of the scientific community will give you odds of one virgin birth in every million. I might give you better than that – say, one in every five hundred thousand births.'

Jonas Wade gazed at the embryologist in astonishment. 'But this is incredible! Why hasn't there been more written up about this, more publicity? This is explosive!'

'For just that reason, Doctor, it *is* explosive. Just as, I think, in time, my own field of research will become too hot to handle. You're talking about human sexuality now, a very touchy topic, and when you broach the subject of virgin births you are stepping on the toes of theologians, moralists, psychologists, and righteous mothers and fathers the world over. You and I, Dr Wade, can sit here and discuss the subject scientifically and objectively, as two scientists. Out there, however, you are walking upon moral, ethical and religious ground, not to mention the very basic structure of our family – and generational – orientated society. Any researcher wishing to bring his theory to the public eye is going to have to make damn sure of himself; he's going to have to defend his findings tooth and nail and he'd better have a ton of evidence to back him up; otherwise he'll be ridden out on the proverbial rail. Do *you* have that much moxie, Doctor?'

Of course she was right. Absolutely any other field of research could be openly discussed and presented to the world for perusal. Except this one. It had something in it to upset just about everyone.

On the other hand, if one man *could* come forth and prove it...

'I still don't see, Dr Henderson,' said Jonas slowly, apprehensively, 'how it could happen spontaneously.'

'Any number of ways, Dr Wade. All you need are the same circumstances that have been created in the laboratory. A stimulus to the cell that will reproduce the same action of the sperm, taking the place of the sperm, as in the case of the cold for the rabbits. Thermal shock did to rabbit ova what rabbit sperm achieve. In mice, researchers are stimulating ova with electricity and, I believe, are producing perfect little fatherless mice. Or possibly a chemical agent, somehow unwittingly introduced into the female's bloodstream and coming in contact with the ovum. In the lab we have shown that parthenogenesis is not difficult to produce artificially. In nature, spontaneously, Dr Wade, all it takes is a similar situation. All you need is an activating agent.'

Jonas thought about this and was reminded of the article in *Lancet*: Dr Spurway's parthenogenic mother claimed that conception had taken place during a bombing raid in the war, that she had been near several blasts and severely jarred. He heard himself murmur, 'Such a big unknown...'

'If, let's say for the sake of argument here, one were to encounter a human female who claimed she had a parthenogenic child, then all it would take is intensive – or perhaps not so intensive, depending on the activating agent – examination to determine what the trigger mechanism had been. Process of elimination should do it.'

Jonas Wade took a long look at the woman seated across from him, then around the laboratory, at the various calendars and posters on the walls, the books lying haphazardly about; he felt behind him the sterile lab, the life that was growing there abnormally, *sterilely*, and he pictured again the cold, dead eyes of Primus.

'All right, Dr Henderson, you have told me that not only is parthenogenesis possible you have said that *spontaneous* parthenogenesis is possible, and not just in lower animals but in mammals as well. As for the activating agent, I don't think that is of as much importance as proof after the fact.'

For the first time, Dorothy Henderson frowned. 'What do you mean by proof after the fact?'

'A woman claims her baby is parthenogenic. What tools are in the hands of science to prove her right or wrong?'

The frown melted into an expression of singular interest. 'A good point, Doctor. With our frogs, we have never needed proof. We saw from the start where they came from. However, working from the end and going backward ... that's not easy. After all, a married woman would have a hard time convincing anyone her child had been virginally conceived, even if she and her husband had not engaged in sex for a long time, and an unmarried woman would have a difficult time convincing anyone she hadn't been "dabbling." You see, Dr Wade, a human parthenogenic birth is more a *moral* question than a biological one.'

Jonas Wade nodded, picturing again the slashed wrists of Mary Ann McFarland.

Dr Henderson went on: 'You have the woman's word against a whole mass of social mores. Say the word sex and people will snigger. Have a girl claim she never did anything and they'll wink. It would be different if she had, say, a stomach ulcer. No social repercussions there; she'd get prompt medical treatment and lots of sympathy. It's not unlike the stigma of venereal disease. If you contract a flu bug, you get sympathy. If you contract a spirochete, you are ostracized. And, all that's different is *how* it's contracted. You bring up anything at all that has to do with the generative organs of the human body and you bang your nose against a wall of indignation and ignorance.'

'I suppose, Dr Henderson, that you and I could discuss this morally and philosophically as long as it takes to determine the number of angels on the head of a pin. What *scientific* proof can be found?'

'Well' – she leaned forward and clasped her long fingers together on the desk – 'the first and most obvious observation one can make is that the offspring will always be a girl.'

Jonas raised an eyebrow.

'No Y chromosome.'

'Of course; I hadn't thought of that.'

'After that, microscopic examination of the chromosomes, skin grafting and, of course, direct visualisation of the daughter.'

'She would be an exact copy of the mother.'

'In every way.'

'And that's all we have?'

'I'm afraid so, until science moves along a little. In a case such as this, all one can do is eliminate those daughters who are *not* virginally conceived. Any found to contain the slightest variation from the mother's genetic composition can be discounted. Those who do exactly match, we can say they are *probably* parthenogenic daughters. In science, Dr Wade, proof lies not in the elimination of something but in its affirmation.'

The two doctors fell silent after this and sat for a moment in private mental involvement. Beyond the glass walls, Dorothy Henderson had all the answers she needed. Science had provided them all. But in here, where all they had were two human brains, she was at a loss.

Jonas Wade's mind was racing with his heart. He had to stop and think; he had to take it all in, spread it out, categorise it, try to fit the puzzle together. Dorothy Henderson had said some disturbing things – things that Jonas Wade had not thought about until now. She had mentioned dermoid cysts. Dr Wade knew all about them, he had seen them in surgery – ugly, gooey masses containing hair and teeth and nerve tissue: an ovum gone beserk, containing all the elements of a complete human being but in the wrong proportions. Allowed to grow, it killed a woman.

Another uninvited memory flashed in his head: in the library, reading about Olson's turkeys. One had not developed normally, had been born with bad eyesight, crooked toes and poor motor coordination. In itself, not frightening, but placed in a human context, disturbing.

Considering all the unknowns, anything could develop from a parthenogenic egg: anything from a dermoid cyst to a child with poor eyesight. Or – the ultimate horror – a living breathing mutation somewhere in between.

The thought so stunned Jonas Wade that he stared openly at the handsome face of Dorothy Henderson without realising he was doing so. And a new idea took hold and jelled into an unfaceable question: Was what was growing inside Mary Ann McFarland indeed a baby?

CHAPTER 9

It was July 1 and the day was scathingly hot. Despite the car's air conditioner, the three people in the Continental sweated and stuck to the leather upholstery. None of them spoke.

It had been a week since Mary had been discharged from Encino Hospital; exactly eight days, and in that time, no progress, with the exception of this morning's trip, had been made. Ted McFarland, having floundered in his efforts to take control of his family again, had spent the week in private mental retreat, passing quiet days in his office and contemplative evenings alone in the den, and had extended his one gym night to four. He had seen little of his daughter and when he had, had been at a loss as to what to say. The gauzes on her wrists and the now-exposed red slashes on her fingertips seemed to be glaring accusations, testimonials to his failure as a parent. Consequently, he had allowed Mary to get through the week on her own, solitarily, moving silently about the house as if she existed on another plane.

Speeding in the fast lane of the Ventura Freeway, Ted now reflected on the one day, last Tuesday, when the three of them had managed to get together for a visit with Father Crispin in the rectory.

It had been warm then, even at nine o'clock in the morning, and Father Crispin's office was not air-conditioned. Maintaining a steady distance behind the car in front of him, Ted pictured again the gravity on the priest's face as he spoke.

'I think it is not only a wise move, Ted, and a beneficial one for Mary, but it is your only move. After all, you can't keep her at home.'

Ted had glanced at his daughter slumped in the chair next to him, her face expressionless, her blue eyes glazed, her wrists hidden by a long-sleeved blouse, and he had wished, for one second, that she would fight them. He had looked to her, in that moment, hoping for a spark of anger, a dash of self-preservation, praying that she would suddenly snap to life and tell them all to go to hell.

'The nuns will take good care of her,' the priest had gone on, studying Mary's face as he made a steeple of his fingers and pursed his lips. 'She will have the availability of a priest at all times, so she can make confession when she finally chooses to. And she can attend Mass every day. Across the street is a school which she will attend in September so that by the time the child is born, Mary will be halfway through the twelfth grade and not have fallen behind. There's no reason why she can't return to Reseda High after that and graduate next June with her regular class.'

Father Crispin had then stood up and come around his desk, sitting on its edge and clasping his hands over one knee. 'The arrangements have all been made. I spoke with Dr Wade and he has also been in touch with them. As a rule, they don't take girls until the fourth month of pregnancy. Dr Wade thinks Mary is at the end of her third, although possibly even farther. However, due to the extenuating circumstances here, both at my recommendation and Dr Wade's they have agreed to take Mary now. Ted, you can take care of the financial arrangements and necessary paperwork when you take her there next Monday.'

Ted reached out and set the air conditioner up a notch. He glanced at Lucille next to him, at the tight profile, the thin line of mouth, and wondered about the six months that lay ahead.

Looking away and watching for the freeway interchange coming up, Ted heard again the voice of Father Crispin.

'About the baby, you won't have to sign anything yet. That can be decided up to six weeks after its birth, whether or not to put it up for adoption.'

Ted had cast a glance at his daughter; Mary hadn't seemed to hear.

At the conclusion of the brief, awkward meeting, Father Crispin had asked Mary to stay behind for a moment, so Ted and Lucille had gone to the car to wait for her. When Mary had emerged a few minutes later, her face had been maddeningly unreadable.

Glancing up now in the rear-view mirror at the same blank expression and resigning himself to the fact that Mary was not going to put up a struggle, Ted did not deny that he was relieved to be making this trip today.

Lucille McFarland had spent the week pretty much as Ted had, barely conscious of the news of the election of Pope Paul VI, and not even watching his coronation on TV. She had called her friends and social groups, complained of the Asian flu, and had kept to herself. Once or twice she had considered trying again to open communications with Mary, but each time she had balked, a little fearful of rejection, but more from a lack of anything to say. Lucille's perplexity was as absolute as her husband's; she needed time to think, to grasp the situation and maybe find ways to mend it.

The one decisive step she had taken was to follow Father Crispin's advice and remove twelve-year-old Amy from the uncertain atmosphere.

The evening after Mary's suicide attempt, Lucille had called a cousin in San Diego and asked if they could take Amy for a few days. The cousin, Lucille's age with a thirteen-year-old daughter of her own, had said she would be delighted. And when Amy had been told, she had been thrilled. The second cousins had known each other for years and had seen one another on sporadic family visits; the prospect of a week in San Diego in the company of a girl her own age was exciting.

Lucille closed her eyes against the sunlight shimmering off

the polished hood of the Continental and thought: I'll make it up to you, Amy. She felt the hysteria start to rise in her; she pulled herself in, held herself rigid, and hung on to an imaginary ballast until the panic subsided. Earlier this morning, however, Lucille had come her closest to totally breaking down.

She had been standing silently in the doorway of Mary's bedroom, watching her daugher pack a small suitcase. Lucille couldn't tell if Mary was aware of her standing there; she gave no indication. Moving like one hypnotised, the girl had slowly taken a few things out of her drawers, folded them neatly, and placed them in the bag.

Lucille had wanted to help, had wanted to tell Mary what to take, for she could see from the doorway that her daughter was packing pathetically little. A few underthings. A nightgown. A summer robe. A Hawaiian muumuu. A diary. And finally a little bottle of water from Lourdes shaped like the Holy Virgin with her crown as the stopper.

Seeing this last go in, Mary's most prized possession, Lucille had turned away and fled down to the end of the hall, where, standing with her cheek pressed to the wall, she had mentally pleaded: For God's sake, Mary Ann, say something! Scream! Shout! *Anything!* Just don't do this to me...

When the anguish started to build in her again, this time threateningly close to erupting, Lucille brought a fist up to her mouth and pressed her knuckles into her lips. This past week had been misery. The whole three weeks, a nightmare. Did Ted and Father Crispin and Dr Wade really think that putting Mary away was going to make the agony go away?

Of the three in the car, only one had no feelings one way or another about this morning's destination. All was the same to Mary; each day like the last, an endless stream of limbos. She had seen Dr Wade twice. The long running suture buried beneath each wrist slash had been removed so that two thin red welts remained. He had also run more blood and urine tests on her and had weighed her. When he had suggested a uterine exam to determine her progress, Mary had submitted, lamblike. He had been friendly and kind and had seemed, on both occasions, on the verge of

111

saying something; but each time he seemed to decide against it and Mary was just as content to let it go; no doubt Dr Wade wanted to lecture her, or ask her again what everyone asked her. Who was the father?

There had been two peaks in the week which should have caught even her momentary interest but did not. The first had been a news film of President Kennedy standing before an enormous crowd and shouting: '*Ich bin ein Berliner!*'

And the second had been when she had been lying flat on her back in bed late one night and had run a hand down her abdomen and into the hollow of her pelvis. There, she had felt a bulge rising.

Gliding along the Hollywood Freeway and seeing the Capital Records Building flit by, Mary reflected again upon the little talk she and Amy had had the night before.

It had been decided that Amy should be told a lie. Mary was going to go to Vermont for the summer to visit an old school friend, after which time a second lie would be fabricated to explain her failure to return in time for school. A broken leg, perhaps, in a hiking accident.

During the week following her discharge from the hospital, Mary had sorely missed Amy; since her little sister had not been allowed to visit at the hospital and then had been spirited off to San Diego, by the time Amy returned, only yesterday, Mary had been hungry for her company.

But twelve-year-old Amy, having not yet been told of her sister's plan to go away the next morning, had run down the street to see her friends and tell them of her week's adventure. By the time Amy had returned, it was suppertime and Mary, nauseated again, was not present at the table.

So it was not until late in the evening that Mary was able to be alone with her little sister.

Against the backdrop of Hollywood as it sped by, Mary pictured again her sister's room.

The haphazardness of it, the glaring contradiction of a handsome Jesus tacked up next to the Kingston Trio. A fluorescent orange 'NIX ON NIXON' bumper sticker on the bulletin board. A plaster statue of the Virgin Mary draped with fresh dandelions. Spread facedown on the bed, the

112

current bestseller, *Moonspinners* by Mary Stewart. Amy's new favourite song for the week, 'Telstar,' twanging on her record player. And Amy sitting cross-legged in the centre of the floor, making an octopus out of pink yarn.

Mary had knocked, thought Amy had heard, and so had stuck her head in. 'Hi. Can I come in?'

'Hey!' Amy had quickly scrambled the yarn and scissors behind her back. 'You're supposed to knock!'

'I did.' Mary glanced at the phonograph. 'That's awfully loud. Can I turn it off for a minute?'

The twelve-year-old pivoted around on her bottom, hiding the octopus behind her as Mary came in, closed the door, and crossed the room to silence the record player.

'You know something?' came Amy's practised sophisticated tone. 'You sure do know how to spoil a surprise!'

Mary turned around. 'What do you mean?'

Amy whipped out the octopus, only two legs braided, the styrofoam ball showing beneath gaps in the yarn. 'I'm making this for you.'

Mary sat down in front of Amy, hiding her hands under her thighs. 'It's pretty. My favourite colour.'

'It's your going-away present. I wanted it to be ready before you left.'

Mary felt a pang but kept a smile fixed on her face. 'There's time. How come you're not watching Soupy Sales?'

Amy returned her attention to the octopus, counting out strands for a new leg. 'Cancelled 'cause of a Dodger game.'

Mary nodded sadly, watching Amy's Buster Brown hair fall forward in her concentration.

'Are you going to miss me, Amy?'

'Sure! Boy, I wish I could go. Wow, Vermont! And for three whole months. I didn't know you had a friend there. Beats me how you're gonna get along without Mike all summer.'

Mary closed her eyes and swallowed hard. Amy, she thought unhappily, I wish I could tell you. I hate lying to you. You should know the truth you really should. After all, what have I done to be ashamed of?

113

Amy's voice faded in and out: 'Me and a bunch of kids are going to Disneyland tomorrow. They've got a new ride called the Matterhorn...'

And besides, thought Mary, you of all people would believe me when I told you I'm not guilty of anything.

Mary felt her heart rush. 'Amy...I want to tell you something...'

'Yeah?' The twelve-year-old lifted her head and gazed at her sister with a look of startling maturity. 'I have something to tell you, too.'

Seeing, for an instant, the childhood fade from Amy's eyes, Mary frowned. 'What is it?'

'Well, I've been wanting to tell you and the folks for days now, but I never got the chance because they've been all upset about your appendix and everything and then I went to San Diego this week and then at suppertime they never listened to me because they were upset about something. You know how they can be sometimes. Anyway, since you're going away tomorrow, Mary, I'll tell you now.'

Mary sighed and waited patiently while Amy carefully put the yarn and scissors on the floor, wiped her hands down her pants, then regarded her sister with casual self-assurance. Amy said softly, 'I'm going to become a nun.'

The words hung in the air as Mary stared at her sister. After a moment she felt the impulse to laugh and ruffle Amy's hair, but when she saw the seriousness in the large brown eyes, the steady determination, Mary felt an unexplainable fear come over her.

'Amy, do you really mean it?'

'Of course I do. Oh, I know, a lot of girls say they're going to become nuns and never do, but I've given it a lot of thought and Sister Agatha has been counselling me. She says she can get me into her order next year, at the convent where I can go to school until I enter the novitiate.'

Mary closed her eyes, trembling. 'Oh, Amy...'

'You know where I first got the idea from, Mary? From you! A couple of years ago you told me you wanted to be a nun because you wanted to help people. I was only ten then so I thought it was sorta dumb to want to be a nun. I mean, all you get to wear is black and no lipstick. But then in catechism, Mary, I've been talking to Sister Agatha and she's been telling me all the neat things nuns do, like be nurses or missionaries, not just the ones that teach grammar school or sew altar cloths.

'And then I got to thinking about what you've been saying about the Peace Corps and how you'd like to help unfortunate people. I got to thinking that I want to do that too, I want to be like you, Mary, only I'd like to do it for Jesus. You know what I mean?'

The wide-eyed innocence mingled with the sudden maturity in Amy's eyes caused Mary to avert her head. She wanted to burst into tears, to run from the big-sister adoration and idealism glowing in Amy's round eyes.

Instead, at a loss for a reply, she looked around the bedroom, at the discarded ballet slippers, the neglected Barbie Dolls, the untouched Nancy Drew books, at the new poster of James Darren recently taped to the wall, the padded bra hanging from the doorknob, and Mary thought sadly: Amy, don't grow up.

'What do you think?'

Finding the strength to smile and keep her voice from wavering, Mary said, 'Wow, it's a big decision.'

'I know, but Sister Agatha says that being at the convent will help me to decide. She says I'd make a great nun, and she says she's already spoken to her mother superior about me. I know Mom and Dad'll be pleased.'

Amy's face then folded into a frown. 'Mary! Is something wrong?'

'No!' Mary gave her best laugh. 'Hey, I'm happy for you!' She reached out and squeezed her sister's arm.

'Mary, why don't you come with me and join the order?'

'Oh –' Her laugh turned to nervousness. 'Now how could I be married to Mike and be a nun too, huh?'

Amy grinned and picked up the yarn and scissors. 'Yeah. I'm glad you're happy for me. What you think means a lot to me. I'm gonna tell Mom and Dad at a special moment; you know, when we're alone and quiet.'

Mary stared down at Amy's nimble fingers as they

115

resumed counting out strands of yarn. Then she heard her say, 'So what was it you were going to tell me, Mary?'

Tears stung her eyes as she said softly, 'Only that I'll miss you.'

'Hey!' Amy looked up, her face beaming. 'That's the first time you've ever said that to me!' She flung her arms around Mary's neck and hugged her. 'I'll miss you, too!'

As Mary became aware of the car slowing down and she saw they had gotten off the freeway and were winding through an old residential neighbourhood, Amy's words continued to echo in her ears. Mary pressed her head against the window and fought back the tears, thinking: Not now, not here. I'll cry when I'm alone...

The car finally came to a halt. All three stared out at the tall hedge protecting a private driveway, and the small unassuming sign that said simply: St Anne's Maternity Hospital.

CHAPTER 10

It was a steamy, smoggy day in Los Angeles; jet trails turned yellow in the sky and palm trees hung limp in the haze. The distant whisper of the building's massive air-conditioning system played at the back of Dr Jonas Wade's mind, a constant subliminal reminder of what sort of afternoon he was soon going to step into. He tried not to think of it, concentrating instead on the balmy evening the rancid day would later miraculously turn into; the fall of night which halted the photochemical process and started the nightly purification of the air. The sky would be plum-coloured and there would be margaritas on the patio while steaks sizzled on the barbecue and friends would be diving into the pool.

But Jonas Wade's mind was not on the coming evening. In his briefcase, under the desk by his feet, was the work he really wanted to turn to: the folder thick with masses of notes, the photocopied articles, the obscure book he had found in a used bookstore, and finally his spiral notebook, full of random thoughts and ideas all waiting to be put into readable condition, all gathered under the tentative title: 'Human Parthenogenesis: A Reality'.

It had been his project for the past eight weeks, ever since his interview with Dr Dorothy Henderson. In that time, Jonas had gone back to the library and painstakingly Thermofaxed every shred, every word of evidence to support his theory; he had visited Dr Henderson's cloning lab again, and had then spent an hour in the Encino Hospital operating room discussing the latest skin-grafting techniques with a plastic surgeon. The burgeoning evidence, drawing him closer and closer to the conclusion that Mary Ann McFarland was a true parthenogenic mother, at the same time made Jonas Wade acutely aware of the fact that it would all fall flat without the inclusion of one vital, missing factor: the girl herself.

He wished now he hadn't been so ready to have her sent to St. Anne's, and, wishing it felt paradoxically guilty, for St. Anne's was for the good of Mary, while having her at home served only the good of Jonas Wade.

A soft tap on his door was followed by the intrusion of his nurse, who stuck her head in and said, 'Dr. Wade? Can you see one more patient?'

He raised his eyebrows, then glanced at his watch. 'But it's four o'clock. I'm about to leave. Is it a scheduled appointment?'

The woman glanced over her shoulder and then came all the way in and softly closed the door behind her. 'It's the McFarland girl. She says she has to talk to you'.

'McFarland? Mary Ann McFarland?' Jonas got to his feet. 'Show her in'.

'Want me to stick around?'

'No, thanks, but call my wife, will you, and tell her I'll be a little late'.

As the nurse went out, Jonas Wade took a deep breath and

117

braced himself. A moment later the girl was standing in his doorway.

He smiled at her, feeling a ripple of excitement run through him. 'Hi, Mary, come in. Have a seat'.

He watched her as she came in, delicately closed the door, set her suitcase on the floor, and then sat down in one of the leather chairs.

A change had taken place since he had last seen her. Mary seemed a little fleshier now, no longer the slim, angular teenager. The rich brown hair, parted in the middle, was hooked behind her ears and fell over gentler shoulders. Beneath the Hawaiian muumuu the contours of her breasts were visible, and just before she sat, he glimpsed the modest protrusion of her abdomen.

The whole effect struck him as a subtle womanisation; she seemed softer now, pliant and more feminine. He shook the thought from his head and sat down. 'This is such a coincidence, Mary. I was just thinking about you. How are you?'

'Dr Wade, why am I pregnant?'

Keeping his face expressionless, Jonas dropped his eyes down to her wrists. The scars were barely visible now; you had to be looking for them. Then he studied her face. The last things he had seen in her wide blue eyes, fear and confusion, were no longer there. Instead she gazed at him with an unflinching self-assurance that startled him and made him wonder what strange transformation had taken place.

'Let me see, I last saw you seven or eight weeks ago. As I recall, Mary, at that time you denied being pregnant.'

She nodded. 'That's changed. Now I know I am. And I want to know why.'

Jonas Wade leaned back in his chair and tried to assume a detached, clinical air. 'So you still think you're a virgin?'

'I know I am.'

'What happened to St. Anne's?'

'I've been there for the past six weeks. I just left today'.

'Oh?' He looked over at her suitcase.

'My friend Germaine came to visit me a couple of times

118

and told me how she did it by taking the Ventura bus to downtown to the Wilshire bus. I simply reversed the process.'

'You came here by bus? All that way?'

'I had to.'

'But ... where are your parents?'

Mary shrugged. 'At home, I guess.'

'Don't they know you left St. Anne's?'

'No.'

Dr Wade leaned abruptly forward and clasped his hands together on the desk. 'You mean you just left St. Anne's on your own and came straight here? Without telling anyone?'

'Yes.'

'Why?'

'Because I didn't want to be there any more.'

'I mean, why did you come straight here? Why didn't you go home?'

'Because I want to know why I'm pregnant and you're the only one who can help me.'

'Mary—' Jonas Wade shifted in his chair, his foot tapped the note-filled briefcase. 'Mary, you have to go home. I can't do anything without your parents' permission.'

'Oh, I know that. I just had to come here first, you know, before I let them know what I'd decided. You were the only person I knew that I could turn to and trust. I can't face my parents alone, Dr Wade, not just yet.'

His eyes settled on her face, on the disquieting little-girl features showing beneath a thin patina of adulthood. Not quite transformed after all, he thought sadly. Merely a child wearing a grown-up's mask.

'You didn't have to leave St. Anne's in order to talk to me. You could have called, I would have come to see you.'

She shook her head vigorously, casting loose the hair from behind her ears so that it fell in waves along her cheeks. 'Yes I did. I want my baby to grow at home. I want to be with my family while this is happening to me. I want them to be part of it.'

'Have you considered what they will think?'

'It doesn't matter, Dr Wade. They're just going to have to accept me. They sent me away because the sight of me reminded them of something that upsets them. Well, I won't be put away like Mr. Rochester's mad wife. Not when I'm not guilty of any crime. Dr. Wade' – Mary leaned forward in her chair, earnestness firming the features of her face – 'can you tell me why I'm pregnant?'

He was held by those crisp blue eyes, the glacial purity of them, their utter frankness; he teetered between telling all and keeping the secret stolidly to himself. 'This may come as a surprise to you, Mary, but I've been thinking about you these past two months, and I, too, have been wondering how you got pregnant.'

'Dr Wade, I knew all along you believed me. That's why I came to you today.'

Jonas had to escape her gaze so he stood abruptly and turned to the floor-to-ceiling window that gave out upon a yellowing valley. He had to take a minute to consider how to handle the situation, how to tell her what he had learned, if indeed to even tell her at all just yet. Mary was so different now from the other times he had seen her, before the mysterious transformation had taken place. Considering this puzzling reversal in her attitude, Jonas Wade studied her pale reflection in the glass.

She was lucky she lived in the valley, where standards of dress were more relaxed, where a girl could wear a muumuu and wedgies without getting a second thought. Today she was a portrait in lavender, he noticed, down to the braiding of her bamboo wedgies; and her eyes seemed to take on an orchid tint in a chameleonlike imitation of the dress below the throat. Her hair was fetchingly shiny, undulled by the hair spray that most women wore these days, and the smooth complexion of her face and arms was tinged pink, as if she had been out in the sun.

Jonas Wade wondered: How do I tell her she might have a monstrous mass growing in her abdomen?

To buy a little more time, he said offhandedly, 'What was it like at St. Anne's?'

He heard her sigh and thought he detected a trace of

impatience in it. 'It was like being at college. In a dormitory. It's a nice enough place, I suppose, not at all like a hospital. I had a nice roommate and the nuns were good to us. But I didn't belong. The other girls, they were all pregnant because they had *done* something, and they knew it. They even talked about it. But I was different. I didn't belong. And I had lots of time to think about it, until I decided I just couldn't sit around anymore. I had to find out why I'm pregnant.'

Finally, he turned around and said, 'The doctors at St. Anne's, Mary, what did they say about your condition?'

Her eyes widened. 'What do you mean?'

'I assume you were examined.'

'Once a week.'

'And did they— ' damn, since when had he had a hard time talking to a patient? – 'say you were healthy, that you were proceeding normally?' No need to alarm the girl; he would request her medical records first thing in the morning.

Mary gave a little shrug. 'I guess. I'm not gaining too much weight, they said, and puffy feet are normal. They didn't talk to me much.'

Jonas felt a tide of irritation sweep through him. He would have preferred to be better prepared for this interview, he needed the facts, he didn't know what to say next.

'Oh,' she added with a smile. 'They did say the baby's normal.'

He gazed down at her blankly for an instant, then: 'What?'

'I heard his heartbeat, too. There was one really nice doctor who...'

Mary's voice faded as his mind began to clamor inside his head. A heartbeat! It has a heartbeat!

'Is something wrong, Dr Wade?'

Jonas blinked down at her. 'What? No. I'm sorry, I was thinking...' His hand reached blindly for the back of his chair.

This was it, the big unknown. It had a heartbeat. It lived...

Jonas Wade forced himself to sit down and calmly fold his hands on the desk. 'Mary, you're not alone in wondering how you got pregnant. I've been trying to solve that riddle myself but found I couldn't do it without your help.'

'How can I help?'

'Maybe by just answering a few questions. Anyway, let's give it a try, okay?'

'Sure. You mean you're not going to call my folks yet?'

Jonas was as stunned as if she had slapped him. So consumed with pursuing his scientific inquiry that he had lost sight of his basic responsibility. The girl was a runaway; a host of people would be worried. Jonas reached for the phone.

Five minutes later, the nuns at St. Anne's had been informed and reassured. There had been no answer at the McFarland house.

'I'll try your parents again in a few minutes. Now, Mary,' Jonas reached for a fresh note pad and slipped his shiny pen out of his lab-coat pocket. 'Let's try to go back to the approximate time of conception. Maybe if we approach it the right way, you'll remember something.'

'I've already thought about it, Dr Wade. Back at St. Anne's. At my last prenatal check, which was a week ago, the doctor said I was sixteen weeks along. He said my conception was somewhere in the first half of April. So I did a lot of thinking about that, and I remember April very well because Mike had houseguests from out of town and we saw each other only twice before Easter. And just once the week following. One time was at the St. Sebastian's spring barbecue and that was during the day, when we were never alone for even a minute, and another time was when we went swimming in my pool at night. The third time we watched "Hootenanny" together at my house, but we were with my folks and were never alone for a second, so how could I have done it with him? Even if I forgot afterward, like everyone thinks, we never had the chance, Dr Wade.'

'I know, Mary. Considering how many pregnant teenagers hotly deny having had sex, I had to explore all avenues, one of them being mental repression. I no longer believe

122

that.' He paused, his mind going back to the Maryland turkeys; the 'unknown contaminant' in the fowl pox vaccine. 'So, Mary, sometime last April, around Easter, did you take medication for any reason?'

She thought a moment. 'No.'

'Did you get a shot for anything – flu, polio, that sort of thing?'

'No.'

His pen moved across the note pad. 'How about vitamins, cough medicine, even aspirin?'

'Nothing, Dr Wade. I was just fine all through April.'

'Okay...' He paused and tapped his chin with the pen. 'Did you maybe step on something, puncture your foot— '

'Nothing happened to me, Dr Wade. I didn't even get a paper cut!'

He put his pen down and wrestled with the idea of bringing out his briefcase. Dr Henderson's notes were in there, and if he could refresh his memory, reread some of the possible 'activating agents' she had suggested; but he didn't want to alarm the girl. All that research, some of the horror stories, massive dermoid cysts the size of basketballs...

'The only exciting thing that happened to me in April, Dr Wade, was when Mike and I went swimming and the pool lights shorted out and I got an electrical shock.'

For the second time in that hour Dr Wade gave her a dumb stare. And followed it with, 'What?'

'It nearly knocked me out, but I wasn't hurt. Mother said a woman had been killed in a hotel— '

'Did you say electrical shock?'

'Yes, why?'

Jonas Wade felt a shock of his own go through him and he suddenly had to drop the pen. He clasped his hands to hide the tremor and said, 'When did that happen? Exactly.'

'A few days before Easter.'

'And...exactly what happened? You and Mike were swimming— '

'I was swimming, Mike was on the board about to dive. It was night so we had the lights on. I don't know, suddenly

123

there was a weird feeling in the water, I can't describe it, and I screamed. Then I couldn't breathe and I vaguely remember Mike pulling me out and pounding on my back. That's all.'

Jonas Wade closed his eyes and clasped his hands so tight they turned white. This was too incredible, too perfect to believe! Could it be that he had it all now, that all the unknowns had fallen into place?

Until this morning Jonas had held himself back, not allowed himself the luxury of giving free reign to his hopes, his dream: the most explosive medical write-up since ... what?

'Dr Wade?'

He opened his eyes. How would he go about it, who would he show it to, which journal would get it—

'Dr Wade?'

He brought his gaze into focus. 'Forgive me, Mary, something you said triggered a memory.' He drew his mouth back in a physician's smile of reassurance. But as Jonas Wade stared at Mary Ann McFarland, his initial excitement of learning of the heartbeat and then of the electrical shock started to turn rapidly into alarm. While completing the foundation of his parthenogenic thesis, the two new factors also created new fears; no longer was it a mass, a tumor to be excised surgically; it had a heartbeat, it was a true parthenogenic foetus, but...was it *normal*?

Jonas shuddered slightly, then impulsively reached for the phone. 'I'll try your parents again, Mary.'

And his mind thought wildly: Bernie. I've got to talk to Bernie.

They sat in the darkening living room. No one made a move to turn on the light. Ted McFarland, his eyes tracing the pattern of the Navaho rug, wondered if he had said everything. Somehow, the silence sounded hollow and incomplete, as if there were more words to be spoken. But he couldn't think of any.

Lucille McFarland, resting back in the easy chair, her eyes roaming the dusky ceiling, cradled a cold fear that too much had been said. And in all of it, the one thing Lucille had most wanted to say – I'm sorry – somehow never got voiced.

Mary, perched on the edge of an ottoman, like an elf squatting on a toadstool, sensed that emotions were being tethered; her parents were constraining themselves. Ted, with his head bowed and fingers interlocked, appeared to be praying, and her mother, Mary thought, looked like the Suffering Servant of God.

It had gone as well as could be expected. Possibly better. They had come to Dr Wade's office effusively polite and grateful, anxious to express their gratitude and to be certain he was aware they held no grudge against him for being the sole recipient of their daughter's trust. They had sat and talked a little while, the four of them, awkwardly and with some embarrassment; Dr Wade, Mary had noted, had seemed a little stiff and stilted, as though he were uncomfortable and anxious to be leaving.

The three adults had tried at first to persuade Mary to return to St. Anne's, then Dr Wade had gone on to give her what sounded like a memorised speech of advice on how the expectant mother should be cared for and had jotted down on a piece of paper the time and day Mary was to come in again.

During the entire agonising hour, Jonas Wade had kept his secret to himself.

Once at home in the living room, the three McFarlands had calmly come to some conclusions.

'Amy isn't to know about this,' Lucille had said. There were little yellow pouches under her eyes.

'How can you keep it from her?' Mary had asked.

'If we can't send *you* away, then we'll send your sister away. Tonight she's at Melody's house. Tomorrow I'll think of something.'

Mary had been about to protest when her father had said quietly, 'Amy is to stay here, Lucille. She has to know. It's time for her to know.'

'No!' Terror had filled Lucille's blue eyes. 'I won't have her exposed to this. She's too young. She's just a child.'

'She's almost thirteen years old, Lucille. It might do her some good to know about this.'

'I won't have Amy spoiled. She's joining Sister Agatha's order next year— '

But Ted had shaken his head and Lucille's voice had died in the twilight.

Then they had talked about other things, touching on school, church, and all other manner of public appearance. Mary had been noncommittal, having not really given any thought to these matters. All she had known was that she needed to be home. Beyond that – going to church, accompanying her mother to the supermarket – she had decided she would tackle each new day as it came.

Now they were finished and the house was dark and no more weary voices rose up, so Mary stirred on the ottoman and came to her feet. Ted brought his head up and seemed, in the smoky shadows, to be trying to smile.

'I guess I'll go to my room now,' she whispered, reaching for her suitcase.

Ted was on his feet at once, grabbing the bag energetically like a bellboy anxious for a tip. Mary turned to Lucille. 'I'm hungry, Mother, what's for supper?'

She used the phone in the kitchen. 'Germaine? It's me. I'm home.'

Her best friend's voice came over the line as clear as if she were in the room with her and Mary was instantly comforted. 'Mare? You're home? Honest? How come?'

She's near, thought Mary, closing her eyes and holding the receiver with both hands. That's what's good about being home. Germaine is near. 'I decided to leave. I came home this afternoon and I'm not going back.'

'Oh, wow, you mean you're going to have it here then, in Tarzana?'

'I want him, Germaine, I want my baby.'

Silence at the other end.

'Germaine?'

A subtle alteration in her voice; caution. 'What do your folks think?'

Mary looked around the kitchen. Pots and pans were not yet washed. A platter of cold spaghetti was clotting on the counter. 'I'm not sure. We've talked a bit, but they don't say an awful lot, if you know what I mean. Dinner was awkward, but I think it's going to get better.'

'Mare, I'm awfully glad to have you back. I've been lonely.'

'Thanks. Germaine?'

'Yeah?'

'Have you seen Mike?'

A pause. 'Only a couple of times at school, Mare. He's taking Chemistry and English Lit. I only see him when I'm on my way to Constitution class.'

'Constitution class?'

'It's new this year. I'm going to take Political Science in September and you have to have the American Constitution as a prerequisite. Old Hat-Peg Nose teaches it.'

'Has he talked to you, Germaine? Said anything about me?'

'Hat-Peg Nose doesn't talk to anyone taller than himself.'

'Germaine— '

'No, Mare, Mike hasn't talked to me. Remember? He doesn't like me.'

'What about the rest of the kids?'

'I really don't know, Mare. Marcie's the only other one going to summer school this year. I guess everyone else is at Malibu every day.'

'Germaine, has anyone ever asked— '

'Not in an obvious way, but I'm sure they wonder. Sheila Brabent of all people called me up a couple of weeks ago and asked me if it was true.'

'What did you tell her?'

'Well, Mare, I had to say yes. I mean, it is true, isn't it? You are pregnant?'

'Yes, it's true, but. . .' Mary heaved a tremulous sigh.

'Mare?'

'Yes.'

'When are you coming over? It's been so damn boring

without you! Rudy's gone down to Mississippi to join the big Medgar Evers protest. Without him or you I have no one. Listen, my mom wants you over for dinner. When can you come?'

After she hung up, Mary felt a little better. But, to her dismay, not a whole lot better, as she had hoped. It would take time, she knew, to get used to this situation. Nearly five more months of finding ways to cope. Thank God for Germaine, acting as if everything were normal; Mary would at least have a friend through the summer.

She dialled three digits of Mike's number and then hung up. Not yet, not on her first night home; she would get adjusted first, then she would confront him and set things right.

Mary leaned against the cool kitchen wall, her hands resting on the gentle rise of her abdomen, and swept her gaze around the room. Two months ago she had made a decision in this same spot and it had been the wrong one.

She looked at the telephone and thought: He's forgotten me.

Mike Holland fumbled for the light switch, hit it, and when the bathroom flared white like a firework, he closed his eyes and made for the sink. The cold water felt good on his hands. Lots of soap. He rubbed and scrubbed, all the way up to the elbows, like a surgeon, and then rinsed and rinsed, all the while avoiding eye contact with the guy in the mirror.

When he was through and roughly drying off with a thick towel, Mike thought sourly: Jesus, what's gotten into me?

Carefully draping the towel over its rack and smoothing it out – all three Holland boys had been taught to keep their own areas tidy for there was no female around to pick up after them – Mike paused to give his face objective scrutiny.

A nice layer of down covered his cheeks, but his chin was still baby-smooth. No sign of stubble yet. He recalled Brother Nicodemas's seventh-grade lecture on the sin of Onan. 'One sure sign that someone is doing it is that his beard starts very late, sometimes not at all. It's a fact, boys, so don't smirk. Touching yourself causes an unnatural release of chemicals that would otherwise have gone into stimulating beard growth. You ask any doctor. Aside from the fact that it's a sin and offensive to God, touching yourself can't be hidden because everyone will be able to see the result plainly on your face.'

'Yeah, sure...' Mike muttered as he ran his fingers over his chin. They hadn't believed it then, the boys of St. Sebastian's seventh-grade class, and they didn't believe it now. Still, it would make him feel more like a man if his beard would grow.

Mike flicked off the light and made his way back to his room. Two things irked him now and kept him from sleeping. One was the fact that he had given in to himself tonight and now it was impossible to take Communion in the morning. The other was Mary Ann McFarland.

Mike slouched on the edge of the bed.

The beard aside, he didn't feel much like a man at anything anymore, not even during football practice when the crunching impact of an opponent's body used to fill him with a surge of masculine satisfaction. He was masturbating more now, more than he ever had when he was going with Mary – and that stuck him as ironical – and he couldn't seem to stop himself from trying to scour the skin off his hands and arms afterward.

Mary...

He lay back on the bed, arms beneath his head, and pictured her, as he did every night, against the black ceiling. He tried, as he also did every night, to analyse his jumbled feelings, to sort them out and make some sense of them. If he could have written a list of them he would have, like separating white laundry from coloured.

He was *angry*. That was evident. But with whom? Mary, maybe. Himself, yes. With the joker that knocked her up, most of all. And he was *unhappy*. He longed for her. He pined. All the golden young bodies on Malibu Beach, thin and smooth and ripe, failed to overcome his fixation that he still belonged to Mary and Mary alone. *Curiosity*. Why had she done it and with whom? *Sexual desire*. Still wanting her as much as ever, his lust increasing, hungering for the forbidden

129

fruit that was even more out of reach now than it had ever been before. And finally, a little in *awe* of Mary herself: the mystique of the pregnant woman.

He was also frustrated with the desire to forgive her, but too proud to take the first step.

He suddenly rolled over and drove his fist into his pillow.

What a blow it had been to hear from his dad that she had come home today. With Mary away at that special home, Mike had been able to fight down his misery and depression; but with her suddenly nearby again, mixed, confused emotions rose up once more. The impulse to call her, kiss her, weep with her. Then fury. That she had lied to him. And then cool objectivity. The yearning to sit down with her and say quietly: Why, Mary, why some other guy and not me?

How often had he started to call her at St. Anne's, dialling the first half of the number and then hanging up. If only he could forget her. Go out with fat Sherry, who clearly had the hots for him and would give him anything he wanted. Or Sheila Brabent with the big tits.

Why Mary?

He punched the pillow again.

Then there were the guys to think about; the god-awful decision he had had to make of whether to take responsibility for her pregnancy, or to tell the truth and admit he'd lied about his conquests with her, a decision he had ultimately avoided making.

And there was his dad, who had been so crestfallen by it all, who continued to insist that Mike stand up for her, marry her, take the man's painful but necessary and old-fashioned duty of honour. And Father Crispin, who pursed his lips and suggested Mike confess his sin of carnal knowledge and who refused to believe it wasn't Mike's fault.

Finally, Timothy, who had hero worshipped his elder brother but who now seemed to regard Mike with something akin to scorn; as if he had been let down.

What Mike desperately hoped for now was that the baby would be given away after it was born and that he and Mary could somehow get back together and take up where they had left off. Because, despite the fact that she had lied to him, hadn't loved him and trusted him enough to be honest with him, Mike still loved her. And he wanted her now more than ever.

Feeling like a coward, and as if the problems of the world pressed down on him, seventeen-year-old Mike Holland finally fell asleep.

CHAPTER 11

The corpse lay on its back on the table, naked except for a cloth draped over its genitals; its left arm was splayed open, revealing muscles and tendons, while eight bearded men looked on in various attitudes of wonder. It was an excellent reproduction of Rembrandt's 'Anatomy Lesson of Dr Tulp' and Bernie could not take his eyes off it.

Sitting across the study, in a high wingback chair and holding a vodka martini, Jonas Wade waited impatiently for his friend to speak. Finally, after ten silent minutes had passed, Jonas prompted with: 'Well?'

Bernie Schwartz forced his eyes from the painting back to Jonas and said with a shrug, 'You've convinced me.'

Jonas relaxed an inch. 'Then I'm not crazy.'

Bernie smiled. 'No, my friend, you're not. You've made a believer out of me. How can I refute all this?' He waved a chubby hand over the papers and notebooks spread on the leather ottoman before him. The geneticist had spent the past half hour reading Jonas's notes, the interviews with Dorothy Henderson, and an extensive bibliography. 'In fact,' he said, 'I'm impressed. I had really thought it impossible. Two months ago, I thought it a crackpot idea. I've come around a hundred and eighty degrees.'

While this should have appeased Jonas Wade, it did not; on the contrary, Bernie's acceptance of his theory only inflamed him all the more. Until now, Jonas had held himself back; with Bernie's imprimatur, his ambitions roared into a full flood.

Pushing himself to his feet and striding across the study, Jonas said, 'It frightens me, Bernie.'

'Why?'

Jonas closed the door to block out the opening theme of 'Mr. Novak' and returned to his chair. He perched at the very edge, regarding his friend in tense earnestness. 'All this time I thought maybe it was only a mass. I was going to contact the doctor in charge of Mary at St. Anne's and let him know my suspicions. In a few weeks, I was going to seriously consider surgery. A dermoid cyst, Bernie, that's what I thought it might be. But then— ' he looked down at his untouched drink, put the glass down and pressed his palms together – 'she showed up on my doorstep and said it had a heartbeat.'

'So? What's frightening?'

Jonas's moist palms slid against one another. 'It's a parthenogenic foetus, Bernie, you know what that implies. God, what form is it taking?'

'You know better how to handle that than I do. X-ray her, Jonas.'

'I can't. It's too soon. X-rays can't be done before twenty-five weeks, you know that; the radiation could harm the foetus.'

'Then all you can do is wait. I'm sure it's a normal baby, Jonas— '

'You are? How can you be sure?' Wade's voice was edged with a touch of anger. 'Electrical shock has produced normal mice in the laboratory. It has also produced mutations.' Jonas held his breath for a moment. '*Mutations*, Bernie.'

'It has a heartbeat— '

'A *monster* can have a heartbeat, for God's sake!'

The word hung suspended between the two men as their eyes met across the dim room. 'It's a big responsibility,' murmured Jonas after a length. 'I have to tell the parents. They have to be warned.'

132

Bernie's voice was soft. 'What are you talking, Jonas? Are you talking abortion?'

Dr Wade's eyebrows rose up. 'That had never occurred to me. And anyway, it's out of the question. The baby only *might* be deformed, and it's too early to X-ray to see if it is or not. By the time we can X-ray, it'll be too far along to abort anyway.'

'Even if it turns out to be a monster?'

'At six months, Bernie, a foetus is legally viable. No court in the country would sanction an abortion on the grounds of deformity. I would have to prove a life-threatening circumstance to the mother.'

'You've got time yet, Jonas.'

Wade stood abruptly and paced back and forth a few times, slapping a fist into his palm. He couldn't wait for the X-rays; that was a good nine or ten weeks away yet. He had to know sooner. He had to know *now*.

Jonas stopped suddenly and said, 'Bernie, I want to do an amniocentesis.'

'What? Oh, Jonas, that's very touchy ground there. Amniocentesis is still experimental and very risky.'

'You do it for Rh-negative mothers, don't you?'

'First of all, Jonas, I don't do anything. Amniocentesis is performed by the hospital and by specialists who know what they're doing and the blood lab does the test. Some people in my department may be experimenting with the fluid, doing genetic tests, but I never see it. And second of all, amniocentesis is done only in life-death circumstances, not merely to satisfy curiosity.'

'But you could do genetic studies, Bernie, if you got hold of the amniotic fluid?'

'You mean look at the chromosomes and tell you if the baby is deformed?'

'Yes.'

'It's not certain, Jonas. I could check for mongolism and other diseases and aberrations that are genetically caused, but if it's a congenital deformity, it wouldn't show. You've got to consider the risks, Jonas. Injury to the foetus. Eclampsia. Premature labour. Infection. And for what?

Inconclusive findings from an untried test. Stick to your X-rays, Jonas.'

'I can't wait that long, Bernie.'

'Jonas, you don't need chromosomatic studies to convince the parents the girl is telling the truth. You have more than enough evidence here. And as for the possibility of it being a monster, the unreliability of amniocentesis plus its dangers far outweigh any shaky proof you might derive from it.'

'Bernie', said Jonas slowly, 'I want that test done. And you have the influence at UCLA to help me.'

The stocky geneticist hoisted himself out of his easy chair and slowly shook his head. 'You know what I think, Jonas? You don't want the amniocentesis because you're worried about the girl's welfare. You want it for yourself.'

Jonas quickly turned away from his friend and picked up his martini. Behind him, he heard Bernie say, 'You're really becoming obsessed with this case, you know? Fine, so you want to defend the girl and convince her parents and friends that she's still pure. But you've got enough here for that. Pushing for amniocentesis at this stage when X-rays will tell you what you need to know is lunacy. It's the action of a man who has other motives on his mind.' Bernie's spatulate hand came down heavily on his friend's shoulder. 'So what's on your mind?'

Jonas turned slowly, took a deep breath and released it as he said evenly, 'I'm going to write it up, Bernie.'

Bernie Schwartz stared for a silent moment, then said, 'You're not serious.'

'I am, Bernie. I'd be a fool not to. With the way science is going, racing toward whole new frontiers in human sexuality, someone's going to broach the area of parthenogenesis. It might as well be me.'

Bernie drew back his hand and regarded his friend solemnly. There was a peculiar tightness, he noticed, to Jonas's forehead. 'You're treating her like a medical curiosity, Jonas. You're losing sight of your responsibility to that girl as a patient.'

'But I'm doing just the opposite, don't you see? By writing it up now, I open the way for future parthenogenic mothers to be accepted. This girl is going through hell, Bernie, she even tried to commit suicide because no one believes her. If I can publish my discovery, *prove* it, and have it accepted as a natural phenomenon, I'll be sparing future Mary McFarlands from heartbreak and desperation!'

The hard, tiny eyes of Bernie Schwartz delved Jonas's face. Beneath the bristly mustache, full lips worked between teeth. Then he said, 'Do you really believe that, Jonas? Or is it an excuse, a safe, ethical out?'

'What the hell do you mean?'

Bernie gazed at him a moment longer, seemed to debate with himself, then shrugged and looked at his watch. 'I have to get going, Jonas. Esther will be wondering where I am. She'll blame the soggy cabbage on me.'

'Bernie, I need your advice.'

'No you don't, Jonas, you've already made up your mind. You made your decision before I got here tonight. You know me well enough to know my feelings on this.'

'What are they? Tell me.'

Bernie walked to the door of the den, Jonas close behind him. 'You'll make a freak out of her and the baby, a public curiosity. So you write it up in a medical journal – very *ethical* of you. But then word gets out and *Life* gets a hold of it. Then the *National Enquirer* and before you know it there will be pictures of the girl and the baby plastered over every magazine and tabloid in the country. They'll be hounded, like the Dionne quins.' Bernie rested his hand on the doorknob. 'Is that what you want?'

'That can be prevented. . .'

Bernie held up a hand. 'All I'm saying, Jonas, is give it a lot of careful thought before you take that step. Examine your motives.'

Jonas walked his friend to the front door and stood on the porch and watched Bernie, in Hawaiian shirt and Bermuda shorts, stroll off into the sultry evening.

A few minutes later, back in his study, Jonas picked up his martini and resumed pacing.

Examine your motives, Bernie had said. *You've invented an excuse, a safe ethical out. . .*But it wasn't an excuse, a rationalisa-

135

tion to give him a clear conscience, it was the truth: Jonas Wade's honest, gut motive was to save future parthenogenic mothers from Mary's suffering.

He placed the glass, still untouched, on his desk and leaned, with his palms down flat on the mahogany and his elbows locked straight, with his head bowed between his shoulders.

Damn you, Bernie Schwartz, for knowing me too well...

Science is racing toward new frontiers and breakthroughs, Jonas had argued. Frontiers, breakthroughs, thresholds...but *whose*? Had Bernie seen through the thin fabric of his mask, seen the soul of Jonas Wade and its tremblings of fear for the future? No, not science's breakthrough but his own, Jonas Wade's last chance to take a seat in the long line of luminaries that had preceded him from Hippocrates to now and that would continue far into the misty, technological future. There weren't many places available in this parade of the famous, the lauded; one had to seize the chance, like a moving chair lift up the ski slopes; another empty one might not pass this way again. At least, not in Jonas Wade's lifetime.

He raised his head with effort and focused his eyes on the certificate newly hung over the desk. President of the Society of Galen. He certainly wouldn't be remembered for *that*. He let his eyes travel: medical diploma from the University of California at Berkeley, graduated magna cum laude; a certificate of completion of residency at UCLA; the Penobscot Award for Outstanding and Meritorious Achievement in the field of general medicine; a letter from the President of the United States. Jonas lowered his gaze and let his head dip again between his shoulders. The dates on those certificates, so many years ago; he had been at the top of every class, a star of the first magnitude, shooting meteorically to the pinnacle of medical success, receiving offers from the top universities and hospitals in the country, a 'hot property,' self-confident, swaggering young Jonas Wade, bursting upon the medical world with his arms full of trophies and honours. And then, marriage to Penny and two babies a year apart and a new office in Tarzana and a mortgage and a succession of tonsils and varicose veins and haemorrhoids and Jonas Wade, somewhere in the clutter of tongue depressors and rectal thermometers, had lost his grip on the meteor. The dazzle and glamour and vain dreams had fizzled into a comfortable rut.

He had forgotten the taste of those dreams – until now.

Jonas pushed away from the desk and gazed up at the Rembrandt. Dr Tulp was immortalised. Just as were Vesalius, William Harvey, Joseph Lister, Walter Reed, Watson and Crick. Who would remember Jonas Wade? He couldn't even look forward to a gold watch upon retirement.

He sank into the high wingback chair, his hands draped over the ends of the upholstered arms, and stared at the pattern in the shag carpet.

For years Jonas Wade had been content, thirty hours a week in the office, ten in the operating room, four on the golf course, twelve watching television; his life was a succession of hours, each one to be 'spent', to be passed, to be gotten through: links of hours, and at the end of the chain, nothing to show for a single one of them. In the nineteen years since graduation from medical school, Jonas Wade had never stopped to examine his life, and now that he was finally doing it, he was questioning it as well.

This was it, his chance to make his mark, to be recognised for something; the man who first described spontaneous parthenogenesis in humans.

'Honey?'

He looked up; Penny, wearing a shift and sandals and holding a can of Metrecal, stood in the doorway. 'I've been talking to you. Didn't you hear me?'

'No...I'm sorry, sweetheart. I was thinking.'

She came in. His desk and ottoman were spread with the papers and notes of his new project. Penny came close, but not intrusively so; when Jonas was ready to tell her about the case that had been distracting him lately, he would.

'I want you to talk to Cortney. She says she wants to move out and get an apartment of her own.'

'What?' He looked up. 'Move out?'

137

'She says she wants to move in with Sarah Long and share expenses.'

'With what money?'

'She says she'll get a job.'

Jonas shook his head. 'Not until after she graduates.'

'She's adamant, Jonas.'

'What's wrong with living here?'

'I don't know!' Penny flung out her thin arms. 'I've tried talking sense to her, but got nowhere.'

'Okay, I'll have a talk with her.'

Penny hesitated before him for a moment, then swung around and hurried out of the room. Jonas returned his gaze to the spread of notes and papers that were going to jell into his bombshell article.

An ethical out, a way to get around my conscience. It's not right, to expose Mary to all that for the sake of my own glory. She would most definitely be exploited, the world wouldn't leave her or the baby alone. Have I that right?

And further: what staggering, far-reaching effects might this parthenogenic theory have? If I detail the cause of her mitosis, then might not some scientists seize upon it, find willing human guinea pigs, and attempt to re-create Mary's circumstance? How many women out there desperately want babies of their own, not adopted, but from their own bodies, want to experience pregnancy, but have no husbands; women in whom the maternal instinct is so strong that it is an obsession yet who cannot even manage just one night with a man? They would do it, oh, yes, they would, willingly. Submit to the Wade-McFarland Technique and reproduce themselves...

Jonas felt a shiver shoot down between his shoulder blades.

Good Lord, carried out to its most far-flung conclusion, this would upset the balance of our most basic social standard and laws of nature; what would happen to sexual customs and rituals if women could reproduce themselves? What would become of men?

I would be opening a gateway to a world without men. But isn't that what Dr Henderson is doing? No, her technique

138

does not exclude males: either sex can be duplicated. In parthenogenesis, men play no part, they are obsolete.

Dear God, where does my obligation lie – to science and enlightenment (write the story) or to humanity and conscience, to save mankind from playing God (kill the story)?

No...someone will do it, eventually, sometime...

Big changes are coming in science and medicine, the world quivers on the threshold of fantastic discoveries and I want to be part of it, I don't want to be left behind in the dust.

Some will hail me, others revile me. Paul Ehrlich with his 'magic bullet' was ostracised for his cure for syphilis; he had defied God's punishments, the world said, for venereal disease was the fruit of fornication. It was as Dr Henderson had said: the man who cured polio was given laurels, the man seeking to cure VD was criticised. And what will I be doing? Placing in the hands of man a dangerous instrument, a weapon perhaps, a key to the doorway of that most fearsome futurological nightmare: genetic manipulation.

CHAPTER 12

'Where's Daddy tonight?' asked Mary as she stood at the sink peeling potatoes.

'He's gone to his gym.'

'But it's Tuesday.'

Lucille shrugged without looking up from her work. She was seated at the kitchen table pasting Green Stamps in little books. Her hair was wrapped in a stained bandana getting a henna treatment.

Mary glanced down at her mother's hands, at the concentration in the sorting and sticking and pounding, and finally had to look away. In all her life Mary had never known her mother to paste trading stamps. That tedious chore had always fallen to the girls, although neither of them had ever reaped the benefits. Lucille had considered Green Stamps beneath her dignity and had, on occasion, made a show of giving them to her friends, saying, 'I never bother with these things.' Yet she had always been a secret collector of the stamps and had always managed to go down to the redemption store and pick up a lamp or an alarm clock.

Mary's thoughts went to Mike. She wondered if he knew she was home. She thought again about her futile starts to call him, which always ended in loss of courage to finish dialling. What had she to be afraid of? He was simply Mike and surely there was a way to get back together with him.

But Mary knew how it would be. Even if he did eventually accept her, he would never relax around her; he'd be like her parents making an effort to act natural and casual. Like people who pretend they're friends with Negroes.

The sound of a car in the driveway brought both mother and daughter to stop what they were doing. Their eyes met for an instant, then Mary whispered, 'Daddy!' She dropped her potato peeler and ran, wiping her hands on her apron.

She stopped short in the entry hall when the front door opened and an orange sunset spilled through with Amy and her knapsack.

The twelve-year-old turned and shouted over her shoulder, 'Bye, Melody! Thanks a lot! Call you tomorrow!' Then she closed the front door, delivering the hallway into darkness again.

'Amy— ' said Mary.

The girl jumped. 'Mary! You're home! What are you doing home?'

'She had to cut her visit short,' came Lucille's voice from the fringe of shadow behind them. 'I thought the camping was going to be for the whole week, Amy.'

'It was.' She picked up her bag, swung it over her shoulder and reached for her sister's hand. 'But Melody's mom got sick so we had to come back early. Mary! How was Vermont! Tell me all about it! When did you get home? Boy, am I glad to see you!'

The two girls swept past their mother and into the chill air-conditioned living room. 'Last Friday,' said Mary. .

'Amy,' said Lucille, her voice edged. 'Why don't you go change? Dinner will be ready soon.'

'Oh, Mom!' She dropped down on the sofa and grinned up at her sister. 'Tell me about Vermont! What's it like?'

'I don't really know where to begin, Amy—'

'Mary,' said Lucille, placing a hand on her daughter's shoulder, 'don't you think we should wait until your father gets home?'

Mary felt the strong brown fingers press firmly into her flesh. 'I guess so...'

'What for?' Amy's deep sepia eyes flickered up to her mother, then rested again on Mary's face. When no immediate response came from either of them, the twelve-year-old crooked her head slightly to one side. 'Hey, Mary, you look different.'

'Do I?'

'Mary, you're getting fat!' said Amy, punctuating her words with a staccato giggle.

'Your father should be home soon,' said Lucille quickly, a little breathlessly.

Mary looked up at her mother; a peculiar, hunted look swept briefly across Lucille's face, then her features softened, saddened. 'Mary Ann, please let's wait till your father gets home.'

'All right.'

Lucille stepped away. 'Amy, go unpack and change your clothes. You probably need a shower, too. Then you can tell us all about the camping trip.'

The twelve-year-old swept up her knapsack and ran from the living room. 'I know why you got fat!' she called back as she ran down the hall. 'It was all that Vermont maple syrup!'

She awoke with a start. For an instant Mary forgot where she was and listened for the gentle breathing of her roommate. But hearing only silence, full consciousness gradually returned and she remembered that she was back at home in her own room.

She gaped up at the inky ceiling and wondered what time

141

it was. The house was still and silent. Not even the air conditioner could be heard.

A slight shift in position brought Mary to discover she was still fully clothed and lying on top of her bedspread.

She strained to remember.

It came back in flashes: Amy splashing in the pool; Lucille clattering in the kitchen; the lights going on as darkness fell; a silent dinner for the three of them; Amy washing the dishes while Mary dried; their mother frequently looking out the front windows for headlights; Amy going to the den to watch 'Dr. Kildare'; Mary feeling tired and lying down for a rest.

She flicked on the nightstand light and saw it was nine-thirty.

Leaving the bed and walking softly to the door, she opened it a few inches and looked out. Dim light crouched at the end of the hall; it was coming from the living room. Mary listened. Muffled voices now. Following their direction, Mary crept like an intruder along the thick carpet, feeling her way along the wall. She passed the den; it was dark and empty. In the living room, the sliding glass doors were open to bring in the fragrance of swimming-pool chlorine. Ted and Lucille were sitting on the couch facing Amy.

Mary remained behind the doorframe unseen and heard her little sister say, 'How can Mary be expecting a baby if she isn't married?'

Mary sank against the wall and thought her legs were going to fail her. In the back of her mouth came the sudden stinging taste of betrayal. You could have waited, she thought angrily; you *should* have waited.

'Well, Amy dear,' came Lucille's voice. 'It *is* possible to have a baby and not be married.'

'How?'

Mary found the strength to grasp the doorframe and peer around, still unnoticed. Her eyes went immediately to her father's face and the look on it made her ache; she had never seen him look so miserable.

'Well, Amy,' continued Lucille awkwardly, 'I know you've been taught in school about...what makes you a girl and why you have you-know-what. It has to do with that.

It's why you have a monthly period. That's what makes you able to have babies. I mean, a man and a woman, they get together and they make love and they produce babies.'

'You mean sleeping together?'

'Yes.'

'And that's what Mary did?'

Before either parent could reply, Mary stepped through the doorway, saying, 'No, I did not sleep with anyone.'

Lucille and Ted snapped their heads up, Amy whipped around. Mary came to a halt a few feet from them. 'I don't care what you think, I didn't do anything with any boy.'

'Then how can you be expecting?' said Amy, her puppyish face puckering.

Mary wavered for an instant, looking briefly to her father for support, and then approached her little sister. Kneeling down beside Amy she looked up into the earnest, innocent eyes and said quietly, 'I can't explain it, Amy, no one can, not even the doctor I'm going to. But a baby started growing inside me for no reason at all.'

Amy's face clouded over, looking very much like it did when she struggled with a math problem. 'But how can a baby grow for no reason at all?'

'I don't know, Amy.' Mary's voice was a bare whisper.

A heaviness descended over the room; a thick, textured atmosphere that had the viscosity of tropical steam. No one could move in it. A silence like cottonwool expanded under the heat and filled the room to all corners. Amy and Mary continued to stare at one another. Lucille took to examining her hands. And Ted sank deeper into the couch, his eyes focusing on nothing.

Movement disturbed the stillness; a soft feminine stirring. Amy and Mary disengaged their gaze, and Lucille, tired of her hands, looked up at her husband.

Amy was the first to find a voice. 'Then if you haven't done anything wrong, Mary, why are Mom and Dad trying to hide you?'

St. Sebastian's was older than it appeared. Now a huge, towering A-frame of white stucco and plate-glass windows with a stylised cross transecting the façade, Tarzana's Catholic church had once been, a long time ago, called San Sebastiano. It had been made of adobe and had crouched humbly in the middle of an orange grove. But that had been before the memory of any living parishioner, going as far back as 1780 when Spanish Franciscans had come to the valley with Father Serra and had built the San Fernando Mission. The rustic little church of San Sebastiano had been an offshoot of the mission, but no trace remained today of the Spanish mind that had been its originator, except for a bronze plaque embedded in one corner of the parking lot, commemorating the spot where the first Indian baptism had taken place in 1783.

A handful of parishioners was emerging from the church and into the warm morning. Mary hastily searched the crowd and spotted Father Crispin crossing the compound behind the church and heading for the rectory.

'Father!'

He halted his stride and swung around. For a moment his small eyes squinted against the early sun, then his face cleared and he offered the girl a broad smile.

'Father Crispin,' she said breathlessly as she came even with him. 'May I talk to you?'

'Of course, Mary. Come in, come in.'

She followed him into the rectory, walking fast to keep up with him; for one so stout, Lionel Crispin was surprisingly agile.

His office was dark and comforting, dressed in wood tones, panelling and leather. Such a contrast to the glaring stucco and glass of the church. Father Crispin's private domain, with its imitation vaulted graystone fireplace, doe-eyed madonnas, and antique icons bespoke his personal preference for medieval and Gothic touches.

He took a seat behind the cluttered desk, puffing a little, the buttons of his cassock straining over his paunch, and said, 'Well, now, Mary, what can I do for you?'

She tried to get comfortable in the straight-backed Elizabethan chair, draping her hands over the wooden arms that ended in paws. 'Well, Father, for one thing, I'm home.'

His face was blank for an instant, then his alert little eyes flickered down to her lap and back up to her face. 'Oh, yes. You were at St. Anne's. So your parents have decided they would rather have you home?'

Mary looked around the room, scanned the veneer panelling that was supposed to give an Elizabethan effect, and rested her eyes on the portrait of a stranger in pontifical robes. 'Is he the new Pope, Father?'

Lionel Crispin followed her line of sight. 'Pope Paul the Sixth.'

She brought her eyes, which today caught highlights of aquamarine from the muumuu she wore, back to Father Crispin and said, 'My parents didn't decide to have me home, Father, I made that decision myself. I left St. Anne's last Friday on my own.'

'Indeed.' His fleshy jowls seemed to firm as he set his face in seriousness. The bright dark-brown eyes, which were like dots of polished jet, became grave beneath the bushy grey eyebrows. Father Crispin pursed his lips. 'And do they want you home now?'

'I don't know. I guess so. They haven't mentioned sending me back to St. Anne's.'

A small furrow started to appear between the eyebrows, deepening with each second.

'Father, the reason I came to you is because I have a problem and I don't know how to work it out.'

'Have you tried asking your parents for help?'

'Well, Father, you see, it involves them. We didn't come to church last Sunday because Mother said she wasn't feeling well. But I really think she doesn't want me out in public. She thinks everyone will stare at me and whisper behind my back. I don't care, but Mother does. I have to go to church, Father.'

His face eased a little, the intensity faded. Now he was remembering. The last time he had seen this girl, in this very office, she had been depressed and irritatingly laconic; she had rejected the Church. His smile became paternal. 'Of course I will help you, Mary. When I see your mother at the Altar and Rosary Society tonight I'll have a word with her.'

'Thank you, Father.'

'Tell me, Mary, why did you leave St. Anne's?'

She cast her eyes down. 'Because I didn't like it there.'

He nodded, puckering his mouth. 'But you do understand that you committed a sin by leaving.'

She jerked her head up. 'How?'

'By breaking the Fourth Commandment. You disobeyed your parents.'

'I hadn't thought of that, Father, I'll be sure to confess it.'

His bushy eyebrows went up. Two months ago she had refused the sacrament. 'I must assume then that Father Grundemann at St. Anne's was some help to you.'

'Oh, yes. He and I had some long talks and I finally went to confession and took Communion every day that I was there.'

Now his face blossomed into a grin as he leaned back in his chair and webbed his fingers across his belly. 'Wonderful, Mary, you don't know how much that pleases me.'

She made an effort to smile back, but was unable to meet his gaze for long. So Mary looked away and scanned the room again. The photograph of President Kennedy over the fake fireplace was the same one that hung over her bed. 'Father Crispin. . .' she began, not looking at him.

'Yes?'

'I do still have that other problem.'

'What problem is that?'

She tried to hold on to the Kennedy portrait, wondered what it would be like to sit and have a talk with him; she knew he wouldn't be as hard on her as everyone else was. He would be sympathetic and he wouldn't condemn her.

'Father, I still don't know why I'm pregnant.'

He resembled a portrait himself, unmoving, appearing not to breathe. Father Crispin was caught in a frame of surprise, and then, when the full meaning of what she had said settled over him, astonishment.

146

'You still don't know why?'

Mary shook her head.

Lionel Crispin slowly unclasped his hands, inclined himself across the desk and said in a half whisper, 'You still don't know why you're in this condition?'

'No, Father.'

His little eyes blinked. 'Mary, you got this way by committing an impure act. Surely you know this!'

'But I didn't, Father.'

His eyes blinked more rapidly. 'But...you went to confession at St. Anne's. You took Holy Communion.'

'Yes, I did. Father Grundemann absolved me.'

'Of what? If you don't think you've committed an impure act, then what did you confess?'

'That I had tried to commit suicide.'

An arctic silence settled over the room, and when Father Crispin spoke, his words fell like snow, each syllable an icicle. 'Mary Ann McFarland, are you telling me that you went to the altar rail and took Communion knowing you had an unconfessed mortal sin on your soul?'

She felt her heart start to race. 'No, Father. I told Father Grundemann all my sins. I said my penance.'

'For what?'

'For trying to commit suicide.'

'And what about the carnal sin, Mary?'

She felt the imitation Elizabethan chair rise up and swallow her. She shrank beneath Father Crispin's formidable gaze. 'I didn't commit a carnal sin, Father.'

He closed his eyes and brought his hands together. The puckered lips seemed to utter a brief prayer. Then he opened his eyes and said with practised patience, 'Mary, are you still persisting in this notion that you are a virgin?'

'It's not a notion, Father, it's the truth. I am a virgin.'

With one elbow on the desk, Lionel Crispin brought up a spatulate hand and cradled his forehead in it, his expression hidden from Mary.

An uncomfortable silence passed slowly as they sat unmoving; it was brought to an end when the priest raised his head and said, 'Are you telling me that you are going to have a virgin birth?'

She flinched as if Father Crispin had physically struck her.

'Mary, you and I and all the world knows that there is only way for a woman to conceive a child. You are not stupid, Mary, and you know that I am not stupid. You got into this condition by having sex with a boy. And since you did not confess it, that sin is still on your soul. And what is more, you took Holy Communion in a state of mortal sin.'

'Father— '

'Mary Ann McFarland, what do you take me for! Make a good confession right now and purify yourself! You are compounding mortal sin with sacrilege!'

She shriveled into the chair. 'Father Crispin,' she whispered, 'I haven't committed sacrilege.'

'Then what do you call taking Holy Communion in a state of sin?'

'But I wasn't— '

Lionel Crispin, although he remained seated, appeared to grow before her eyes. He became a composite of layers upon layers of flesh; he towered, swayed, glared down at her with unbridled rage.

'Father Crispin, I swear! I never did anything— '

'Mary.' He got to his feet, came around the desk and held out his hand. 'Mary, come with me now to the church.'

She recoiled.

'Not to the confessional, but to pray. If you're frightened, we must pray to God for guidance. I don't know what forces you to keep silent, Mary, whether it's to protect the identity of the boy – although I have an idea who it is – or because you're ashamed to admit to having committed the sin, but the time has come for you to turn to God for help. Come now, Mary, we'll pray. Open your heart to God. Let him come in. Let him guide your conscience. Ask him, Mary, God will have the answer.'

She crushed her fingers together until the knuckles hurt, hoping that physical exertion would make the prayer more clearly heard. Beside her, Father Crispin knelt stiffly, his balding head bowed over folded hands. With her eyes firmly closed, screwed tight, she heard him breathing, felt his nearness.

The church was empty. The warm air was redolent of incense and smoke; flowers choked the altar, colours streaming through the stained glass washed the pews and marble floor in floods of rainbows. Mary felt her knees begin to sweat on the vinyl pad. She tried to concentrate, tried to scream with her mind to force God to hear her. She imagined a rosary in her hands, pictured each bead going through her fingers. The Apostles' Creed, a Lord's Prayer, three Hail Marys.

It didn't feel right. She bowed her head in deeper concentration. *Glory be to the Father, the Son, and the Holy Ghost. As it was in the beginning, is now and ever shall be, world without end, amen.*

She launched into a string of Hail Marys. In her mind the litany sounded meaningless; an endless repetition of words, vowels, consonants. She lost control of the mental image of the rosary. One Hail Mary melted into the next.

Finally, her heart aching with despair, lacking the vision and the path by which to communicate with God, Mary opened her eyes and raised her head. She searched the altar. Fixing on the body of Jesus hanging on the cross, she started again. *O my God, I am heartily sorry for having offended thee, and I detest all my sins because of thy just punishment. . .*

Her concentration faltered. It wasn't going right. It was all wrong. Beside her, Father Crispin remained piously bowed. Mary sucked in her lips, held fast to the crucified Jesus and tried again.

Lord have mercy on me! cried her mind. *Christ have mercy on me! God the Father of Heaven have mercy on me! God the Son, Redeemer of the world, have mercy on me!*

Mary's eyes strayed to the statue of the Virgin to the left of the chancel.

God the Holy Ghost, Holy Trinity, One God have mercy on me!
She swallowed hard.
Jesus, Son of the living God, have mercy on me!

Jesus, splendour of the Father, have mercy on me!
Jesus, brightness of. . .brightness of. . .

Mary bit her lower lip. Her eyes moved away from the Virgin, tracing their own involuntary path.

Brightness of eternal light, have mercy on me!
Jesus, king of glory, have mercy on me!
Jesus, son of justice, have mercy on me!

When her eyes stopped before they reached the First Station of the Cross, Mary felt a peculiar anxiousness grip her. Unaware of what her eyes beheld, she stared unblinking and struggled with the words in her mind.

'Oh, God!' screamed her thought. 'Tell me what's happening to me! Tell me *why!* Tell me *how!* No one else but you can help me! Dr Wade doesn't have the answer. Father Crispin doesn't have the answer. Only you, God, you know why this happened. God, help me. . .'

Her heart pounded beneath the strain her mind was putting on her body; a reaching out, a struggling with her conscience and spirit that blurred her vision and caused her to tremble. Mary closed her eyes, tried to open her mind, tried to lift the boundaries of her consciousness, tried to reach out to the heavens with her thoughts. She took in a deep breath, held it, *trembled*, then let it out, slowly. . .

She opened her eyes. This time they focused. She was suddenly aware of what she had been staring at.

St. Sebastian.

Forgetting her frantic prayer, Mary gazed curiously, hypnotically, at the arrows piercing his muscular body; she studied each bleeding wound; the tight sinews of his naked thighs; the rippled abdomen and chest. Her eyes roamed the twisted, tortured body and paused at last in fascination at his agonized yet ecstatic, handsome face.

And then she remembered.

And in that instant, a sweet, comforting peace descended over her. . .

CHAPTER 13

Jonas Wade had a difficult time concentrating. It was almost noon and the McFarland girl would be there any minute.

'Okay, Timmy, that's it!' He clapped a hand on the youngster's head. 'You took it bravely. All ten stitches are out!'

The little boy beamed proudly at the red scar on his knee and said in a small voice, 'Thank you.'

With the nurse helping the child off the exam table, Jonas Wade went straight to his office, closing the door behind him. He did not remove his lab coat as he usually did on Fridays at this time. Nor were his thoughts filled with the habitual weekend plans. Instead, Jonas Wade sat anxiously at his desk and stared unseeing at the open chart before him.

He had decided to tell Mary everything today.

The intercom buzzed.

Jonas Wade was rapidly scribbling in Timmy's chart when Mary softly entered, closed the door, and took a seat. At the periphery of his vision he could see her, waiting patiently, hands folded in her lap.

He kept writing as long as he could, flipped back through Timmy's chart to see if there was anything else he could comment on, to stretch out the time, to mentally prepare himself for this girl, and then finally had to close the folder and slip the pen into his breast pocket.

He offered Mary his most charming smile. 'Well! What a nice surprise! I haven't see you in four whole days!'

She laughed silently, blue eyes flashing. 'Hi, Dr. Wade. Thanks for letting me come over.'

'How did you get here? Is your mother with you?'

'No, she let me take her car.'

'You drive?'

151

'I've had my license for six months. She lets me take the car to the grocery store and the library and places like that. I told her I absolutely had to see you today and since she was going shopping with Shirley Thomas, she let me have her car.'

'So what did you want to see me about?'

She hesitated, her face bright with anticipation and excitement. Then she said in a rush, 'Dr Wade, I know why I'm pregnant!'

A stunned pause, then: 'What?'

'I know why now, and I also know *how* it happened.'

He shifted uneasily in his chair. 'Well, Mary, this sounds interesting. Tell me about it.'

She described briefly her encounter with Father Crispin two days before and their subsequent visit to the church to pray together.

'But I couldn't pray, Dr Wade!' she said breathlessly, her hands flying. 'I've never had trouble praying in my whole life, but just then I did! I mean, I could recite the words and everything, but they had no *meaning*, they were just words. It was like I was reciting a foreign language.'

She moved to the edge of the chair. 'I started to panic. I really did! I mean, it must have meant something, right? When a Catholic suddenly can't pray. I got scared. I thought: what if this is what it feels like when God stops listening?

'I got really scared then and I started to shake and I was afraid Father Crispin could tell I was having trouble praying. And *then*, Dr Wade—' Mary's eyes glittered— '*then*, for no reason at all, I stopped praying to God and started *talking* to him. I'd never done that before, you know, just talk to him.

'And it was while I was talking to God, just pouring my heart out to him, that it happened.'

Jonas blinked, mesmerised by her animation. '*What* happened, Mary?'

'I remembered the dream.'

He didn't know why, but a small alarm went off at the back of his head. 'Dream?'

'It was the night just before Easter. I had a very strange dream, Dr Wade, you know, *bizarre*. I'd never had anything like that before. It was, well' – she gave an embarrassed shrug – *'sexy*. St. Sebastian came to me in this dream.' Mary's words slowed now; they came out carefully chosen, measured. 'I dreamed that St. Sebastian made love to me and the dream was so real that it was like, you know, it really happened.'

Jonas Wade's fingers toyed with the cuffs of his lab coat. 'So you remembered this dream in the church. . .'

'Yes, while I was asking God to help me. All of a sudden the dream came back to me, as if God had put it in my mind.'

'Is that what you think? That God heard your prayer and answered by making you remember the dream?'

'Yes, but not just the dream, Dr Wade. I mean, a plain old dream, even a sexy one, I wouldn't think is very important, but this one had something *special* about it. There was a physical part to it, something I've never experienced before. *That* was what I remembered in the church, Dr Wade.'

His forehead gathered into a deep frown. 'Physical part?'

'It was the neatest thing I'd ever felt in my whole life and it was so strong that it woke me up. And after I was awake I knew something had happened to my body because, well' – her voice dropped – 'I felt around myself and discovered that something had happened to me, you know, *down there*.'

He stared at her for a moment, then said, 'Mary, don't you know what that was?'

'It was the feeling of St. Sebastian visiting me.'

Jonas found himself blinking stupidly. 'St. Sebastian *visiting* you?'

'Well, the dream did take place at the right time, you know, in the second week of April, like you said. And if the Angel Gabriel visited the other Mary, then why couldn't St. Sebastian do the same to me?'

Dr Jonas Wade sat suspended before her, his eyes blank, his face frozen. As the girl's words swirled around in his brain

153

and began to coagulate into a meaningful statement, he slowly sank back into his chair and whispered, 'Oh, my God...'

Her voice came from far away. 'You told me conception took place somewhere in the first two weeks of April, probably closer to the end of the second week.' Mary's face was bright with an inner radiance, her cornflower-blue eyes alive and shimmering.

Jonas felt a devasting chill come over him. 'Mary,' he said gravely, 'are you saying you think this saint actually came to you in your sleep and impregnated you?'

'It's what happened, Dr Wade, because God made me realize it.'

He suddenly leaned forward, his hands clenched on the desk before him. Jonas felt a tightening of his bowels and wished desperately he hadn't put off telling her about his research. 'Mary, what you felt at the end of that dream was nothing more than an ordinary physiological response. You had an orgasm.'

Her face flushed instantly. 'Women don't have those!'

His eyebrows shot up. 'You are greatly mistaken. Women certainly do have orgasms, and it's not uncommon to have one in your sleep. Mary, you're calling a normal body reflex a religious experience, and it wasn't.'

Mary's smile suddenly dropped away and her eyes hardened. 'Dr Wade, God wouldn't make me remember a dirty thing like that while I was praying to him. I know what my dream was, God told me.'

Jonas Wade stared in helpless bewilderment. This sudden unexpected turn had derailed him; all his preparations suddenly fled him. He should have told her sooner, gotten to her before the Church had; he might have thwarted this delusion. Mary had been frantic for an explanation, and since he had offered her nothing, a shrug of the shoulders, she had seized upon *this*.

'Mary, you're claiming a religious miracle. You're comparing yourself with the mother of Jesus.'

'Because it's true. If it could happen to her, why can't it happen to me?' The seventeen-year-old's voice was chillingly calm. 'No one believed her then, not until the baby was born. If millions of people can believe it happened to one girl, why should no one believe it can happen to another?'

'Mary, have you told anyone else about this? Father Crispin?'

'No one, not even my parents. I wanted to discuss it first with you because I thought you'd understand. *You* couldn't find the answer, Dr Wade, so I asked God and he told me.'

'Mary, you gave that answer to yourself. I know definitely why you're pregnant. I've been doing some research. You have a very rare condition, but it *can* occur— '

'Dr Wade,' her voice was metallic, her eyes wintry. 'Father Crispin told me I was walking around in a state of mortal sin. He told me I had committed a sacrilege by taking Holy Communion. Well, now I know he was wrong. I am pure Dr Wade. God sent St. Sebastian to me and put this baby in my womb. Just like Gabriel came to the other Mary. I haven't committed a sin and there is nothing *scientifically* wrong with me or my baby.'

'Mary please listen to me.' Jonas eyed the girl with some trepidation, uncertain of where to begin, fearful of having her run away from him, of losing her. 'Mary, I've been looking into this and I've made some startling finds.' He reached down for his briefcase.

'I don't think I need you anymore, Dr Wade.' She eyed him coolly as she rose. 'Sebastian will take care of me from now on.'

Jonas Wade watched her go, a feeling of utter helplessness keeping him in his chair. When a long, thoughtful moment had passed, he finally stirred and reached into the stack of charts on his desk, withdrawing the one marked MCFARLAND. Opening to the biographical sheet at the very front, Jonas Wade found the phone number of St. Sebastian's.

'Mother?' Mary poked her head through the door. The kitchen was cool and dark.

She entered the dining room, looking out onto the sunny patio, crossed the living room, and called out again, 'Mother? Anybody home?'

155

She heard sounds in the den and looked in. The TV was on but no one was watching it. Mary walked over to the set and clicked it off, extinguishing a news film that showed a picket sign which read: MARLON BRANDO IS A NIGGER-LOV-ING CREEP.

Mary listened to the house. It was still and quiet. She went into the hall and headed for the bedrooms. Amy's door was open. Mary stopped and smiled. 'Hi! Where is everyone?'

Amy was sitting on the bed with her back to the wall and her knees drawn up to her chest. She didn't look at her sister but continued to pout in the direction of the wall opposite.

'Amy? What's wrong?'

The twelve-year-old shrugged.

Mary came in and sat down on the white painted chair that matched her sister's desk. 'Amy, you all right?'

'Yeah...'

'Where's Mother?'

Amy shrugged again.

'Is she still out shopping with Shirley Thomas?'

'Guess so.'

Mary studied her sister's mouth, how the corners turned down. 'How was the movie?'

'All right.'

'What did you go see?'

Amy stuck a finger in her hair and started to twist it, as if making a ringlet. 'Frankie Avalon and Annette Funicello.'

'Amy, what's wrong?'

'Nothing.'

'What, Amy?'

Finally the twelve-year-old turned her head and a spark of belligerence danced in her eyes. 'Dad was supposed to pick me up this afternoon from the show and he never came. I stood there and stood there and he never came. So I called his office. They said he was on another line, talking to *your* Dr Wade, so I called Mom and there was no answer. So I had to take the bus and walk five blocks up the hill in ninety-degree heat, that's what!'

Mary sat back in the chair, regarding her little sister in mild surprise.

'And another thing,' Amy went on, 'I don't like the way things have changed around here. Even when you were supposed to be away in Vermont I knew something was wrong because Mom and Dad acted funny and I heard Mom crying at night.'

'Oh, Amy...'

A petulant lower lip emerged. 'And when I told them my important news about joining Sister Agatha's order, they weren't even interested! And then *you* came home and now nothing's right!'

'Amy—'

The younger girl sprang off the bed. 'They've forgotten I exist all of a sudden. I don't count anymore!'

'That's not true!'

'Sure!' Amy stood with her hands on her hips. 'You're the big deal around here because having a baby is more important than becoming a nun! That's all Mom and Dad care about! And that's all *you* care about, having Mike's baby!'

'*Amy!*'

The twelve-year-old swung around and marched out of the room.

Mary stared after her for a moment, then jumped up and ran after her, catching Amy by the arm. 'Don't run away from me, please!'

The girl snapped around, yanking her arm free, and glared at her older sister with tear-filled eyes. 'I've been waiting and waiting,' she cried, 'for the perfect moment to tell Mom and Dad and all they say is we'll talk about it later!'

'Amy, I'm so sorry—'

'Yeah, *you're* sorry! You get all the attention around here and it's not like you did anything good to deserve it!'

Mary fell back a step.

'I know what you did!' continued Amy, a tear tumbling down her cheek. '*Everyone* knows. The kids are all talking about it. And I don't think it's anything that deserves getting you treated like a princess or something! And what's it going to be like around here after the baby's born and all everyone can do is pay attention to *it*?'

Mary wrapped her arms around herself and turned away from Amy. 'I'm so so sorry,' she moaned. 'I truly am. But it's going to get better, I promise you. I didn't do what you think I did, what the kids are saying. The baby isn't Mike's. Something beautiful and wonderful has happened to me, to this family, and in a little while, Amy, you'll understand and rejoice with me.'

The sound of the front door slamming brought Mary to turn back around and find herself alone in the dark hall.

'Yes, Mrs Wyatt, the annual St. Vincent de Paul drive will be held in September, like it has been every year for the past twenty years. And yes, Mrs. Wyatt, we would very much appreciate the use of your station wagon. I'll let you know. Thank you, Mrs. Wyatt. Good-bye.'

Father Lionel Crispin curtailed the impulse to slam the receiver down, instead dropped it gently onto the cradle, then scowled at the instrument as if it were the cause of his irritability this afternoon.

He sat alone in his pseudo-Gothic office, alone with his icons and fake Tudor panelling and piles of letters requesting charity and a memo from the bishop reminding him that politics were to be kept out of the pulpit.

Politics! Father Crispin could not care less about politics; the memorandum was a printed sheet, distributed thoughout the diocese, aimed particularly at young radical priests who were preaching racial integration instead of the Gospel. The bishop was upset; last month three of his priests in the East Los Angeles area had been reprimanded for helping student groups to organise antisegregation demonstrations. Photographs in the news of priests carrying picket signs.

Politics! That was the least of Father Crispin's troubles; he kept his pulpit neutral and avoided controversy. The hottest issue he had ever touched upon was the fiery split between St. Peter and St. Paul. Lionel Crispin had other worries, and they were more frightening, more immediate than the debate of whether or not coloured people should drink from a white water fountain.

Looking back, he could see that it had been a long time coming – this feeling of obsolescence – but it had only been lately that he had felt its sting. The McFarland child had brought it to the fore, stripped away the protective patina he had worked so hard at layering over his fears, and laid bare the stark truth that Father Lionel Crispin was, in fact, a very unnecessary and ineffectual priest.

At least, this was what he had been thinking the past couple of days, ever since he had had no influence whatever on Mary's Catholic conscience. And then yesterday, angry that she had not confessed, he had visited the Holland house, had had a long and serious talk with Nathan and had tried to get Mike to admit his sin of sex with Mary so that she could stop compounding mortal sin upon mortal sin. To no avail. Like the girl, Mike had protested his innocence even though, prior to the pregnancy he had published abroad, freely and boastingly his sexual adventures with Mary.

Crispin had left the house frustrated and defeated; and all the subsequent evening and sleepless night he had come to see the McFarland problem as just a symptom of the whole perishing mess. If he couldn't make two teen-agers confess a single sin, then what effect was he having on the congregation as a whole?

Father Crispin could say only one good thing for himself; he was good at organising charity drives.

His rancour deepened, first with the phone call from Dr Wade, then with the doctor's impending visit. Somehow, Crispin was certain, this man was directly tied in with Mary's stubborn refusal to confess; possibly even he supported her.

Jonas Wade knocked on the door, then entered. He paused as he closed the door behind him to let his eyes adjust to the interior, and when he could see better tried to mask his surprise. Father Crispin's office was a glaring contrast to the glass-and-stucco church. It was almost as if the priest had constructed for himself an enclave of medieval Catholicism to stave off the encroaching modern age. Good Lord, the statues and Gothic madonnas and crucifixes and candles; did anyone really believe in all these trappings?

'Good afternoon, Dr Wade, won't you have a seat?'

Jonas made himself as comfortable as possible in the hard, straight-backed Elizabethan chair and kept his briefcase on the floor between his feet.

'I presume, Doctor, you are here to discuss Mary McFarland?'

'We have a serious problem on our hands, Father Crispin; I'm here to enlist your aid.' Jonas Wade took a quick inventory of the man before him: the jowls mapped with fine blood vessels, the little eyes glinting like chips of jet, the set expression – a scowl – and suspected he was not going to have an easy time of it.

Briefly, he recounted his visit with Mary, her delusion of having been impregnated by a saint, and when he was through, he waited for the priest to react.

It took Father Crispin some minutes to fully digest what the doctor had said, and when its impact hit, he felt a new fury roil within him: he was apparently more ineffectual than he had supposed!

'This is getting out of hand, Doctor. I shall most certainly have a talk with the girl.'

'I think we should work in this together, Father.'

'What do you mean?'

'I have found the reason for her pregnancy but she won't listen to me. I'm hoping that if it came from you— '

'I'm sorry, Dr Wade, I don't know what you're talking about.'

Jonas reached down for his briefcase. 'I've been doing some extensive research over the past few months, Father, and I've come up with an explanation for Mary's condition. 'He opened the case and withdrew a neat stack of papers, held together by a paper clip.

When it was placed on the edge of Father Crispin's desk the priest seemed almost to recoil. 'What is this all about?'

'I'm talking about parthenogenesis, Father, virgin births.'

'You're what!' Father Crispin's eyes flared volcanically.

'But you just said we have to talk the girl out of that notion and now you're supporting it?'

'Not Mary's theory, Father, but the scientific one. Certainly I don't believe St. Sebastian visited Mary in her sleep, but I do believe the baby she carries was virginally conceived. Now this draft is a compilation of my findings—'

'Dr. Wade.' Father Crispin inclined himself forward, fixing a pontifical glare on the physician. 'Mary Ann McFarland had sex with a boy. That's how she got pregnant.'

Jonas regarded the man in brief, mute surprise. Then he said, 'It would appear so on the surface, but when you've read what I— '

'I'm not going to read that Dr Wade.'

Jonas blinked at him.

'You are asking me to condone Mary's delusion of sainthood. You want me to support her in her admonitions of holiness, of being a second Virgin Mary. Surely you can't be serious!'

'Father Crispin, what I have written here has nothing to do with holiness or the Second Coming. It's a simple scientific explanation of how an ovum inside Mary started to divide and mature into an embryo on its own.'

'Then you insist she's a virgin?'

'Yes, I do.'

'Dr Wade.' Father Crispin drew himself up to look down upon his visitor, the buttons of his cassock straining over his belly. 'You are making my job even harder with this.'

'Quite the contrary. Father, I have simplified it. If you would just read—

'And how did this ovum start dividing?'

'I believe an electrical shock was the cause.'

'I see.' The priest turned away and went to stand at the garden window, his back to Wade. 'So the baby inside Mary Ann McFarland is the result of a physiological...quirk.'

'Yes, it is.'

'Then are you also saying,' when Father Crispin turned around his face was solemn, grave, 'that the Mother of Our Lord suffered the same fate, that in fact Jesus Christ was a biological fluke?'

161

Jonas sat in stunned silence.

'Dr Wade, if what you say is true, that a virgin can become pregnant by a simple shock to the body, then what does that say for the Blessed Virgin?' Father Crispin released a reedy sigh and leaned on the back of his chair. 'Dr Wade,' he said tiredly, 'what do you take me for?'

Now it was Jonas's turn to be angry, but he tethered himself. 'Father Crispin, my intent in coming here was not to debate theology with you but to make you aware of a very serious concern we have on our hands. Whether or not you choose to believe me, it is my province to see to Mary's physical and medical welfare, and since I know how the baby was conceived I am aware also of the inherent dangers. This is why I came to you, to put you wise to the crisis we might be facing.'

'And that is?'

'Father Crispin, there is a good chance the baby is deformed, a monster in fact. There is also a good chance that at the time of delivery Mary's life will be in danger. I have no way of telling just yet, not until I can take X-rays, and even that will not be conclusive. What I am saying, Father, is that the foetus inside Mary Ann McFarland is not a normal one and therefore lays us open to serious problems. This is what I want you to think about.'

Father Crispin's acute little eyes scrutinised the face of the doctor. He did not speak.

'You might be called upon,' continued Jonas, 'to make a life-or-death decision, Father, and I only wanted to prepare you for it.'

As Dr Wade reached for his manuscript, the priest said, 'You have to understand, Doctor, that as a priest I cannot accept your parthenogenic theory. Surely you realise it undermines the very foundation of Catholicism.'

'Father Crispin, I was not raised in any kind of faith, I have had no religious training. My parents were atheists, I am an atheist. What I believe in is what I have here' – his finger tapped the paper-clipped report – 'scientific proof of her condition. I don't mean to attack your religion, Father, I came here out of concern for Mary.'

162

Behind the polished little eyes a lot of deliberation went on; they flickered briefly down to the report, then returned to fasten onto the doctor's face. Father Crispin's voice was as stonehard as his stare. 'I will listen to you on one point alone, Doctor, and that is the fact of a possible deformity in the child. As to its causes, I will not give ear to your preposterous claim. But you are the girl's physician and if you caution me about dangers in the pregnancy, I have no choice but to honour your advice. How certain are you that the baby is deformed?'

'I'm not certain at all. It's only a possibility. Father Crispin, Mary McFarland should be under very careful medical supervision; I have to monitor her progress closely. However, with this new delusion she is entertaining, I have lost my sway with her. She's now under the impression that St. Sebastian will take care of her and the baby and that I am no longer necessary. I need your help, Father, to convince her otherwise.'

Lionel Crispin straightened up and clasped his hands behind his back. Pursing his lips, he rocked a little on his heels. This was incredible: the doctor was asking him, a man of God, to counsel one of his parishioners *not* to seek the protection of a saint!

'Dr Wade, I cannot countenance your request.'

'But surely you see she needs medical supervision!'

That was the damnable part: Father Crispin *did* see that. 'Dr Wade, I cannot reconcile your advice with the advice of the Church. We believe in seeking the protection and guidance of our saints.'

Jonas seized the claw arms of the chair. 'Is that what you tell all your pregnant parishioners, to avoid doctors and pray to saints?'

'Come now, Dr Wade— '

'The girl needs medical help!' Jonas shot to his feet. 'She may be in serious danger!'

'I am not arguing with you, Dr Wade. *Please*'. Father Crispin held out his hands. 'Certainly I agree she should continue to be under your care, but I will not instruct her to turn from her devotion to Sebastian. What I will do,

163

however, and what I must do as her priest is counsel her against this lunacy that it was Sebastian who impregnated her. Surely, Doctor, there is room for compromise.'

Jonas relaxed his hands, which had been curled into fists so that his nails had left white half moons in his palms. 'Forgive me for shouting, Father, I'm worried about Mary. I know the influence you have over her; I'm asking you to tell her she should continue to see me. The rest – St. Sebastian – is up to you.'

Father Crispin tried to smile, but it came out more as a grimace. Influence over the girl? How wrong you are, Doctor, how very wrong! 'I will have words with her right away, Dr Wade. And as for the possible abnormal development of the child, I would appreciate it if you would keep me informed.'

'I will, Father.' Jonas replaced his report in the briefcase, snapped it shut, and held out his hand.

The handshake was firm, self-assured, as the priest said, 'We have to put our trust in God.'

CHAPTER 14

Nathan Holland guided his car into the space between Father Crispin's old green Falcon and a red Cadillac which he assumed belonged to Dr Wade; the McFarlands had parked their two cars on the street so that there was enough room in the driveway for their three visitors. Nathan turned off the motor and looked at his watch, afraid he was late, but saw that the others were early. It was exactly noon.

He didn't know what this was all about – only that Dr Wade had said it affected Mike and that the two should be present. The boy was quiet and unspeaking on the seat next to him, but Nathan had an idea of what was going through his son's mind. Nathan Holland hoped this meeting would help lift the cloud that had descended over their house since the day Ted McFarland had first brought the news about Mary; everyone had suffered, not only Mike, whose summer-school grades had slipped and whose usual summer energies had flagged, but Timothy as well, who seemed almost scornful now of his older brother, once worshipped; it was as if the fourteen-year-old had suffered a disillusionment. All his friends knew what Mike had done and found it a great butt for their adolescent teasing. Matthew, on the other hand, seemed not to have been touched by it, seemed in fact not to care, and that disturbed Nathan most of all. Whatever, today was probably going to be a show-down of sorts, a day of decision making, and since Mike was the likeliest candidate for paternity, then no doubt the McFarlands and Jonas Wade wanted to discuss marriage. Nathan still wasn't, after three months, prepared for this eventuality, although he had known it was inevitable; he was thankful Father Crispin would be on hand for guidance.

Mike, knowing what his father was thinking, faced this meeting with trepidation; it would be the first time he had seen Mary since before she had gone away. He was afraid, not of her, but of himself, afraid that he would fail himself, break down, show how weak he was. Away from her, out of her presence, Mike could steel himself against the pain she had caused him; but near her, looking at her, hearing her voice, all his convictions would dissolve. He would be her victim again.

Mike, unlike his father, was not heartened to see Father Crispin's car; he had already gone a round with the priest on this score; primarily, the priest had urged him to confess his sin of having had sex, and secondarily to protect Mary's honour and give the child a name. Mike had fought both points.

'Let's go in, son,' said Nathan softly.

Lucille met them at the door, smiling and shaking hands with Nat and relieved that the last two had finally arrived, for now they could begin and she would be forced to face the problem and maybe even a path could be found back to Mary again. They had become two strangers, mother and daughter, and although Lucille didn't know why, she suspected Mary blamed her for the suicide attempt. Lucille had tried several times to approach Mary, to open the way to communication; they needed to sit down and talk and air emotions, but Mary was different now, no longer the girl Lucille knew, so her mother was unsure of how to handle her, what to say.

Not much had changed, on the surface, because of Mary's condition; life went on as before, and yet Lucille felt the undercurrents and they made her uncomfortable. These came mostly from her friends, who all knew now, from one source or another, of Mary's pregnancy. Every Saturday morning at her weekly gourmet cooking class at Pierce College, Lucille sensed a subtle difference in the other women; an unspoken sympathy seemed to hover over them, a veiled look in their eyes that was like the look one sees in the eyes of someone who wants to express condolences over a death but is too timid. They were especially nice to her now, her friends; Lucille found herself, every Saturday morning, ending up at the workbench by the window – the one everyone wanted, with the best light. But somehow it was now always Lucille's. And they praised her crepes when she knew they were soggy, and even the best, most seasoned veterans to cooking were now asking her for basic culinary advice.

Lucille's social life had, not by her own doing, expanded; she received so many invitations lately – to luncheon, the movies, evening lectures, drives to Oxnard – that she couldn't possibly accept them all. They were killing her with kindness and sympathy, her friends; it was as though someone had said, Lucille is going through a difficult time right now, let's be nice to her.

She led Nathan and Mike Holland into the living room and offered them frosty glasses of iced tea. Father Crispin stood at once and shook hands with Nathan. Then he scowled, reflexively, at Mike.

The priest had been displeased since his afternoon talk with Mary just the day before, when he had come upon her in the empty church, kneeling before the painting of St.

Sebastian and praying to it. He had asked her to come to his office and had then heard for himself the incredible delusion she was harbouring. He had been patient at first, then irritated, then angry, and had drawn upon his twenty years' experience as a parish priest to shake the girl out of her insanity.

'Mary Ann McFarland, you're speaking blasphemies,' he had said. 'You are compounding your sins with this foolishness. You had a dream, Mary, and that's all.'

'A *visitation*,' she had protested. 'I know, Father, because I *felt* it. I felt St. Sebastian place his seed inside me. You don't *feel* dreams, do you Father?'

'It was just a realistic dream, child!'

'Now I know why *she* kept Gabriel a secret.'

'She?'

'The Blessed Virgin. She knew people wouldn't believe her so she kept his visit a secret, which is what I should have done.'

'This is preposterous, Mary, comparing yourself with the Mother of God. I won't stand for it; this has gone on long enough. You have managed to get yourself coddled by your parents and Dr Wade, but I have the responsibility of your soul, Mary, and I will not sanction this childish dilly-dallying. You're a Catholic, Mary, one of the privileged group that has the promise of heaven and God's love if you but follow his laws. You have the privilege of confession and penance, not something just anyone can take advantage of and certainly not something to be taken lightly. Confess this abomination right now, Mary Ann McFarland, for the sake of your immortal soul.'

But fear tactics hadn't worked. And then on the subject of Dr Wade: 'You are abandoning the welfare of the unborn child.'

'God will take care of it,' she had rejoined with damning calmness.

'God has given us physicians, Mary, so that they can carry out his work here on earth. It is his will that you continue to see Dr Wade; you must not neglect the health of the baby!'

Father Crispin had ended the futile visit with something close to a plea: 'Mary, make confession now. Let Mother Church take away your pain.'

But she had been as immovable as the Blarney Stone, and if he, her priest and confessor, couldn't shock some common sense into her, what in creation did Jonas Wade hope to accomplish here today?

Jonas himself wasn't sure; two objectives had brought him here: to clear up the question of Mary's innocence, and to get permission from the parents for an amniocentesis.

At her last checkup – before the disastrous visit, when she had said she wasn't coming back to him – Jonas had done a uterine exam. To his touch, the foetus seemed to be developing normally, the fundus the prescribed length. But it wasn't enough. Only last night Jonas had taken out Eastman's *Williams Obstetrics* and had reviewed the chapter 'Abnormalities of Development.' In it, he had come across a shocking statistic: three quarters of all monsters such as anencephalics (foetuses without heads) and hemicephalics (half-headed) were female. He had sat in his study, staggered by the significance of this fact, ignoring Penny's call to dinner, drawing to the chilling conclusion that some of those horribly deformed creatures might be the result of partheno-genic conception.

He couldn't bear it, that Mary might have such a monster inside her. Jonas Wade wanted the amniocentesis – and all its inherent dangers – so badly he was prepared to fight for it.

Mary was in her bedroom combing her hair when she heard Nathan Holland come in and be introduced to Dr. Wade. The voices were muffled, but she thought she detected Mike's among them. While the thought of seeing him again gave her a pang, Mary knew she would be in control of herself. Mike was like Joseph; in Matthew it said that Joseph had first wanted to put Mary away privately, break their engagement, and then Gabriel had appeared to him and explained everything. That's what was going to happen to Mike. God would see to it.

She wondered why Dr Wade had arranged this meeting.

168

It didn't matter. If it made her parents happy (the two of them had seemed so *relieved* to hear he was coming), then that was enough. She knew her mother and father were uncomfortable with the miracle of St. Sebastian; Mary was content to let Dr. Wade offer something for their troubled hearts.

On the dresser next to her mirror was a stack of library books waiting to be returned. The one on the bottom, *Queen of Heaven*, had been the first read: a large, overstuffed study of the Virgin Mary. Despite its thousand-and-some pages, the book had offered little in the way of concrete facts or new material; it was comprised mostly of medieval and Renaissance attitudes toward the cult of the Virgin. Stripped down to its basic New Testament story, the life of the Virgin was frustratingly scant. Mary Ann McFarland had learned only two things from the book: that the Virgin herself had been conceived when her mother St. Anne had been kissed on the cheek by St. Joachim (the Immaculate Conception) and that Mary, when delivering Jesus, had had a clean, painless, and bloodless birth.

The other library books dealt with a similar theme, only outside the framework of Christianity: classical mythology. In these Mary had read of other instances of virgin birth – Leda, Semele, Io – mortal women who had been visited by gods and had given birth to divine offspring. Plato and Pythagoras and Alexander the Great were believed to have been born to virgin mothers. History was full of such instances; Mary learned that she was not alone. And in learning such, drew comfort from it.

Dropping the comb onto the dresser, Mary took a moment to close her eyes and pull in a deep, sustaining breath. She thought: I am Vesta, I am all virgins; I am Isis, I am all mothers; I am Eve, I am all women...

Just as he knew it would happen, the instant Mary came into the living room, Mike fell in love with her all over again. She was so changed! The maternity smock with little ducks and rabbits on it only emphasized her new fecundity rather than hid it; her face was rounder, softer, her breasts large, her hair shiny and straight, her eyes like window panes over a

169

glowing blue light. Mike felt a lump gather in his throat and congeal there; he wanted to take Mary's hand but his palms were sweaty.

'Hello, everybody,' she said with a smile.

Jonas Wade wasted no time. With everyone seated around him – Lucille and Ted on either side of him on the sofa, Father Crispin in the easy chair, the Hollands on two dining room chairs, and Mary on the ottoman – he opened his briefcase, removed several blank pieces of paper and proceeded to give them a brief lesson on human conception.

He drew a circle on the paper, with a small circle and some squiggly lines in it. 'This is a human egg, and these lines here are its chromosomes, forty-six in all. When the egg comes out of the ovary during ovulation, it begins what is known as the maturation stage: it divides, the chromosomes pull apart so that there are two pairs of twenty-three, and this half of the egg' – he drew a squat hourglass and slashed an X over the top half – 'known as the second polar body, is expelled. The matured egg now has only twenty-three chromosomes and is ready to accept the other twenty-three contained within the sperm. If, at this stage, intercourse takes place, the sperm penetrates the vitelline membrane, becomes a spindle-shaped mass known as the male pronucleus, and fuses with the twenty-three female chromosomes in the centre of the egg. Segmentation is triggered and the egg starts dividing, multiplying itself until it becomes a cluster of cells, and then, an embryo.'

He looked at the faces around him. Lucille said, 'Why are you telling us this, Doctor?'

'In preparation for what I'm going to say next. I want to be certain we all have the same foundation, that nobody is left in the dark.' Jonas looked from her to Ted, who nodded, to Nathan and Mike Holland, and lastly to Father Crispin, whose lips were pursed in displeasure.

'The reason I came here today,' said Jonas, 'is to give you all a clear understanding of why Mary's pregnant.'

'Surely, Dr Wade,' interjected Father Crispin, 'you aren't persisting in that preposterous theory!'

'It's not preposterous, Father, as you will soon see.'

'What?' said Lucille. 'What is he talking about?'

'I'm talking, Mrs. McFarland, about parthenogenesis.'

As the seven around him listened in silence, their faces a range of masks, Jonas Wade slowly and carefully, after defining the term, recounted the step-by-step research he had done, including his talks with Bernie and Dr Henderson, the data he had compiled, and the startling conclusion he had arrived at. The talk took only thirty minutes, but it seemed much longer, as Jonas Wade's voice filled the living room; the small circle of people closed in on itself, shutting out the dazzling noon sun rebounding off the white patio floor and the speckling of pool reflections playing the walls and ceiling. As each listened to the tone of authority, saw the photocopied articles emerge from the briefcase, heard the facts and statistics and ultimately was drawn to the staggering end, each ingested and absorbed the material in his or her own way.

When Jonas was finished, five of the seven were not the same people as half an hour before.

Nathan Holland leaned back and drove his hands through his mane of white hair. His unreadable grey eyes moved slowly over the sheets spread before him on the coffee table, from the pencil drawing of an ovum and sperm, to the magazine articles with their unique headlines (all contained the word 'virgin') and lastly settled upon the ink sketch of a human egg dividing, its chromosomes separating, then coming back together. He believed it, every word.

Lucille McFarland, continually brushing straying strands off her forehead, stared at the same papers and drawings and thought: Impossible!

'What amazes me,' came Father Crispin's pulpit voice, 'even more so than this farfetched idiocy, is that you expect us to believe it.'

Before Jonas could respond, Ted said, 'I don't know, Father, it's pretty convincing— '

'Then I'm even more amazed!' The priest rose to his feet with a grunt and walked around the easy chair, trying to pump life back into his portly body.

Jonas looked up at him with a mingling of impatience and regret, and thought: You're only fighting this because you think it attacks your faith. You hear me implying Jesus might have been a biological fluke! While all I'm really saying is, I think Mary McFarland's baby is.

'Dr Wade,' came Ted's soft voice, 'is it really possible?'

'Mr. McFarland, look at the case of the Dionne quintuplets in Canada. Do you know what the odds are on the birth of fraternal quintuplets? At least fifty million to one. A fifty-million-to-one chance of five babies developing from one egg, and yet they did just that. And all the world accepts it. Mr. McFarland, the birth of the Dionne quins was in effect a scientific miracle – far more so than what has happened to your daughter – no one believed it could happen. And yet no one contested it, no one fought it; the quins are recognised and accepted for what they are. Now I'm saying that the chances of a parthenogenic birth are much greater. If you can accept the Dionne quins, why not Mary's virginity?'

Ted nodded slowly, mesmerised.

In the lengthening afternoon shadow, Father Crispin took hold of the back of the easy chair and, leaning on it, said quietly, 'Very well, Doctor, let us discuss Mary's virginity. You examined her, did you not?'

'Of course.'

'And the maidenhead?'

Jonas Wade regarded the jowly face of the priest. 'Mary's hymen was tough and unbroken, with an opening the size of a dime, just enough to allow for menstrual flow.'

'Is this conclusive evidence of virginity?'

'No, but a damn good case for it.'

'Can the maidenhead be stretched to allow a one-time admission and then return to its virginal shape?'

'In some cases, yes.'

'Would one penetration rupture it?'

'Not necessarily.'

'And would you say, Dr Wade, that Mary's maidenhead had never been tampered with?'

Jonas glanced reflexively at the girl, her face stonelike. 'No.'

172

Father Crispin leaned back from the chair in triumph, his lips puckered again.

'Tell me again, Dr Wade,' came Ted's heavy voice, 'why you think the baby will be a girl.'

'I'll show you.'

'Incredible. . .' whispered Ted a minute later, shaking his head over the diagram Dr Wade had roughly sketched.

Lucille, leaning forward, studied the illustration without comment, taking in the X-labelled egg and Y-labelled sperm and the simplified genetic equation Dr Wade had made of them.

Jonas Wade left the papers in their hands and rested back in the sofa. 'The sperm determines the sex of the child. It carries the Y chromosome which would make the baby male. Since there was no sperm, and there are only the X, female, chromosomes in the egg, then the baby has to be female.'

Finally Lucille looked up, her frosty eyes blank with wonder. Her resemblance to Mary made Jonas think: this is what *she'll* look like in twenty years.

Then he looked at Mary and wondered what was going on behind those crystal eyes.

She was thinking: He's wrong. . .

Lucille spoke in a breathy voice, 'Dr Wade, the electricity, the shock from the pool lights, you think that's what did it?'

'Yes.'

'But' – there was confusion in her eyes – for an instant, Lucille looked younger, more childlike than her daughter – 'can it have a *soul?*'

This was uncertain territory for Jonas Wade, who, confident in the scientific analysis of the situation, had been able to speak with assurance and conviction; now he faltered. Reflexively he looked to the priest for help.

Seeing the look in the doctor's eye, Father Crispin said quickly, 'Of course it has a soul, Lucille!'

'But. . .it wasn't conceived in the normal way.'

'All the same, it is a life, and all life comes from God. He chooses his instruments and his ways for his own mysterious reasons' – Father Crispin suddenly caught himself and blinked – 'not that I believe this nonsense,' he added hurriedly. 'But even if it were true, Lucille, it would still be a child of God.'

The priest's voice had stumbled; the support Jonas had hoped to secure from Father Crispin was not there. He moved cautiously. 'The child will be normal, Mrs. McFarland, there's no reason it shouldn't be. In a few weeks I'll be able to X-ray and then we'll be able to actually *look* at the foetus.' Jonas Wade glanced at Mary who continued to sit like a statue. 'There is, however' – he tiptoed through a mine field here – 'the slim chance that there might be a problem, so just as a precaution— '

'Problem?' said Lucille. 'What sort of problem?'

'I have no idea. I'm just saying that this case is unique, it might have unique considerations. And just as a precautionary measure I would like permission to run a special test on your daughter.'

'What sort of test?' asked Ted.

'It's called amniocentesis and it involves drawing out some of the amniotic fluid surrounding the foetus and examining it microscopically. It's being done now on mothers with Rh-negative blood to determine if the baby is in any danger from the mother's antibodies. We can take a look at the chromosomatic structure of the baby' – careful, Wade, don't alarm them – 'to ensure that its development is taking a normal course.'

'How reliable is this test?'

'Right now it's in the experimental stages, but— '

Lucille shook her head. 'No experiments on my daughter. She's been through enough.'

'Mrs. McFarland, amniocentesis is performed on hundreds of women every year in hospitals by reputable physicians— '

'Is it safe?'

'I beg your pardon?'

'Are there any dangers?'

'Well, yes, but you have those in any— '

'No, Doctor, no tests on my daughter.'

Jonas Wade felt himself constrict, his voice became tight.

'It's for your daughter's own good, Mrs. McFarland, and for the welfare of the baby.'

She held her glacial eyes on him. 'And if the baby were found to be abnormal?'

He stared at her.

'Dr Wade,' came Ted, 'I think what my wife is saying is that since nothing can be done about the baby anyway, why run risky tests? I mean, if it were found to be deformed, your course of care for Mary wouldn't change, would it?'

Jonas considered this, evaluated the defensive look in Lucille's ice-blue eyes, then said, 'No.'

'Dr Wade...'

All eyes turned to Mike, who startled them by speaking. His face bore a clouded aspect. 'What will it look like?'

'I beg your pardon?'

'The baby, what will it look like?'

'Well,' Jonas shifted uncomfortably, wondering what the youth was thinking, 'Mary's chromosomes separated and then linked together again. Since there was no sperm to introduce new traits, the baby will look exactly like Mary.'

Mike slowly turned his head, his grey eyes misted, and regarded Mary queerly. 'Like a replica?' he said.

'Yes...Mary is, in a sense, giving birth to herself.' And at the back of Jonas Wade's mind a voice echoed: 'These frogs are not offspring of Primus, they *are* Primus...'

Long sheets of sunlight slanted through the sliding glass doors; the dust of summer floated on the beams, diffusing the living room in an unearthly, halo glow. Seven uncertain and perplexed minds continued to wrestle with the day's revelation, with the exception of one, Mary, who sat bathed in an inner peace that protected her from the coldness of reality.

Father Crispin's struggle was the greatest, for, unlike the others, who were straining to find it in their hearts to accept Wade's scientific theory, the priest fought against it with all his might.

'So you see,' said Jonas Wade after a pause, 'there was no crime committed. Mary was telling the truth.'

Lucille gazed at the doctor with a small glow of gratitude

in her eyes but still could not bring herself to look at her daughter. Then she tried to smile at Ted; there was relief in acceptance.

'After the baby is born,' said Jonas, gathering up his papers, 'I'll be in a better position to confirm all of this with a few simple diagnostic tests— '

'No, Doctor.'

'These are not dangerous tests, Mrs. McFarland. A blood sample is all, to study the baby's genetic composition, and a patch skin graft transplanted from the infant to— '

'That's not what I meant,' said Lucille, rising to her feet and rubbing the back of her neck. 'We won't be keeping the baby.'

Jonas gaped up at her in astonishment.

'We've talked about it, Dr Wade,' came Ted's voice as he also rose. 'We think it's best for Mary if the baby is put up for adoption.'

Jonas looked at Mary, whose face was infuriatingly impassive, and then back at Lucille. He felt a small rise of panic and fought it down. 'Are you sure? It's early yet. It might be traumatic to separate mother and child— '

'I have to agree with the McFarlands,' said Father Crispin. 'Mary's only seventeen; what kind of mother would she be, not yet out of high school? The baby is better off in an adoptive home where it can be raised in a loving family atmosphere.'

Jonas cast wildly about for an argument, but could think of nothing other than the truth, and that one he could not voice: that giving up the baby for adoption would make completion of his write-up impossible. To finish his article and publish his theory he needed the genetic studies of the child and the skin graft. Losing the baby would dash all the plans he had made. Also, if the baby were to be adopted, it wouldn't be fair to reveal who the real mother was, or the strange circumstances of birth. But he had already arranged for Dr Norbert, the plastic surgeon, to do the grafting.

'Well,' he said, snapping shut his briefcase and standing. 'There's time yet to think about it. I'm sure you'll change your minds.' He gazed down at the girl squatting on the ottoman. 'I can't imagine Mary wanting to part with her baby.' He looked hopefully at her, but she seemed not to have heard. 'Anyway, in a couple of weeks I will X-ray Mary's abdomen and will continue to monitor her very closely.'

They went out the front door and into the hot furnace of the afternoon. Nathan Holland shook hands with Ted, grateful to have had the responsibility lifted, and Mike, still puzzling over all he had heard, discovered that he could not give one last backward glance at Mary. In fact, what Mike found in the place of the warm devotion and affection he had once felt for Mary was a queer awe of her; a curiosity laced with a little bit of cold fear, and while he would not allow the word 'freak' to come to mind, Mike Holland found himself suddenly 'turned off' by Mary Ann McFarland.

Father Crispin left angry, for two reasons: that everyone had believed Wade and that the doctor had more influence than he, their priest, had. Again, another symptom...

After the front door closed on them and the cars drove off and Mary could be heard going into her room, Lucille slipped into the comforting circle of her husband's arms, laid her head on his chest, and whispered, 'Oh, Ted, I don't know whether I'm relieved, or more frightened than ever.'

CHAPTER 15

While Tarzana slept through the hot August night, a light glowed in a window of St. Sebastian's rectory. Father Lionel Crispin, working by the light of one lamp and taking an occasional sip of brandy, was trying to write tomorrow morning's sermon. He was having difficulty.

A lot of his parishioners had been expressing concern lately over the ecumenism of the new Pope and feared great upheavals in the Church. The ultraconservative archdiocese of Los Angeles looked warily upon the convening of the

Second Vatican Council and could not deny the fact that some sort of change was coming. Father Crispin had decided to use his Sunday sermon as a vehicle for explaining the issues to his congregation, and tried, in his writing, to avoid a slanted, personal view.

He found he could not concentrate.

Picking up his brandy and walking to the window, Lionel Crispin parted the curtains slightly and looked out at the deserted parking lot.

For the first time in many years Father Crispin thought about his old dream, the one he had so cherished thirty years back when he had been in the seminary. Back then, young and idealistic Lionel Crispin had dearly wanted to enter the Franciscan Order. The simplicity, the poverty, the brotherhood with all of God's creatures, had so appealed to him that he had gone as far as taking formal steps to enter. But then his rich Bostonian family had intervened, shocked that their son should wish to demean himself and have no aspirations to the bishopric. Both his parents had had blazing visions of their son wearing the purple grosgrain sash of office, and when young Lionel had seen how shattered they would be if he carried out his plan, had abandoned his Franciscan dream and had accepted an assignment as a local parish priest.

He turned away from the window and went to stand at the desk.

The idealism was gone now, the youthful drive to minister to the world's poor and afflicted. All that was left of the young visionary was a balding, potbellied middle-aged priest who had long ago lost sight of his values.

Why, O Lord, he thought ruefully, am I thinking these things now?

He knew why: it was the McFarland girl.

Father Crispin walked wearily to the one easy chair in the office and sank into it, his eyes staring at the grey stone medieval fireplace that would never have a real fire in it, and he thought: I shouldn't have done that tonight. I shouldn't have walked out of that confessional. I as good as abandoned the girl.

He reflected briefly again, as he had several times during the evening, on that cataclysmic moment in the confessional: Mary had recited an average, unremarkable list of sins – eating meat on Friday, using the name of God to curse, forgetting to say prayers before going to sleep – but had omitted the one sin Father Crispin had wanted her to confess. When he had pressed her for it, they had argued – in his confessional! – he had slammed the window shut, turned to the next parishioner, and when he had returned to the other side, had heard Mary's familiar, protesting whisper. A second time Lionel Crispin had turned away from her, admonishing her to search her soul and not return to confessional until she was ready to confess her sin, and when he reopened the grate, there she was, damnably stubborn, insisting on her innocence, refusing to confess. And he, Lionel Crispin, in a pique of anger and lack of control, had gotten up and marched out of the confessional.

He sipped his brandy but didn't taste it.

Why? Why does she frustrate me so? He slammed a fist on the arm of the chair. If only she didn't seem so rational. If only he could believe she was truly mentally unstable – a psychiatric case – and not merely lying! But he couldn't risk it. Her soul was at stake.

His thoughts went back to the meeting at the McFarland house with Jonas Wade a few days before, and Father Crispin felt his anger rise with the memory. Yes, that was it; the crux of what bothered him.

How could he, a man of God, be expected to accept such a preposterous notion! He refused to believe it, *had* to disbelieve it for the sake of his faith. Because if this 'spontaneous parthenogenesis' can happen to a Tarzana teen-ager, then what about that other Mary two thousand years ago? The Catholic Church, the faith of millions, all founded on a biological fluke?

Overwhelmed with the significance of Mary's claim, that another girl named Mary a long time ago had been just as innocent, just as bewildered, and just as anxious to latch on to a dream about an angel, Father Crispin fell to his knees where he was, dropped the empty brandy glass, and bowed his head in prayer.

Father Crispin was deep in thought as the altar boys helped him to get dressed in the sacristy. Father Ignatius and Father Douglass had done the earlier Masses, leaving Father Crispin with the one he preferred, the one that was always fullest.

The altar boys thought their pastor was mentally rehearsing his sermon as he dressed quietly, washing his hands first, then taking the amice from them, kissing it, placing it on his head for a moment, and lastly draping it around his shoulders. He didn't joke with them as he usually did.

Father Crispin had slept very little that night; his mood was dark and distracted. How on earth to handle the McFarland girl? Her parents were adamant about that scientific malarkey. They had been so easy to convince, so ready to accept any half-baked placebo that came down the pike! Why Wade's side and not Crispin's; why so eager to absolve the girl?

Father Crispin took the alb from the altar boys and draped it over his head, fluffing it out and away from his cassock. They bound his waist with the cincture, after which they hung on his arm the narrow silken maniple.

The girl was either lying or psychotic. The problem was, how to find out which. Mental instability could be tolerated, but the purposeful concealment of a mortal sin could not. For the sake of Mary's soul, Father Crispin had to find the truth.

Mary took a moment to lift her head and look around the church. It was so crowded that people stood at the rear. She looked at all the clasped hands and bowed heads, at the way some people made Gothic spires of their fingers, how others had intermingled and collapsed fingers, still others prayed with one hand draped over the other.

When Father Crispin and the altar boys emerged from the sacristy, the whole congregation rose. He turned to them and made a benediction, and they all crossed themselves.

All through the service Mary tried to concentrate on the miracle of the Mass. She had never really thought about it before, how during the Mass Jesus Christ actually went through the entire cycle of Incarnation to Ascension, how he was born on the altar, how the priest turned mere bread into the flesh of Jesus, and how Jesus died and rose from the dead. All before the eyes of the congregation, all within an hour.

Father Crispin also had to force himself to concentrate, to remind himself what he was doing, to remember that he held in his hands the Body and Blood of Jesus Christ. His voice rang with uncharacteristic sharpness.

'*Kyrie eleison.*'

He knew that his distraction this morning was not just the McFarland girl; it was those confounded memories, welling up from locked recesses of his mind, robbing him of sleep and forcing him to relive, through the night, the long forgotten visions of his seminary days. At dawn he had risen unrefreshed and bitter. And now, nearly shouting the Introitus to keep his mind on the Mass, Lionel Crispin could not keep from thinking that the large crowd behind him, the overfed, overdressed, self-righteous suburbanites were the cause of his lost idealism.

'*Credo in unum Deum Patrem omnipotentem, factorem. . .*'

Too many years spent in cosseting socialites, in arranging bingo games and carnivals and raffles, in doling out penances for plastic fast-food sins.

He turned to face them. '*Dominus vobiscum.*' There was not a drop of ethnic blood in his parish; all skin colour had been gotten by the sides of pools. '*Sanctus, sanctus, sanctus. . .*'

Mary lost track of the Mass, her concentration dwindled. She held her eyes on the naked, tortured body of St. Sebastian.

'*Agnus Dei, qui tollis peccata mundi, miserere nobis.*'

Then the bells rang and Mary's fist thumped her chest.

'*Mea culpa, mea culpa, mea maxima culpa. . .*'

It was time to receive the Body. As the congregation quietly rose and started to file down the centre aisle toward the altar, Mary got up and joined them.

She knelt at the rail, crossed herself, and started to pray.

181

Under her lashes she saw Father Crispin moving slowly along the line of gaping mouths, dropping wafers on the protruding tongues.

When he was three people away from her, aided by an altar boy who held the gilt paten beneath each chin, Mary bent her head back and opened her mouth.

She felt a breeze, that of someone walking near her, and heard a voice whisper, 'May the body of our Lord Jesus Christ preserve your soul to everlasting life, amen.' Then she felt the person next to her push away from the rail.

Feeling but not seeing Father Crispin pause before her, Mary's heart raced. Her throat was dry and she wanted desperately to swallow, but she kept her head back, her eyes tightly shut, her mouth wide open.

Then the moment passed and Father Crispin, having skipped Mary, served the next parishioner down the line.

Humiliated, Mary snapped her head down and squeezed her knuckles together until she wanted to cry out with pain. She sucked in her lips and bit hard on them, tasting blood. *No!* screamed her mind. *Don't run!*

Father Crispin, at the end of the line and turning around to start again, scowled at the girl who remained stubbornly at the rail. The altar boy, trying not to let his amazement show, kept his eyes on the paten and so tripped on his cassock, falling against the priest and sputtering, 'I beg your pardon, Father!'

She felt him breeze by, going to the other end of the line to come back again, and firmly held her ground. She clutched the rail as if she were on a roller coaster and forced down rising nausea.

Father Crispin came down the line, giving the Host and blessing each parishioner. His fingers grasping the stem of the ciborium were a bloodless white. His lips were thin and angry; his voice rose a little and could be heard over the shuffling feet.

When he was three people away again, Mary threw back her head and forced her mouth open, even though fear made her gag. She stuck out her dry tongue and pressed her elbows close to her sides; she trembled so violently that her entire body shook.

Beneath her slightly open eyelids she saw the white hem of Father Crispin's alb come to rest before her.

A fine sweat instantly washed over her; Mary was afraid she was going to retch.

A plea went through her mind: Help me, God, help me, God, help me, God—

And then the touch, the tickle, the delicious whisper of the wafer on her tongue.

Throwing herself forward, nearly bending double over the rail, Mary sobbed with relief and joy. A chorus of angels burst in her head and an organ bellowed its deep tones throughout the church. The choir was singing and the last of the parishioners walked away from the Communion rail.

CHAPTER 16

Her feet were up in stirrups again, with her naked thighs parted and exposed to the cool air of the exam room. If she lifted her head slightly, Mary could see Dr Wade between her legs, his attractive face set in seriousness. She could hear the rubber glove snapping over his hand. Mary lay expectantly, ready.

She felt his arm brush her inner thigh as he positioned himself. Mary took a deep breath and relaxed. His fingers slid comfortably into her vagina. On her naked abdomen, his other hand massaged her skin, pressing here, there.

Mary closed her eyes. She hadn't noticed it before, how much she enjoyed the feel of Dr Wade's fingers inside her.

Then he moved slightly, altering his position, and Mary felt the hand on her abdomen slowly move up toward her chest. The fingers gently lifted her gown, bunching it up around her neck so that her naked breasts were exposed to the air. She kept her eyes closed, wondering what he was doing.

His fingertips explored the contours of her breasts, touched the nipples, pinched erotically, all the while the fingers in her vagina massaging and manipulating.

Aroused, wanting to do more than lie passively, Mary opened her eyes and saw that it wasn't Dr Wade who teased her breasts but Mike, who for some reason was wearing only swim trunks and was bending over her.

While Jonas Wade continued his delicious exploration between her legs, Mike Holland lowered his head and took one of her nipples in his mouth.

Mary heard herself cry out in pain and ecstasy, trying to move her arms, which she discovered were tied down to the table.

Dr Wade's probing grew rougher, his fingers no longer exploring but thrusting now, pounding. Mike's hungry feasting on her breasts became more violent; he encircled her with his muscular arms and sucked her nipples, her neck, her shoulders.

Between her legs, which were strapped to the stirrups and unable to move, Mary felt the jabbing fingers increase momentum.

Mary struggled. The straps held her arms fast, her legs wide apart. She wanted to scream, to fight off her attackers.

In the instant her eyes snapped open she recognised the wave that was about to inundate her; gaping at the black bedroom ceiling she felt it coming, starting with her curled toes, rippling along her legs, swelling in her buttocks and drawing her abdomen tight. She clenched her teeth and screwed her eyes shut as the rapture spilled over her, causing her to groan and release a long, quivering breath.

Exhausted, Mary blinked in wonder. She knew without examining herself that there would be wetness and swelling. The lingering throb was startlingly familiar.

'Sebastian. . .' she whimpered into the lonely night. Then she rolled over on her side and cried for a very long time.

'In a couple of weeks, Mr. McFarland, I am going to X-ray Mary and I would like you and your wife to be on hand. Since it will have to be done on a weekday, I thought you might need a little advance notice so you can arrange your schedule around it.'

'Certainly, Dr Wade, what day?'

Jonas reached for the Bank of America calendar on his desk, shifting the phone to his other ear. 'Any day in the week of the twenty-first. I think it'll be safe by then. Talk it over with Mrs. McFarland, then give my office nurse a call and she'll arrange an appointment with the X-ray lab.'

There was a short silence, as though Ted were writing himself a note, then he said, 'Dr Wade, how great *are* the chances of its being deformed?' Unflinchingly to the point, Ted McFarland seemed to be facing up to the situation.

'I'm afraid I can't say. I only want you and your wife to be there when the films are developed just in case there is something wrong with the baby. Mary will need the support.'

Ted's voice came through curiously thin and strong at the same time. 'And if it is a monster, what will you recommend?'

Jonas closed his eyes. 'I can't say right now, Mr. McFarland. It depends on so many things. If it should happen that the baby is grossly abnormal, then you'll want to discuss the matter with your priest.'

There was a pause before Ted said, 'You're thinking of an abortion, aren't you?'

'If there's a real threat of danger to Mary's life, yes.'

'But she's six months along. Isn't it. . .a baby by now?'

'Yes.'

'I see. I appreciate your being honest with me, Dr. Wade. Lucille and I will be there. Thank you for calling.'

Jonas hung up and remained at his desk, staring at the red folder which contained the first draft of his article. The last chapter was all it needed. He had briefly considered approaching Ted McFarland on this matter – both parents would have to give permission – but had, at the last minute, changed his mind. The poor man had enough to contend with right now – Jonas hated having to tell Ted about the possibility of deformity, but the man had to know – so Jonas had decided that the matter of permission to do the write-up could wait. After all, if the X-rays showed a hopelessly deformed foetus, then the article would not be finished anyway. But if the films showed a normal baby, then Jonas would find a diplomatic way to approach the McFarlands...

Jonas gently massaged his face as his mind revolved in endless circles of solutionless quandaries; there was so much more to this case than surface appearance, it was consuming him. Another problem which Jonas was facing and which he was soon going to have to tackle was this business of giving up the baby for adoption. He was going to have to find a way, in clear conscience, to advise the McFarlands to keep the child; but that was the hitch: *in clear conscience*. Jonas Wade was stabbingly aware that he worked in self-interest on this issue; if both Mary and her parents felt it was better to give up the baby, and if Father Crispin backed them up, then it *was* the best course to take and Jonas Wade had no business advising otherwise. And yet, with the baby removed, his article could not be finished; while he had laid a firm base to support his theory, without the 'proof after the fact' to back it all up, he might as well abandon the whole plan.

Jonas rose from his desk and looked around the study. Unanswered correspondence was strewn on the leather couch; untouched medical journals; new books still in their UPS wrappers. Good Lord, had he become *so* absorbed in Mary Ann McFarland?

A staccato rap on his door brought him out of his internalising. On the other side, Penny's voice: 'Jonas?'

He opened the door.

'I thought you were going to talk to Cortney tonight.' There was a trace of impatience in her manner, so unlike Penny; she looked past him and into the den. There was the red folder, the one she had seen in his hands so often lately; at breakfast, on the patio, even during TV. He would open it frequently, scratch out a word or line and rewrite above it. Paper clips held three-by-five notes to the pages; sheets of photocopy paper were inserted at intervals. Penny knew it was an important project to Jonas – he had told her about it, had let her read the first draft – and she agreed that it was without a doubt dynamite material. Still, she couldn't see why it preoccupied him so.

'Cortney says she's moving out the end of this month. Jonas, she won't listen to me, you have to talk to her.'

'All right,' he said, coming all the way out of the study and closing the door behind him. 'Where is she?'

'Good God, Daddy, I'm eighteen! A lot of girls work and put themselves through school! You let Brad do it, why not me?'

'Cortney, it's only for three more years, then you'll have your diploma and you can get the job you really want. What would you do now, work at Thrifty's?'

'What's wrong with that? Sarah works at Taco Bell. We're going to split the rent and food costs and we'll take our bikes to school. She doesn't live far from the campus.'

Jonas sank back into the cushioned lawn chair and watched dead brown leaves, like ancient galleons, twirl on the surface of the pool. It was a peculiar evening for October. While the yearly Santa Anas blew their familiar hot breath through the valley, alternately fiercely and gently, carrying in whirlwinds decayed leaves and empty walnut shells, tonight the gusts were laced with an unusual edge of cold, as though it were a hint of a harsh winter ahead.

'I can't stand it,' Cortney went on. 'You and Mom make me come home from a date by eleven o'clock. Jesus, Dad, I'm eighteen!'

'You keep saying that like I've forgotten.'

Cortney's face hardened, aged twenty years. 'I think you have. I'm not a baby anymore. I want to go out and fend for myself.'

Jonas could not help, fleetingly, comparing Cortney with Mary Ann McFarland; they were only a year apart but Cortney was so mature, so adult, while Mary was still, in many ways, a child. Cortney had her mother's self-sufficiency, Penny's survival streak: an ability to take command

187

of herself and her life and weather any gale. At times like this, when Cortney was asserting herself, she looked more like Penny than ever.

As he listened to his daughter's pragmatic outline of her plans, Jonas could not help studying her face. The voice, the words faded away as the facial features came into sharp, almost exaggerated clarity until Jonas felt he was looking at her for the first time.

He had never before realised how strongly Cortney resembled her mother. But it went beyond the long straight nose with the narrow Nordic nostrils, beyond the thin strip of mouth, the bare slant to the eyes, the line of chin and cheekbone – all Penny's. Cortney had inherited her mother's mannerisms, her habit of closing her eyes when emphasising a point, of chewing on the inside of her right cheek while thinking of a word; the lips moved the same way Penny's did, the musculature beneath was not Cortney's, it was Penny's. And the more Jonas saw this, for the first time, the more he felt a chill and a tremor of anxiousness rush through him.

A haunting whisper brushed the back of his mind: *Put a wedding gown on her and you are looking at the girl you married.*

He found himself searching her face for evidence of himself; tried to twist the Penny features into ones that matched his. God, was it his imagination or was there none of him in Cortney? Would a stranger see any of Jonas Wade in her or would the stranger see only a young Penny?

They are not offspring of Primus, Dorothy Henderson had said, *they* are *Primus*...

'Daddy?'

Jonas experienced a passing moment of revulsion, of horror: My own daughter, what if she were – the result of some freakish 'activating agent' rather than a love embrace? Lord, was Father Crispin right? Would she have a soul?

Then it passed, the paroxysm, and was replaced by profound guilt and remorse. Jonas Wade had been grandstanding to get everyone to accept Mary Ann McFarland's baby as a normal human being, and here, for a moment, he rejected his own daughter as a soulless entity.

Hypocrite, whispered his mind.

'Daddy?'

He narrowed his eyes, trying to hold his attention on her. It was happening again, so much lately, this preoccupation with Mary Ann McFarland stealing him from his other responsibilities. Penny had commented on it a few times lately; now Cortney noticed a distraction in her father.

Guilt seemed to be his natural state now: guilt about the article, guilt about his ethics to protect Mary, guilt about robbing his family of his attention. Still, it didn't stop him from pursuing his course: the article was nearly finished; later, after the birth of the child, when he had proof, he would submit the write-up to the *Journal of the American Medical Association*.

'Cortney, your mother and I want only what's best for you. We think your studies would suffer if you were to move out.'

She sighed irritably and tossed her head back (another trait of Penny's). 'Honestly, Daddy, there's more to education than books! I want to learn about life, too. You're sheltering me and I don't want to be sheltered. You've got to let me go!'

Jonas didn't want this battle, not now, not with Mary Ann McFarland tugging at his mind for attention. He knew where resistance would lead: the same place it always led when he came up against Penny's determination – a deadlock. And then Cortney would be miserable and the household upset and she'd move out eventually anyway...

Jonas reached over and patted her hand. 'All right, Cortney, we'll give it a try. If it works out, fine, if not you can always come back here.'

'Thanks, Daddy!' She jumped up, threw her arms around his neck, then dashed into the house, calling her mother and leaving Jonas to stare at the rippled surface of the wind- and leaf-swept pool.

Lionel Crispin kept his gaze fixed on the world beyond the reflection in the window; he forced himself to watch the October wind maraud the street, stripping the trees and tipping over trash cans, so that he could avoid looking at

189

himself in the glass. Fall was coming unusually early this year. Southern California generally enjoyed balmy autumns, but there was an uncharacteristic rage to the fury outside, a *bareness* to the scene, that made Father Crispin sense the advent of a difficult winter.

'Lionel. . .' came a gentle prompt from the man behind him.

Father Crispin turned away from the window. 'Forgive me, Your Excellency.'

The man in the brocaded easy chair, with his feet on a footstool, watched his visitor intently. 'Is that it? The whole story?'

'Yes, Your Excellency.' Father Crispin took up his pacing again, walking in and out of the hemisphere of warmth created by the fire in the fireplace.

'And you haven't seen the girl since?'

'No, Your Excellency.'

'Did you go to her house or make any attempt to contact her?'

The priest stopped in the middle of the elegant living room and tried to control his voice as he said to the bishop, 'I couldn't! I couldn't face her again!'

'Why not?'

'Because she defeated me!'

'Lionel,' said the bishop quietly. 'Come, sit down.'

Father Crispin took a seat opposite the prelate. The two men sat with one side of their faces reflecting the fire's glow, the other side in darkness; their profiles were distinct in the contrasting light: Lionel Crispin was a collection of roundnesses, full cheeks and fleshy nose; sixty-year-old Bishop Michael Maloney's face was made up of sharp angles and flat planes, like a portrait in cubism.

'You and I go back a long way, Lionel,' came the bishop's nasal voice. 'I remember when you first came to this diocese. I was only a parish priest then. Do you remember those days, Lionel?'

'Your Excellency, I failed that girl. I literally ran out on my duty to her soul.'

Bishop Maloney made a spire of his hands and tucked i

under his firm chin. 'All right, let's talk about that. Why did you give the girl Communion if you didn't think she deserved it?'

Father Crispin's hands contracted into fat fists. 'Because I was embarrassed.'

'What do you mean?'

Lionel avoided his old friend's eyes, turned his gaze into the dancing flames, not blinking. 'I felt the whole congregation watching me.'

'Were they?'

'I don't know, but that's how I felt. All eyes were on me, even my altar boys'. It was so mortifying' – Lionel ran a dry tongue over his lips – 'to turn around and see her still kneeling there. And I knew, when I saw the look on her face, that she was going to stay there, after everyone had gone back to their seats and I was to commence with the *Postcommunio*, that Mary Ann McFarland would continue to kneel at the rail with her head back and her tongue sticking out. I did it' – he brought his face back to the prelate – 'I did it, Your Excellency, to get rid of her!'

Bishop Michael Maloney took in Father Crispin's words, his taut voice, his hunted expression, and the jerkiness of his manner with a calm, unreadable look. The fingers remained propped under the sharp chin as the bishop recognised that his priest was not yet telling him what he really came here for tonight.

'So,' came the nasal voice, 'you thought the girl to be in a state of mortal sin and you gave her Communion. Have you confessed this?'

'Yes. To Father Ignatius.'

'Then your own sin has been expunged. Now we must work on the problem of the girl.'

Father Crispin bowed his head and looked at his hands. He was still not at peace. He had gone to old Father Ignatius because the man was partially deaf and gave out light penances; Lionel Crispin was no better than his parishioners.

'About the girl, Lionel. It would seem to me she truly believes herself to be innocent, in which case she committed no sin. If she cannot remember it, or for whatever psychological reason. After all, Lionel, we do not damn the mentally afflicted.'

'I don't believe she has a mental problem, Your Excellency, and what's more, neither does her physician.'

'Ah, yes, what did you say the man's name was?'

'Wade.'

'This Dr Wade claims Mary is perfectly sane and in control of her faculties. So it would seem then that she would be lying. However, there is the matter of this parthenogenesis business. What you told me is very interesting. I should like to hear more about it from Dr Wade.'

Father Crispin snapped his head up. 'Surely you don't condone it, Your Excellency!'

'I do not know yet, Lionel, I haven't all the facts, but from what you've told me—'

'Forgive me, Your Excellency' – the priest started to rise – 'but this parthenogenesis nonsense undermines everything we believe in!'

'Lionel, please stay seated, and tell me how it undermines all we believe in. On the contrary, I find it quite in harmony with the Faith, after all, aren't we founded on just such a tenet? Was not Eve created without sexual intercourse, and the Blessed Virgin herself?'

'Your Excellency, I cannot believe my ears! Surely you must see that if a virgin can become pregnant by a simple shock to the body, then what of the Mother of Our Lord?'

'Oh, Lionel, is your faith so fragile? Cannot the two be separate phenomena? Two thousand years ago God spoke to one named Mary and called her Blessed. As Catholics, we must believe this. Now, in nineteen hundred sixty-three, another named Mary is subjected to an electrical shock and is suddenly with child. What, pray, has one to do with the other? Father Crispin, the first Mary was chosen by God. Mary McFarland is the victim of biology, how can she pose a threat to your faith? Is your faith so vulnerable?'

Father Crispin quivered as he sought to control himself. 'It's just the opposite, Your Excellency! My faith is stronger now than ever! I am unshakable!'

Bishop Maloney narrowed his eyes and observed the cracks in Lionel Crispin's solidity. He felt himself grow alarmed. 'If your faith is so strong, Lionel,' he said slowly, 'then why should this case frighten you? The man clad in armour has nothing to fear from wooden arrows.'

Lionel Crispin rammed his fists together so that his knuckles gave out a loud crack. He couldn't put into words the turmoil in his heart: the haunting fear that Wade was right. What if the girl *was* a virgin. And what if she had a boy...

'Lionel, what else is troubling you?'

Father Crispin fought for a moment to calm himself and heard, above the crackling of the fire, the howling October winds outside. 'Dr Wade said there might be a problem with the child. It might be deformed.'

Bishop Maloney's forehead gathered into a frown. 'Deformed how?'

Lionel Crispin could not meet his friend's eyes. 'Badly. A monster.'

'I see...'

The lonely wail of the wind seemed to intensify; it tunnelled through the empty streets of Los Angeles. Summer was being blown away. Lionel Crispin turned to the small glass of sherry on the table by his chair. The bishop had poured it when he had first come in over an hour ago; now Father Crispin picked it up for the first time. Sipping it and listening to the wind he thought: Soon it will be All Saints' Day, then Christmas, then the New Year, and January...

It struck him as ironical that the biggest Christian holiday, Christmas, celebrating new life and new hope, was held in the middle of the deadest, most hopeless season. No, that wasn't true. Easter was the biggest Christian holiday, the celebration of the Resurrection. At least it was supposed to be. But people didn't turn out for Easter the way they did for Christmas; for some reason they preferred to focus on the birth of Jesus instead of on his conquest over death—

'Father?'

Lionel shook his head. 'Forgive me, Excellency, I was thinking.'

'What is your trouble with the McFarland baby?'

Father Crispin searched about for the right words. How to express it, the cold fear that held his heart in a vice? *You might be called upon to make a life-and-death decision,* Jonas Wade had said. Lionel Crispin was remembering a nightmare in his life, not many years before, when he had been called to the home of a parishioner. The woman was delivering prematurely and was bleeding so profusely that there had been no time to get her to the hospital. Father Crispin had arrived in time to give the poor woman last rites and to baptise the baby; only...only it had had no head – just a grotesque stump of neck with two bulging eyes and a wicked gash of a mouth. And it had been alive, writhing in the pan the obstetrician had dropped it in while the mother haemorrhaged to death in the bed, and Father Crispin had nearly vomited, just as the memory sickened him now.

'I'm afraid,' he said softly.

'Of what?'

'Of the decision.' He met the bishop's eyes squarely, and Michael Maloney was taken aback by the look of naked fear. 'Dr Wade said her delivery might be difficult and I might be called upon to decide between the mother and the child.'

'Surely, Lionel, this can pose no problem to you. You know where your duty lies.'

I know! cried his troubled heart. But I don't want the responsibility! How can I let that beautiful girl die in order to baptise something that won't live a minute and that won't have a head and that didn't deserve to be alive in the first place? Echoing Lucille McFarland's anguish, he said, 'Your Excellency, can it have a *soul?*'

Feeling some of Lionel Crispin's anxiety infect his own soul, the bishop got up from the chair, rose to a tall and lanky height and absently toyed with the heavy ring of office on his right hand. 'The baby has a soul, Lionel, no matter what its physical origin. And you have a duty to send that soul to heaven. You must not look at the bodily aspect of the child, however grotesque it might be.' Bishop Maloney, slender and towering in his long black cassock and purple sash, cast a distorted shadow across the oriental carpet. He seemed to fill the large room. 'Lionel,' he said gently. 'No one told you a priest's lot would be an easy one. Being responsible for people's souls is no simple job. It takes courage to face decisions such as this. In my lifetime as a priest,' the bishop sighed almost mournfully, 'I have been called upon to make such decisions, and they have troubled me forever afterward. Lionel' – Michael Maloney strode over to his friend and dropped a comforting hand on his arm – 'I know what you are going through, and I am convinced that this is a test put before you by God. Pray to Our Lord and his holy Mother. They will guide you. Trust me.'

Lionel Crispin turned back to the cold pane of glass in the window and the formidable October wind that marauded the street and he thought: Please, Lord, let it be normal. Give it eyes and a nose and a mouth and a real head...

He felt his heart shiver. It was a premonition. Mary Ann McFarland's baby would be horribly grotesque, monstrously deformed, and he, Lionel Crispin, would be expected to baptise it into a state of undeserving grace...

The house wasn't dark enough for Mary.

She had closed her curtains to block out the moon, had turned off the night light, but as she lay on her back with the covers pulled up to her neck and could not even make out the dim shapes of her bedroom furniture, Mary wished it were darker yet.

How far away do you have to hide, she wondered, how dark does it have to be before you don't feel like every eye in the world can see you?

She was naked. Her nightgown lay crumpled on the floor. She had drawn the bedspread, normally removed at night, over the covers and up to her chin.

How much darkness, how many covers, how much silence do you need before you can be alone with your own body? It was not the nakedness itself. It was what she was going to do with it.

Mary heard her mind whisper involuntarily: Forgive me. She felt silly. I'll ask forgiveness afterward, not now.

Why can I touch my arm or leg without feeling guilty?

Why do I have to feel bad about wanting to discover myself? After all, it's *mine*, isn't it? Mine to touch, to explore, to enjoy?

'A good Catholic girl keeps her thoughts and hands busy.' Sister Michael, sixth grade.

'Whenever you're tempted to touch yourself, think of the Virgin.' Sister Joan, eighth grade.

'Thinking of an impure act is as sinful as committing that act.' Father Crispin.

'Touching yourself makes Jesus cry.' Sister Joan.

But I have to know, pleaded Mary with the darkness around her. I thought Sebastian had done it, but Dr. Wade said *I* did it.

I have to know...

She closed her eyes and pictured St. Sebastian. She pictured him standing before her, the loincloth lying on the floor around his feet. She saw how the moonlight highlighted the hills and valleys of his beautiful hard muscles. How trickles of blood oozed from his many wounds. How his eyes, deep and brooding, gazed sadly and lovingly down at her.

Her hand, hesitant and uncertain, slid over the crest of her thigh.

Her mind whispered again: *Forgive me...*

CHAPTER 17

The wind scudded down Collins Street in a fury that set telephone lines to swinging. Neighbourhood cats, their fur charged with dry electricity, leaped from fence to fence, backs arched in Halloween fashion, ears pressed back, yowling at the wind as if to drive it away. The Massey house was dark and locked up tight; in the driveway stood Lucille McFarland's Impala.

The two girls were alone in the living room, ensconced in

a small circle of light that emanated from the bayberry candle that burned between them. Mary, lying on the lumpy sofa with her eyes closed, listened to Germaine's soft voice as, sitting close by on the floor, she chanted: 'Oh this, this only stirs the troubled heart in my breast to tremble!' She was reading from a paperback book, opened out between her knees, while Mary, every so often, stirred herself and refilled their paper cups from the bottle of purple wine that stood by the candle.

'For should I but see thee a little moment,' recited Germaine, hunched over the dog-eared book, 'Straight is my voice hushed; Yea, my tongue is broken, and through and through me, 'neath the flesh, impalpable fire runs tingling.' She paused, her eyelids fluttering, then she resumed in a softer, more melodic tone: 'Nothing see mine eyes, and a voice of roaring waves in my ear sounds; Sweat runs down in rivers, a tremor seizes all my limbs, and paler than grass in autumn, caught by pains of menacing death, I falter. . .lost in the love-trance. . .'

'That's beautiful,' murmured Mary, shifting her awkward weight on the sofa. With Germaine's parents out for the evening, the two girls enjoyed the silence and compelling darkness of the house and, after an hour, half of the litre of wine. 'What is it?'

Germaine did not raise her head but remained bowed over the book, her silken hair streaming down to hide her face. 'A poem by Sappho.'

'Who?'

'She was a woman who lived in ancient Greece and she wrote love poems.'

'Who was the lucky man?'

Germaine picked up her Dixie cup, took a long draw on the sweet wine, then said in a breathy voice, 'She wrote it for a woman named Atthis.'

Mary's eyes finally came open. 'You're kidding. She wrote a love poem to another woman?'

Germaine hesitated over this, alternately staring at the worn book and her cup of wine, then, drinking down the last, she impulsively slapped the book closed and tossed back her head. Her smile was glowing. 'Refill me, Mare!'

Mary grunted as she reached down for the bottle, uncapped it, and spilled some into each cup. She was unaccustomed to wine and found it to be a deliciously euphoric treat.

'So...' came Germaine's velvety voice, 'when did you say you get X-rayed?'

'Next week.'

'How much will you be able to see?'

'Mostly the baby's bone structure.'

'Does it scare you, Mare?'

'No, I don't think so...Oh!' Her hand flew to her abdomen. 'She's very restless tonight! Must be the wine. Here.' Mary took hold of Germaine's hand and placed it on her belly. 'Feel her kick?'

'Yes.' Germaine quickly drew her hand away.

'You know, we still haven't bought any baby things. Mother and Daddy want to put the baby up for adoption, but I'm not sure. I could take care of her and still go to school.' She picked up her cup, drained it and reached for the bottle. The room seemed to grow increasingly warm. 'Maybe you could help me with her. Would you do that?'

Germaine looked down at the book in her hands, seemed to trace with her eyes the face of the woman on the cover, then said distantly, 'I don't know anything about babies, Mare. I'm not the maternal type. I doubt I'll ever have kids.'

Grunting onto her side and propping her head up with one hand, Mary gazed at Germaine. There were so many things she wondered about her friend, things that had for a long time gone unspoken and understood and that Mary had never questioned. But now she was curious and the wine was making her feel free.

'You and Rudy really have a lot of sex, don't you?'

'Yes.'

'How do you keep from getting pregnant?'

Germaine's eyes sparkled with reflections from the flame. 'I use a diaphragm.'

198

'What's that?'

'Leave it to a Catholic not to know! It's just a form of contraception. Saves Rudy the hassle of rubbers.'

'Oh—'

'I know, you don't believe in contraception.'

'Well, it isn't natural, is it? Sex is for making babies, isn't it?'

'Sex is for fun, Mare, and contraception makes women free. We should be able to have sex as often as men do and enjoy it as much as they do. What law says we have to hate it and be constantly worried about pregnancy?'

Mary's voice fell to a whisper. 'Do you enjoy it?'

Germaine paused, drank her cup dry, and said, 'Yes.'

Mary rolled onto her back, watching shadows dance on the ceiling. 'I envy you. Your parents are so liberal and you're so free. You don't suffer a single pang of guilt. That must be great. I wish I knew what that was like.' She let out a short laugh. 'I wish I knew what a lot of stuff was like!'

She closed her eyes and thought of the wonderful discovery she had made alone in her bed and how she was able to unfailingly reproduce the miracle of orgasm almost every night. The fact that she had to confess it to old Father Ignatius every Saturday evening didn't detract from the pleasure of it.

She wondered if Germaine did it. Wondered how often she and Rudy had sex. What it was like. Envied her for being able to enjoy it and not have to whisper about it to a hidden priest on Saturdays. Mary envied Germaine her liberal mother who allowed her to use the new Tampax; Lucille had forbidden it, saying it would break Mary's hymen. She envied her for Rudy, for being able to make love to a real man. Then Mary thought of Dr Wade.

She leaned over, picked up her cup, and drank noisily from it. Germaine was gazing hypnotically at the candle flame and softly humming 'We Shall Overcome.'

In discovering her own sexuality, Mary had started to wonder about it in others. About her parents. Why her mother said, 'No nice girl wants it.' Why the nuns had taught her that for a woman sex was a duty, while in a man the 'urge' was natural.

The girls soon grew silent and let their stares fall into the shadows of the living room. It was a wonderfully intimate moment, embraced in the halo of the flickering light, feeling the effects of cheap wine. 'Mare?'

'Yes?'

'Mare, this business about it being a girl. . .'

'Yes?'

'It's hard to believe.'

'Not really. Not when you hear Dr Wade explain it.'

Germaine looked out of the corner of her eye, quickly, furtively, at Mary's puffed-out belly. 'I guess I just wonder what it's like.'

'Well, if you really want to know, stop using that diaphragm or whatever it's called.'

Germaine bowed her head as she inspected the threadbare carpet. With her face obscured, she said in a soft voice, 'Mare. . .I gotta tell you something.'

'What?'

'Well, it's not easy to say.'

Mary tilted her head and reached out to touch her fingertips to Germaine's arm. 'What is it?'

She emitted a brief, dry laugh and then raised her eyes, looking directly at Mary, her face white in the candle's glow. 'I wanted to tell you long before this, but somehow, I never could.'

'Germaine, you can tell me anything.'

'Yes, it must be the wine. . .Mare, it's about Rudy.'

Mary held her friend's gaze.

Germaine said, 'He doesn't exist.'

The sounds of the October night rushed in to fill the momentary void, then faded away as Mary, trying to sit up a little but failing, said, 'What?'

'I said he doesn't exist. There is no Rudy. I don't have a boy friend at UCLA.'

'I don't understand.'

'I made him up, Mare. There is no poli-sci student named

200

Rudy and I don't have a boy friend and I don't have sex all the time like you think.'

'But...I don't understand.'

'I made him up, for God's sake!'

'Why?'

Unable to look at her friend's astonished face any longer, Germaine dropped her gaze back to the candle and drank some more wine. 'Because at first it was just you and me and it was really neat. And then Mike came onto the scene and I didn't have you all to myself anymore. I don't know, I guess I was hurt or envious or something.' Her soft voice filled the circle of light. 'And then you started going steady with him and I guess, I don't know, maybe I wanted to show you that I could do it, too, you know, have a boy friend and go steady.'

Germaine fell silent and Mary found herself listening to the rhythm of her own breathing. The room was dark and close; the wine made her head swim. She blinked at her friend. 'I'm sorry,' she said softly.

Germaine tossed back her head and avoided looking at Mary. Refilling her cup and drinking it all down without a breath, she thought: There's more, but you wouldn't understand.

The fact was, Germaine didn't understand it herself and so was unable to put it into words for her friend. It had to do with not liking boys and desperately wishing she could and being frightened of her own sexuality and of the shocking dreams she'd been having lately – or were they fantasies?

Germaine shook her head and stared sadly at the little flame. She wanted Mary to put her arms around her and let her cry on her shoulder, to feel important to her, to try to find a way to say how much she cared...

'You didn't have to make it up,' she heard Mary say. 'I don't care if you have a boy friend or not.'

But you don't understand, cried Germaine's mind, struggling through the wine to reach an idea she had been struggling for months to grasp. I didn't want you to think I was weird or anything, that there was anything wrong with me...

But the idea, as it always had, as it always would until later years when she came to fully understand the truth about herself, eluded Germaine. Afraid of herself and repulsed by what she suspected, Germaine said unhappily, 'Actually, Mare, I've ...I've never done anything at all with a boy...'

The night seemed to go on forever. Mary felt hot, dreamy. Had she been sober, she might have seized upon the subtlety of her friend's words, might have saved Germaine the anguish of having to try to make plain something she didn't even understand herself. But Mary was drinking wine and feeling transparent and heard only what had been said. Sipping a little more, she watched Germaine's long black hair cast back the candlelight; she wanted to reach out and touch it, stroke the silkiness, run her fingers through it—

'So anyway...' said Germaine with a heavy sigh. 'That's it. Now you know my deepest darkest secret.'

Mary smiled and murmured, 'I'm glad you told me.'

Germaine returned the smile, but her eyes were full of sadness. 'I guess it's silly for us to have secrets, Mare. You and me, we're real close, aren't we?' She lifted her dark liquid eyes. 'Mare?'

'Hm?'

'Why don't you tell me about, you know, the baby.'

With eyes closed, Mary relished the feeling of the wine enveloping her body. 'What do you mean?'

'You know. What was it like? Doing it, I mean.'

Her head came up with a start. 'What are you talking about?'

'Did you like it, Mare, did you like sex with a boy?'

There was a sudden tightness in Mary's bowels, a creeping rigidity that she hadn't felt in months, not since the night she had taken her father's razor blades out of the medicine chest. Suddenly the wine dissipated. 'Germaine, I told you how I got the baby.'

Her friend's voice was flinty. 'Yes, I know, but what I mean is, you can tell me the truth, you know? God, parthenowhatchamacallit. You did it with Mike, didn't you? You let him fuck you. What was it like?'

202

Mary's fingers drove hard into the sofa, boring into the stuffing to give her something to hold on to. In a tight voice she said, 'Germaine, I told you the truth. The baby started on its own. And that's why it's going to be a girl. I told you all that. And you said you believed me. I never did anything with anybody. Least of all Mike!'

Her friend's voice came from very far away, like through a wad of cotton. 'Mare, don't be mad, but I did tell you about Rudy and I've never told anyone that. Even my mom thinks he exists. You're the only one who knows the truth.' Germaine's words fell over one another breathlessly. 'I know what you've told Dr Wade and I'm sure he believes you. And so does your priest and your folks, but Mare, you can tell *me* because I won't tell anyone and it'll be just between the two of us, just like my secret about Rudy. Mare!' Germaine's hand shot out and took hold of Mary's arm. 'Tell me you did it with Mike!'

Something rose up inside Mary. It started from the deepest part of her, struggling to get out, and found its way through her throat. 'Oh, my God—'

'Mare!'

Shaking free of Germaine's hold, Mary writhed to a sitting position, struggled to her feet, and with some effort stood without falling back down.

'Mare, wait! I'm sorry! I didn't mean—'

But she ran. She didn't think she could, being this heavy and clumsy, but Mary ran, and managed to find her way through the darkness and out of the front door.

Mary wanted to talk to her father, sit down with him and spill everything out; but she couldn't wait for him to come home, she had to talk to him now. And it was Wednesday.

She knew where he would be.

Pulling into the parking lot of the health club, Mary felt no hesitation about walking in and asking to see him. She had visions of Ted dropping whatever he was doing, changing into his clothes, and taking her out for a Coke.

But what Mary had not anticipated was having the T-shirted attendant at the front desk say to her, 'Ted

McFarland hasn't been here since his membership expired, oh, two, three years ago.'

She stood in stupid amazement. 'Are you sure?'

His flat gaze flickered down to her abdomen. 'Sure am, miss.'

'Does he go to another gym, do you know?'

'Couldn't say.'

Five minutes later she was behind the wheel of the Impala, going aimlessly up and down streets, oblivious to the neon lights of Ventura, to the traffic around her, even to driving. Her consciousness went to a faraway place while her hands and feet, like those of a robot, manipulated the car, braking at red lights, signalling at corners. There was nowhere she wanted to go except to be going.

Mary traced a zigzag pattern along the streets of Tarzana – up this one, down the next – until she was driving over the unsurfaced dirt and bumps of Etiwanda Avenue. She had turned right when she came to the library and followed this dark rural street that bordered a large, mossy storm ditch. A lot of streets in the valley were still unpaved; the jolting potholes did not snap her out of her hypnotic state.

But something else did.

When the green Lincoln Continental reached a responsive centre in her brain, Mary slowed her mother's car and rolled to a stop in front of the next house. Turning off the motor, she swivelled around with a grunt and looked back at her father's car.

It was parked in the driveway of a boxy little house not unlike Germaine's, with a few leaves from the sheltering sycamore spotting the vinyl roof and polished hood.

Mary gazed for some minutes at the car, knowing it to be her father's and puzzling over its being there.

It was not unusual for Ted to visit the home of a client, spending an evening going over a stock portfolio. Perhaps this was one such case.

However. . .

Mary gnawed her lower lip. What had the muscle man at the gym said? Her father hadn't been there in two or three years.

Then where was he going every Wednesday night?

Mary's eyes roved the little house, took in the yellowed lawn, the faded stucco paint, the pale light behind the closed draperies. It was an old tract house, but neat and well kept.

There was a name on the mailbox, spelled out in adhesive-backed reflector letters: RENFRO.

Thinking for a moment about what to do, Mary started the engine and drove away.

Her mother and Amy were fast asleep when she heard him pull into the driveway. Mary was sitting in the living room, the glow of one lamp incandescent around her head. She had been sitting like this for two hours without moving.

Immediately upon returning home, Mary had gone through the telephone directory. The only Renfro listed was on Lindley Avenue. But there was a Renfroe on Victory Boulevard and another on Kittridge. Beneath them she found: RENFROW, G, 5531 Etiwanda Av

Not knowing why she did it, Mary dialled the number. A woman answered.

'May I please speak to Mr. Renfrow?'

'Sorry,' said the woman, 'no Mr. Renfrow here.'

Mary had spoken calmly and maturely. 'Then may I please speak with Miss G. Renfrow?'

'This is Gloria Renfrow, who's this?'

'Well, I'm – uh – selling magazine subscriptions and— '

'I'm sorry, I have all the magazines I need.'

A click and a dial tone had left Mary holding the phone and staring stupidly at it.

Then she had gone into the living room to sit and wait for she didn't know what.

'Hey,' murmured Ted, closing the front door quietly and coming into the living room. 'What are you still doing up, kitten?'

She didn't raise her eyes. 'Waiting for you, Daddy.'

'Waiting for me?' He came around to her line of vision and sat on the sofa opposite her. Mary saw him place his Pan Am carry-on, which contained a towel, gym shorts and tennis shoes, on the floor by his feet. 'What's wrong, kitten? You feel all right?'

Mary was amazed at her ability to bring herself to look at him. 'No, I don't,' she said softly. 'I'm sad and depressed and I wanted to talk to you.'

'What about? What's wrong?'

'Germaine let me down. I found out that all this time she's been thinking I was lying. I thought she was the only one I could really trust and it turned out I was wrong.'

'I'm sorry to hear that.'

'Yes, it's amazing who you can't trust anymore.'

'Hey.' He leaned over and patted her knee. 'Want to share some hot chocolate with me?'

She gazed at him with chilling steadiness. 'Daddy...'

'Yes, kitten?'

'I wanted to talk to you tonight. I went to the gym.'

His hand hovered for an instant, then slowly drew back.

'They said you hadn't been there for years.'

Ted took in a deep breath and let it out slowly. 'That's right.'

'So I went driving. I went down Etiwanda Avenue— '

'Oh, my God,' he whispered.

'It was by accident. I wasn't looking for you. I was just lonely and unhappy and had no one to go to so I just drove around. Daddy, who's Gloria Renfrow?'

He fell back on the sofa and rested his head on the cushion, staring up at the ceiling. 'What do you want me to say, kitten?'

'Tell me she's a client, Daddy, and that you went there just for tonight and that you really do go to a gym every Wednesday only now it's a different one but you forgot to tell us. Tell me that, Daddy, and I'll believe you!'

He slowly brought his head up and regarded his daughter with great sadness. 'I won't lie to you, kitten. I respect you too much for that.'

'Daddy, *please*!' Tears rose in her eyes. 'Tell me she's just a client, Daddy!'

'I think you know better,' he whispered.

'How could you, Daddy!' The tears spilled down her cheeks.

'Mary, can we talk?' he asked softly.

'I don't see where there's anything to talk about.'

'You don't?'

'Daddy, how can you do this to Mother?'

'And what,' he said wearily, feeling suddenly very old, 'am I doing to your mother?'

'It's such an awful' – she hiccupped – 'dirty thing. Daddy, *you* of all people!'

A brittle laugh escaped his throat. 'Me of all people. What am I supposed to be? St. Francis of Assisi? I'm a man, Mary, that's all.'

'Just tell me why, Daddy.'

'Why?' he spread out his hands and shook his head. 'I don't think I can tell you why. I don't even think I know why myself.'

'Who is she?'

'A friend.'

'Have you. . .known her for long?'

'For almost seven years.'

Mary blinked at her father. 'And you've been going there. . .'

He nodded. 'For seven years.'

'Daddy!' Her hands flew to her lips.

He reached for her, but Mary was amazingly quick to her feet. 'I'm going to be sick!' she cried, backing away from him.

'Mary— ' Ted started to rise. 'Mary, don't hate me, *please*.'

And then she was gone.

She said she wanted to go to the library so Lucille let her have the car.

Mary didn't know why, but it was important for her to look her best, so she put on her newest and most becoming maternity outfit and brushed her hair until it gleamed. She also didn't know why she was going or what she expected to find at the other end. All she knew was that something had to be done. She and her father hadn't spoken for two days; she wasn't eating, and the house was filled with uncomfortable silences. It was time to take a step.

She sat in the car for some time, watching the boxy little house, trying to imagine seven years of Wednesdays here, wishing it was a palace so she could understand her father's attraction to it. Then she got out, walked past the mailbox with its missing W, marched up the steps, and rang the bell.

CHAPTER 18

The wind joined her on the front step and whipped around as if to carry her away; it was the hot October Santa Ana but was for some reason edged tonight with a biting chill. Mary drew her sweater tighter about herself and, after ringing the doorbell, slid her hands into her sleeves. With her belly sticking out and her feet so swollen they looked like bread loaves and her hair snapping away from her head in thin ropes, Mary felt ugly, like a trick-or-treater come a week too soon and hoped, in defiance of her desire to meet this woman face to face, that the door would never open.

When it did, a homely yellow light spilled out, silhouetting the woman across the threshold, and causing Mary, for an instant, to squint. 'Mrs. Renfrow?' she said thinly.

A deep, throaty voice came from the silhouette. 'You must be Mary. Come on in. Lord, what a night!'

As she was swept in and the door closed and suddenly the roar of the wind was cut off and her hair fell limp around her face, Mary tried to give her face and voice a mature set as she said, 'How do you know who I am?'

'Ted told me about the other night. I had a feeling you'd be coming by.'

Mary was disappointed with the looks of Gloria Renfrow,

felt, in fact, cheated. Her imagination had not prepared her for a short, plumpish woman in her forties whose hair was undyed and whose face had no makeup. Ted's mistress was startlingly plain, like a woman behind a counter.

'Come inside, honey, I'll put some coffee on.'

Mary was led from the little entry hall into a cracker-box living room that had the appearance of its owner. The furniture was worn and unmatched: there was a black bookcase, dusty with paperbacks and magazines; a blond coffee table with stick legs; and the TV set was housed in a maple cabinet. A Robert Wood forest scene in its Woolworth's frame hung over the sofa; a bowl of plastic fruit, the seams clearly visible, sat on the coffee table; and on the TV set crouched two shiny black panthers with green glass eyes. In the corner stood a birdcage with a parakeet in it; lining the bottom, a front page with the headline: DODGERS WIN SERIES IN FOUR STRAIGHT GAMES.

Mary suddenly felt uncomfortable. This was not what she had expected; the floozy and love nest she had hoped to rail against were not here. Mary felt robbed.

'Take but a few minutes,' said Gloria, coming into the living room. 'Let me take your sweater.'

'No, thanks.' Mary pulled it around herself.

'Okay. Let's sit down, shall we?'

After Gloria took her place in the armchair by the Chinese bookcase, Mary eased herself into the overstuffed chair next to it and found it deceptively comfortable.

'Push back, honey, push back on the arms.'

Mary did so and the chair reclined a notch, with the padded footplate swinging up under her calves.

'That's gotta be better. I know when I was pregnant with my first my feet got so swollen it felt like I was wearing hip boots full of water. And cramps! Talk about Charlie-horses!'

Mary looked at her feet, swelling out of her pumps like rising bread dough.

'I'll tell you what's good for it,' said Gloria. 'A cup of Epsom salts in a bucket of hot water and a long soak. I learned that with my second. And eat lots of asparagus, it's a natural diuretic.'

Mary kept her hands on the arms of her chair and watched her toes as she tipped them toward one another, then away again – anything to keep from looking at Gloria Renfrow.

They sat in silence for a while. Once, Gloria commented on the weather, saying that it was a sure sign of a miserable winter; the occasional cheep of a parakeet and his scuttling around the cage were the only sounds to be heard above the wind. Then a high-pitched whistle tore the air, startling Mary and causing Gloria to jump up. 'Water's ready!' She shuffled toward the kitchen, then paused and turned to say, 'Or would you rather have tea? I've got some Constant Comment.'

Mary nodded, although she had no idea what that was, and continued to stare at her feet while she listened to noises coming from the kitchen.

Then, a few minutes later, Gloria returned with a TV tray on top of which were two steaming cups, a creamer, a bowl of sugar, and a plate of Sara Lee pound cake, generously sliced. She placed it between the two easy chairs, then sat on the arm of her own chair and poured cream into her coffee. 'Sugar, Mary? Or do you like it English style, with cream?'

Mary finally pulled her gaze away from her feet and looked at the cup. 'Two sugars, please,' she murmured, studying the hands, which were red from wear and had uneven finger-nails.

After Gloria moved the cup so that Mary could reach it and placed a slice of cake on a napkin next to the cup, she settled back down into her own chair and started to sip her coffee.

After a moment, Mary picked up the tea and, bringing it to her mouth, inhaled the heady aroma of spices.

'So,' said Gloria softly, 'how far along are you now?'

Mary had to clear her throat. 'Six months.'

Gloria smiled in admiration. 'Six months and already so big! She's going to be a healthy baby.'

Mary eyed the woman with catlike wariness.

'I had four of my own,' continued Gloria. 'My oldest is a

210

lawyer in Seattle. My second is a sergeant in the Air Force in Mississippi. My third goes to the University of California at Santa Barbara, and my fourth died of leukemia when he was three.'

Mary's cup halted at her lips. 'I'm sorry,' she said.

'I know. We all are.' Gloria gave Mary a wistful smile.'Have you got a name for her yet?'

Again the cup froze at her mouth. 'Did my – did my father tell you it's going to be a girl?'

'He told me all about it, honey. I've been following the story of Mary Ann McFarland ever since June, like watching "As the World Turns."'

Mary shot her an indignant glance, but saw only a smile of patient amusement on the woman's face. Mary put her cup down. 'He told you *everything*?'

Gloria nodded.

'He had no right.'

'Don't be silly. Of course he did.'

Mary's look turned to one of defiance. 'It's none of your business!'

Gloria's unplucked eyebrows went up. 'I beg your pardon. Whatever affects your father is my business.'

'Why?'

'Because I love him.'

'Don't say that.' Mary tried to push the recliner back to its original upright position, but it did not budge.

'Mary,' said Gloria in a firm voice, the smile gone, 'don't you think it's time we talked? We owe it to your father.'

Mary flopped her legs up and down. 'I don't owe him anything.'

'Sure feel sorry for yourself, don't you?'

Mary continued to struggle with the chair. 'I...have...- good...reason...'

'Take hold of the arms and pull. Lord, you look like a turtle on its back!'

Mary seized the arms and pulled so hard that the footrest slammed down with a clang.

'I hope you haven't broken my chair.'

She glared at Gloria, her fingers digging into the spaces

211

where the upholstery leaked some stuffing. 'A turtle!' she said. And then, before she knew it and without knowing why, tears welled in her eyes and Mary started to laugh.

'Honey, if you could have seen yourself! Listen, my third was so big that in my ninth month people used to stop me on the street and ask me if I was express or local. I'm not kidding! And I once got stuck in the turnstyle at Gelson's so they had to call the fire department to come and get me out!'

Mary laughed harder until she had to wipe her eyes with the cuff of her sweater. When it subsided, she regarded Gloria Renfrow in confusion. The woman said gently, 'If you don't want to talk, honey, then why did you come here?'

Mary dug her knuckles into her eyes. 'I don't know. To see you. To see what Daddy— ' She dropped her hands. 'I don't like the idea of Daddy telling everyone about me.'

'First of all, he didn't tell *everyone*, and second of all, don't you think your father has some rights? Look, honey, the world doesn't revolve around you!'

Mary pulled her arms into her sleeves and curled the cuffs over her fists, like mittens. 'You don't know what it's like for me.'

'Oh, honey!' Gloria broke off a piece of pound cake and popped it into her mouth. 'You are not the first woman to get pregnant and you're also not the first unmarried one to get pregnant.'

'But my case is different!'

'Is it?' Gloria broke off another piece. 'Seems to me, from what your Dr Wade says, there's been a few of your type around, maybe even right now, so even with a parthenogenic baby, you're still not the first and only.'

Mary stared at the woman as she popped the second piece into her mouth, chewed, and washed it down with coffee.

Others? thought Mary. Others like me? Right now?

'In fact, honey, you're a *lucky* one. You have Dr Wade to defend you and a wonderful daddy who believes you. What about other girls in your spot who aren't as fortunate? Yes, I can see that never occurred to you. Drink your tea, honey, it's too expensive to waste.'

212

Mary took a mechanical sip and found it to be delicious.
'Good, isn't it?'

'I've never had it before.'

'I keep it for special occasions, like when I have cramps.
It's a good diuretic, too.'

Mary shifted back into the chair and, holding her cup so
hot to spill, pushed back a notch. Her lumpy feet rose up.

'So,' said Gloria in a softer voice, 'have you got a name for
her yet?'

Mary studied the steam that rose from the surface of her
tea, swirling up in a gossamer eddy like steam on hot
pavement after a summer rain. She whispered, 'I want to call
her Jaqueline.'

'That's a nice name.'

Mary's fingers curled around the hot cup as she tried to
understand what had triggered the confession; it was her
deepest locked secret, something she hadn't even told Amy
or Dr Wade, because the baby was going to be taken away
from her anyway and given another name by its new parents.
But Mary knew, in her heart, that in the years to come she
would always privately think of the baby as Jaqueline.

'What's wrong, honey?'

Mary lifted moist eyes to Gloria and her lip quivered.
'Nothing. I just...'

Gloria put her cup down and reached out to touch Mary's
shoulder. 'You want to keep her, don't you?'

She swallowed painfully. 'I don't know. My folks say it has
to be put up for adoption and so does Father Crispin and I
guess I agree with them. Only...'

'Only what?'

'Only she's a *special* baby, she wasn't made in the normal
way, and her new parents won't treat her special, and I get
these strong feelings that I should be with her.' Mary's eyes
started to move rapidly around the room. A new and
startling thought was beginning to form in her mind,
something that had been there all along, but dormant,
hidden, unknown to Mary until this moment when it
suddenly came to her: 'I should be with her in the years to
come!'

Gloria nodded. 'And so you should, honey. She *is* a special baby and only you would understand that.'

'I didn't know before now...' Mary struggled with her words. *It's me*, said her mind, *the baby's me and I'd be giving me to strangers.* 'It's just been a baby up to now that would be born and then gone. But suddenly I see it as a little girl learning to walk and learning to talk and going to school and dating boys and I want to be there when it happens! Oh—' The tears came up again and before Mary could help herself, she was blubbering into her hands.

After a minute, she gulped it all back and said with her fists in her eyes, 'I'm sorry.'

'That's all right, honey, let it come out.'

'I don't know why I came here. I was so mad at Daddy and I had to see what...what...'

'What he came here for?' Gloria picked up her cup and started sipping again. Gazing over the rim of her cup at the stack of yellowing *National Enquirers* under the coffee table and making a mental note to call the elementary school to find out when their next paper drive would be, she said quietly, 'I envy you, honey. I always wanted a little girl but had four boys instead. After the first two I was frantic. I even bought girls' things before my third was born, as if that was going to guarantee a girl somehow! They say it's the man who has the sex-determining chromosome, so I guess it was Sam's fault.'

Mary looked around the room.

'He was my husband. I'm a widow. Sam died very suddenly seven years ago of a heart attack. We were loading the car for a camping trip up to Sequoia. He came inside for a flashlight and never came out. Johnny was the one came in the house and found him. Sam was forty-one years old.' Gloria turned her bright, gold-flocked eyes to Mary. 'That's how I met your father, when I had to liquidate Sam's portfolio to cover burial expenses. Your father had been Sam's broker. Your tea's getting cold.'

Mary looked down at the cup in her hands as if she wondered how it got there, then she returned to Gloria Renfrow's eyes: the peculiar hazel irises rimmed with black, and the fluctuating gold flecks, like the changing colours in a theatre screen during the intermission. Suddenly, a hundred questions stood on Mary's tongue.

'What's it like?' she asked.

'What's what like?'

'Having a baby.'

'Oh,' Gloria released a short laugh. 'Honey, it's different for everyone. My first, the one who's a lawyer now, had what the doctors called cephalopelvic disproportion, which meant his head was too big for my pelvis so they had to do a Cesarean section. The doctor told me that once you have that with one baby, all the rest will have to be sections, too. But I wanted the next one God's way, so I insisted. We pushed and pulled, Johnny and I, and sweated and farted all through the night until I thought one of us was going to die, then he slithered out like a bar of soap and after that, the next one came so easy it was like passing gas.'

Gloria paused a moment, then laughed at a private memory before continuing. 'It all depends on your condition and the baby's and on your doctor. Some hospitals put you right to sleep so you have no awareness of the experience. Some give you a spinal so you can at least watch. Now I hear there's something new being done in some areas where women are having babies completely naturally without anaesthetic.'

Mary's eyes widened. 'Is that possible?'

Gloria's face creased in amusement. 'Of course! Women were doing it for thousands of years before anaesthetics were invented. What do you think, the ancient Greeks used ether?'

Mary's forehead folded into a frown. 'I never gave it any thought...'

'I wish I could be there with you when it happens. The baby, I mean. Childbirth is such a marvellous experience. Well, no woman can tell you what it's going to be like, it's something you have to experience for yourself to appreciate it, like Disneyland.'

Mary placed her cup on the TV tray and dropped her hands to her abdomen. 'I'm being X-rayed tomorrow,' she said distantly. 'Dr Wade says there's nothing wrong, he just wants to monitor the baby's progress.' She lifted her cool, winter-sky eyes to Gloria. 'Is that normal procedure, X-ray?'

Mary caught the sudden shift in Gloria's face just before she turned away. 'Honey, it's been so long since I was pregnant, I don't know what's normal procedure these days.'

'They think there's something wrong with it, don't they?'

Gloria toyed with a chunk of cake, turning it end over end between her fingers, then dropped it back onto the napkin. 'Honey, you've got a unique baby there. Your doctor is just taking every precaution he can to make sure both you and your daughter are doing all right. It's nothing to get alarmed about.'

Listening to the husky voice that sounded as if it belonged on a farm, and watching the square, comfortable face, Mary was put at ease. She picked up her cup and, drinking down the last of the tea and wondering if she should ask for a second cup, was suddenly reminded that, in Gloria Renfrow's steadying presence, she had forgotten her initial reason for coming here.

She turned a bold gaze to the woman next to her and said, 'Are you a Catholic?'

The question seemed not to surprise her. 'Why? Would it change anything for you?' Gloria's voice dropped. 'Would it ease your father's sin?'

Mary didn't answer; her fingers were webbed over her belly, like a protective shield, while nebulous ideas and feelings and concepts swirled in her mind.

'I'm not going to speak for your father,' said Gloria softly. 'That has to come from him. But for myself. . .I was a widow and lonely and struggling with three teen-aged boys and your father entered my life when I most needed someone strong. But please don't think of me as some temptress who lured him into my parlour. I came into his life when *he* most needed someone, too. These things go both ways. Mary, it's not easy being a married man's mistress.'

Her voice softened, became fragile. 'Although I love him with all my heart and being and want to do everything for him, I must take a secondary place in his life. It's something like living in a constant shadow; like purgatory. I can never call him when I'm feeling sad. I can never expect to see him on week-ends or holidays, or go out in public with him, or take trips with him. If I give him a present, he can't take it home with him. We must play a game of pretend and I must be content with spending a few hours a week with him. And if you have any ideas that I'm a kept woman, you can forget them. I have a job and earn my own living. Your father doesn't give me a penny. All I want from him is himself.'

Mary felt her eyes betray her as they started to burn. 'If he hates my mother so much why doesn't he leave her?'

'But he doesn't hate her. Maybe you can't understand this right now, but your father loves us both. Only in different ways. You don't know much about men, honey, and when you get to be as old as I am you still won't know much.' She emitted a curt, bitter laugh. 'And they call *us* the mysterious sex!'

'Do you...really *love* him?'

'Broaden your brain, honey, a man can be loved by more than one woman. And he in turn can love more than one.'

Mary was fighting back another flood of tears as Gloria continued: 'Don't be angry with him. I hope you'll understand when you get older.'

Words suddenly broke loose, tumbled out: 'But how *can* he! He's a good Catholic—'

'Mary, why do you think your father comes here? I know what you're thinking, and you're quite wrong. Oh, there was sex at first, I won't deny that, and a lot of it. Somehow, desperately lonely people find that the easiest avenue to console one another. But that was seven years ago. Do you know what we do every Wednesday night, Mary? Your father comes in, takes off his shoes and watches "Have Gun, Will Travel" with me. Sometimes we play cards. Or he fixes a leak in the kitchen sink. Or we sit in the backyard and watch the sun go down. And then, once in a long while, we go to bed together.

'Mary, I know why you came here. In fact, ever since your father told me about the other night, I've been sort of expecting you. Your father used to be a saint in your eyes and now he's just a man. You're mad at him, and me I guess, for doing that to you. You came here hoping to get the saint back, hoping I would deny everything and reinstate your father's holiness. I know, I was a daughter once myself...But I can't do that for you, Mary.

'Please don't despise me. That's not a luxury you've earned. At least not until you have some experience and maturity under your belt. My life is a lonely one because I'm in love with a man I can never have. And I've resigned myself to the years ahead. Maybe you should, too.'

Mary felt a pain shoot through her; she curled her hands into fists.

'I'm going to tell your father you came here. If you want to tell him about it, fine, that's up to you. Mary, your father has secrets, things about his past that he's told only me, not even your mother knows. And they all have to do with why he comes here. But they're for him to tell you about, not me.'

Wiping her hands down her face, Mary finally found her voice. 'I don't know what to think. It's like...nothing's the same anymore.' She thought of Mike and Germaine and her parents and her own rudely altered future. 'Everything's different.'

'You're right, honey, and nothing ever can stay the same, no matter how much we wish it would. When I saw Sam lying there on the kitchen floor, as peaceful as if he'd curled up to take a nap, it was like I was standing at the edge of a great, black ocean. And sometimes, if I let myself do it, I'm at that shore again and I start doing stupid things like feeling sorry for myself and thinking there's no reason to go on. But— '

Mary was stunned to see a tear fall down Gloria's cheek. Impulsively, she reached out and rested a hand on the woman's arm.

Gloria forced a smile and squeezed Mary's hand. 'I'm not like some women, who can cry silently without a tear or a red eye. Me, I slobber and wail and my nose runs and my face swells up all out of shape, and God knows my face can't afford to look any homelier than it is! Now look, your cup's empty. Ready for a refill?'

Two and a half hours later, Mary was quietly easing her mother's Impala into the driveway. She turned off the motor and sat for some minutes staring at the bulb softly glowing over the front porch.

She opened the front door quietly and tiptoed through the dark living room to the open doorway of the den. She was not surprised to find her father sitting alone by the light of a single lamp, in his pyjamas and sipping a drink. Ted McFarland looked old and discarded.

She watched him unseen, fascinated by her new perspective. Mary found herself wondering what he was like as a lover, in the same way she had wondered about Fabian; her own father was suddenly in the category of *men*, and it did not shock Mary that she should be sexually curious about him. She should have noticed it before, yet she saw it only now; how handsome and appealing he really was. Muscular and firm even at forty-five, with a rugged face and a magnetic smile. Even though he was her father, a daddy, Mary knew he must be attractive to women, and she saw now why Gloria Renfrow had so easily fallen in love with him.

But now, sitting alone in the middle of the night with no company but a glass, his virility was gone. And it suddenly gave Mary a pang.

'Daddy. . .' she whispered

Startled, he looked up.

Mary took a tentative step forward. He put the glass down, staring at her.

Then, in a rush, she went to him, dropped to her knees and flung her arms across his lap. 'Daddy,' she murmured. 'I'm sorry. I'm so sorry. . .'

They talked until well past midnight; Ted's words came out soft and metered, like a prayer, while Mary sat at his feet. He spoke of his relationship with Gloria, then confessed the secret that not even Lucille knew.

Ted McFarland thought he had been born in a tent

outside of Tuscaloosa but wasn't sure; whatever, his earliest memory was of a clapboard house on a hot, steamy night when the air was thick with the stink of alcohol and the cries of a woman in the next room. He must have been very young, for he sat on the floor, while a tall, gaunt man, who had struck him as Abe Lincoln reborn, paced in and out of the milky light muttering to someone named Lord. Neighbour women, hushed and fretting, had dashed in and out of shadows and had, at the end of the long clammy night, emerged with a limp bundle and wails raised to the sky. Thus had Ted's mother died, giving birth to one child too many.

Hoseah McFarland was a 'preacher man' and, after the death of his wife, had packed his few bags and started a circuit around the southern states with his sons. Tents became their way of life, with evangelical Hoseah spewing fire and brimstone at credulous sharecroppers and passing a hat that invariably came back full. The boys were the hat-passers, and when it occurred to the haunted, driven Hoseah to cash in on the healing business, they became his 'recipients of God's manna'. Ted was thirteen when his father handed him a set of crutches and instructed him on how to hobble into the tent, listen to the sermon, then throw off the crutches and rush forth to the platform.

Ted was good at it; the poor blacks and 'white trash' responded riotously; Hoseah increased his wealth; and when, on occasion, young Ted went to the back of the tent after the service for a word of appreciation from his father, he was shut out because Hoseah was seeing to the personal salvation of a young southern miss.

Then, one night, somehow, the tent caught fire and Hoseah McFarland was able to slip out the back way and save himself but a lot of people were killed in the panic and one of Ted's little brothers was trampled to death and Ted had run for his life and had grabbed the first train passing by the cotton fields.

He had ridden the rails north to Chicago and had managed to survive by wits and brawn when, in the year 1932, in the middle of the Depression, he had been caught by the police for mugging an old man and had been thrown into St. Mark's Home for Wayward Boys.

That was where he had found Catholicism.

Mary, not understanding the Catholicism was something people *found* but something they *left*, had asked softly, 'Do you know where they are now, your father and brothers?'

Ted didn't know and didn't care, for the Church had become his family. He hadn't spoken to Lucille of his boyhood because he had been twenty-two when he had met her and had, at that time, been too proud to talk about his shameful past. Lucille had come from a fairly well-to-do family and had had a sheltered upbringing; Ted had been so much in love with her that he had feared mentioning his sordid past would drive her away. So he had kept it a secret, intending to reveal the truth at a later time, and telling her that St. Mark's had been an orphanage. But then, as the months went by, Ted never got around to telling Lucille the truth of his past until it became convenient to forget it altogether.

But he had been able to tell Gloria; he had to tell someone, since of late the memories had been coming back and he needed to be relieved of them.

Hearing this from her father, Mary had wondered first: What can Gloria give you that Mother can't? Then she had wondered: What can she give you that I can't? Then Mary had understood that what had caused her the most pain upon first learning about Gloria Renfrow was not that he had been unfaithful to her mother but that Ted had been unfaithful to *her*.

'Daddy,' she said, 'why is Mother the way she is? Sometimes I think she cares more about other people than she does about us. All that charity work she does, visiting people in hospitals, collecting clothes for Mexicans. Her committees mean more to her than we do.'

Ted placed a hand on his daughter's head. 'Mary, were you ever taught in school about a man named Goethe? He once said something to the effect that there is redemption from sins through good works.'

'Mother? She doesn't sin.'

221

'Maybe she thinks she does.'

'Daddy, she drinks a lot. Did *I* do that to her?'

'No, you didn't. Drinking is, well, a *need* of hers. She's done it for a long time, Mary, you just weren't aware of it.'

'Why do you let her boss you around?'

'I guess because it's easy. I don't know for sure. That's another need of your mother's and I'm content to let her have it. Mary, I never knew my own mother, she died before I was old enough to appreciate her. Then, in the South, there were my brothers and my father. At St. Mark's I was surrounded by all the other boys, the priests and the lay teachers, who were all male. There was a glaring absence of females in my life, you see, so who knows? Maybe I want to be dominated by women.'

Ted got up and strode to the bar. He started to refill his glass, then stopped, putting the bottle down. He turned and looked down at his daughter. 'You want to know why I let her boss me around. Well, maybe its because I'm at peace, Mary, and I'd like your mother to be at peace, too.'

With those words came a revelation to Mary, like a bright flash suddenly illuminating the den, for she suddenly saw her father as a priest. And seeing this, Mary realised she had always seen this quality in him until now, fully understanding everything, she thought of her father as more priestlike than Father Crispin.

Ted came back to the chair and Mary felt at ease again. She wondered what it must have been like for him, a young seminary student joining the Army and going to the South Pacific to fight a bloody war and then returning to find his old ideals shattered and then meeting Lucille and falling in love and marrying and turning his back on the call. . .

'You really love God, don't you, Daddy?'

'Let's just say I admire him.'

They talked about Catholicism for a bit and Mary confessed that she had always thought, until tonight, her mother the better Catholic of her parents and Ted gave her a queer smile. Then, somewhere near dawn, father and daughter stared at one another in silence as if they had just fallen in love.

222

Ted said, 'It's late, kitten, and we have to be at the X-ray lab early.'

Mary buried her face in his lap and murmured, 'I'm scared about tomorrow, Daddy...'

CHAPTER 19

She clutched the flaps of her flimsy paper gown as she was helped onto the cold metal table by a smiling technician. Mary thought it must be freezing in the room because she shivered so badly, but then she saw that the young technician, barely older than herself, was wearing a thin, short-sleeved uniform of cool robin-egg blue. Then, admitting that she was nervous – worse, scared – Mary tried to focus her mind on something other than the awesome X-ray machine that descended upon her.

An hour earlier, upon leaving the house with her parents, Mary had been surprised to find a gaily wrapped package on the front doorstep. In it she had found a hand-crocheted baby set of pink yarn – bonnet, sweater, and booties – and a note in Germaine's handwriting:

> Mary I'm sorry.
> Don't shut me out
> I love you.

She had rushed back into the house, while her father warmed up the car, and called the Massey residence. Germaine was at school but Mary had left a message with her mother: 'Have her call me when she gets home, please.'

Mary's spirits had been temporarily lifted by the prospect of being reunited with her friend but had then collapsed as Dr Wade's medical building had come into view. Now she lay on her back on the cold slab of an X-ray table, recognising the fragrance of Right Guard as the technician leaned over her to adjust the machine.

'You'll have to lie perfectly still now.'

'It's uncomfortable.'

'I know.'

'It hurts my back.'

'I'm sorry. This won't take long.' The technician stepped behind a lead screen. 'Hold your breath, please, and don't move.'

The machine clicked, hummed, and clicked again and the girl came back to the table. Removing the cassette from beneath Mary and sliding another one in, she said, 'One more front view, then two laterals. Can you shift your hips an inch or two to the right?'

As she moved, the back of the gown spread open and Mary felt the icy metal against her bare back. The technician went back behind the screen. 'Hold absolutely still now,' then click, hum, click.

'Okay, on your left side now, please. Let me help you.'

When Mary emerged from the dressing room a few minutes later, she found her parents hovering anxiously at the door. 'We're to go right up to Dr Wade's office,' said Ted, and Mary noticed an ashen colour about his lips and nostrils.

This wasn't going to be easy. Possibly the most difficult, most crucial moment, in fact, in all the years he had been in practice. So much hinged on those films – not the least, his medical write-up, lying on his desk at home, waiting for that last chapter. An hour of decision making. For everyone. Father Crispin, he knew, was waiting for the X-ray results in his rectory. If the baby was anencephalic, Jonas would have to call. But what if it was simply armless or legless? What if the aberrations didn't warrant drastic measures? How to prepare Mary for that eventuality?

Jonas felt, as his hands contracted into fists, his fingernails dig deep into his palms.

A turning-point day. And it all, ultimately, rested on him. Jonas Wade was about to play God.

When his nurse ushered the three McFarlands into his office, Jonas saw the naked anxiety on their faces and felt, for an instant, pity for them.

He didn't waste time. As soon as they were seated, Jonas flipped the toggle switches of his X-ray – viewing boxes and two dark films – one frontal, one lateral – flared whitely.

'These are the best films of the series. The foetus is clearly outlined as you can see.' Taking his pen out of his pocket and using it as a pointer, Jonas traced the ethereal outlines of the little cobweb creature. 'You can see here the ribs, the curve of the spine, the arms and legs. This,' he drew an invisible circle around a fleecy cloud, 'is the head.'

He dropped his arm and turned to face them. 'She *appears* to be normal.'

Seeing relief wash over the two women, with Lucille awkwardly reaching out to give her daughter's hand a congratulatory squeeze, Jonas saw that Ted had not relaxed; indeed, the face of Mary's father, Jonas suspected, was a mirror image of his own new concerns.

Jonas Wade had expected that, with the confirmation of a normal foetus, he would be instantly relieved; however; upon crossing one hurdle, he had discovered more, unseen hurdles on the other side. Physically the foetus looked all right, but X-rays were vague; didn't show hands and feet or facial features. Or the condition of its brain...

Ted cleared his throat. 'So everything's all right then, Doctor?'

Jonas thought: What will its face look like? Will it have hands and feet? Will its brain be a gooey mass—

'Everything appears to be all right,' he said, and cleared his throat. 'So'—walking away from the viewing boxes, Jonas took a seat behind his desk, clasping his hands and said—'so, have you given any more thought to whether or not you'll keep the baby?'

Both Mary and her father opened their mouths, but Lucille came first with: 'We decided that issue long ago, Dr Wade. We haven't changed our minds.'

He looked at Mary. Her face seemed to crumple. 'But you have to admit, Mrs. McFarland that certain factors have changed. There are fewer unknowns now. I thought you might reconsider.'

'Nothing has changed, Doctor. We don't want the baby.'

He looked hopefully at the girl. 'Mary? How do you feel?' But she remained maddeningly silent. He thought: Come on, Mary, speak up! Fight for what you want, for what we both want.

'Besides,' came Lucille's crisp voice, 'I don't see why you should concern yourself about it, Doctor. It's not as though we're asking you for advice.'

Jonas had to run through a rapid mental deliberation; the outcome of the X-rays had been the determining factor as to how and when he was going to broach the subject of his write-up. He had hoped to get started on it today, on the campaign to convince them to give him permission to publish it. Now he saw he should put it off. None of these three would be the least bit receptive today. But time was rapidly running out...

Joan Crawford lifted the cover off her dinner and, seeing the dead rat on the plate, shrieked.

Because the windows of the car were fogged, like all the car windows in the back row of the drive-in, neither Mike nor fat Sherry witnessed the horrific scene; but the scream came sharply through the tinny speaker and pierced the silence. Grunting, Mike reached over and turned off the volume.

He and Sherry were wrapped in a wool football blanket against the blustering, windy night, and although they had been necking heavily for the past hour, enough to steam the windows to opacity, neither was receiving much satisfaction.

'I'm hungry,' muttered Sherry as Mike's hands explored under her sweater.

'Jesus,' he murmured, burying his face in her neck. 'You've had two tamales and a jumbo box of buttered popcorn.'

'I can't help it, going to the movies always makes me

hungry.' She leaned forward and wiped a porthole on the fogged window.

'Come on, Sherry, forget the movie.'

'I gotta do something, I'm bored.'

'Christ!' He pulled away from her and pounded the steering wheel with a fist. 'We were going pretty good there for a while, what did you stop for?'

'Because,' she turned her tawny eyes on him and said coolly, 'The least you could do is get a hard on.'

'Come on, Sherry, I'm trying. But you have to help.'

'I've been helping you for an hour, Mike. Boy, you sure can't tell a package by its wrapping.'

Tossing the blanket off, Mike slid away from her and pressed his perspiring forehead against his window. Fat Sherry was his third attempt this month. First it was Sheila Brabent, who had come on strong and eager but who, at the last minute, had demanded a new pair of skis. Then there had been Charlotte Adams, the class treasurer, who had always seemed to have a thing for him, but who had told him as they parked on Mulholland that he could only touch her breasts and nothing more. Desperate, he had turned to fat Sherry, who, having broken up with Rick during the summer, had started playing the field.

'You know,' she said now, watching the movie as she talked, 'sex isn't what it's cracked up to be anyway. Rick wasn't good at it either.'

'I don't wanna hear about it.'

'Well,' she hoisted her husky shoulders, 'don't be disappointed. We can try again some other time.'

He folded his arms and glared sullenly at the steamed windshield. Bette Davis was singing 'Baby Jane.'

'I know what's wrong,' said Sherry, exploring her chin for a pimple.

'What.'

'You don't really want me, you want Mary.' She turned to face him. 'You don't have to pretend with me, Mike, I know you didn't ask me out because I make your blood boil. You're just not getting it from Mary any more so— '

'Shut up.'

227

'Yeah, right, you never did it with her in the first place. Okay, I believe you. Besides, everybody knows it was Charlie Thatcher that got her pregnant.'

Mike snapped around. 'What! Who said that?'

'Charlie Thatcher.'

'Jesus— '

'Serves her right. I don't hold it against her, though, anyone can make a mistake. I wanted to invite her to my pyjama party last month but it was my mother who said no – Hey! What're you doing?'

He rolled the window down, tossed the speaker out, then started up the motor.

'But the movie's still on!'

Mary was in her room when she heard a car pull into the driveway. When the doorbell rang, she turned down Bobby Vinton and opened her door a few inches. Hearing, softly, Mike's voice, she opened it all the way. Then she saw him, standing at the end of the hall, a slump to his shoulders, uncertainty on his handsome face.

Mary took a step forward, held out her hand, and whispered, 'Mike. . .'

CHAPTER 20

Southern California was in the grip of an unusually cold December with biting winds ripping through the San Fernando Valley and angry black clouds gathering over the Santa Monica Mountains. The air was charged with hostility and uncertainty; a violent storm was building.

It was Wednesday evening, Christmas was a week away; decorations were already up and illuminating the McFarland house. Ted was out for the evening, Amy was at Girl Scouts, Lucille was getting ready for Altar and Rosary, and

Mary was in her room wrapping presents. There was a movement in her abdomen – a swilling, an eddy, something turned and tumbled – and when her hands went down, she felt that things had shifted. As Mary put down the Scotch tape and wondered if this was what Dr Wade had called 'the head being engaged,' she felt a gush of warm moisture spread over the seat of her pants.

She slowly rose from her chair and remained standing for a moment when a sharp cramp closed down on her abdomen, then passed. Mary walked calmly to the door of the master bedroom, from where she could see her mother struggling with the zipper of her dress. Mary said, 'It's time.'

Lucille said without looking up, 'Time for what?'

'The baby.'

Lucille froze, her arms bent back over her head, the dress half zipped. Then she slowly let go of it and turned around. 'What?'

'The water broke and I had a contraction.'

'But it's too early.'

'I can't help it.' Then she wrapped her arms about herself and said, 'Here comes another one— '

'Are you sure? It could be false labour.'

Wincing, Mary shook her head. 'Dr Wade told me what to expect, how it would feel, and my pants are wet.'

'The first contraction, what did it feel like?'

'Cramps.'

Lucille studied Mary's face for a moment, then said, 'Sit down, Mary Ann, and I'll call Dr Wade.'

Mary plopped down on the vanity stool while her mother went to the phone on her nightstand. Mary gazed at her reflection in the mirror as Lucille looked up the number in her little book, dialled, and waited for an answer.

It's too early, Mary thought, there's something wrong...

'Mary Ann?'

She lifted her eyes. Reflected in the glass was Lucille sitting on the edge of the king-sized bed in bare feet and a half-zipped dress. 'Are you all right?'

'Yes , Mother.'

'His exchange said they don't know where he is, but since

229

it's an emergency, they'll try to find him for us. In the meantime, Mary Ann, I have to get you to the hospital. It was Encino he said he was going to send you to, wasn't it?'

Mary closed her eyes and thought: This is it. What we've been waiting for. The reason for everything...

'Mary Ann?' Her mother was suddenly at her side, looking down in concern. 'Are you sure you're all right? Another contraction?' 'No'

'All right then. We have to pack you a bag and get you to the hospital. I'll give them a call so they'll know we're coming.'

She walked back to the phone as she talked. 'The contractions usually come about ten or fifteen minutes apart at first, and it's usually a while before you're even near delivery with the first child, so we have time.'

Mary continued to stare at the girl in the mirror as though she were a stranger. 'You know, I thought I felt her turn around. Her head isn't up here anymore, it's down here. Dr Wade told me that would happen, too, so I guess this is really it.'

Lucille dialled Information. 'I'd like the number of Encino Hospital, please.' She jotted it down on a note pad.

Mary watched in the mirror as her mother pressed down the button and listened for a dial tone. When she started to dial, Mary said, 'Don't call them, Mother. I'm not going.'

The dial whirred as Lucille's finger snapped each number. 'What are you talking about?'

'I mean, Mother, that I'm not going to the hospital. Please put the phone down.'

Lucille looked at her daughter for a moment, then hung up the phone.

'I don't want to have my baby in a hospital. I don't want to be asleep while it happens, while strangers bring her into the world. It's something I have to do myself. I started it, I have to finish it.'

'What on earth are you talking about?'

'I want my baby here.'

Lucille shot to her feet. 'You can't be serious!'

Mary also rose with difficulty. 'I will not go to the hospital and you can't force me. I'm having another...contraction. Are they supposed to be this close together?'

'My God, child, don't you understand? The baby is premature! You have to go to a hospital. Any number of things could go wrong. I'll call an ambulance—'

'No!'

Lucille started dialling.

Mary moved as quickly as she could, one arm clutching her stomach. She snatched the receiver out of her mother's hand and dropped it onto its cradle.

'You can't mean it!' cried Lucille

'She has to be born here. Don't you understand—'

'Mary Ann, listen to me.' Lucille took hold of her daughter's shoulders. 'You cannot have the baby here. It isn't safe, for you or for the child. You need a proper delivery room. You need sterile things and a proper doctor and anaesthesia.'

'Why? Women have had babies for centuries without any of those things.'

'Yes, and how many of them died! Listen to me, Mary Ann, things happen during childbirth! Complications! Mary Ann' – Lucille gave her a shake – 'the baby's coming too soon. That means there's something wrong.'

'No it doesn't, Mother. It's simply her time to be born. My back hurts. That's where the pains are. I want to lie down. And my pants are uncomfortable.'

'Let me call an ambulance—'

'No.' Mary sank onto the edge of the bed. 'I feel all right between contractions. Mother, you can't force me to go. And if you try, I'll fight and scream all the way.'

'Oh, Mary Ann...' Lucille sat next to her. 'Not here, not like this. *Why*, for God's sake?'

'Because I want to be part of it. I want to *feel* it.'

Lucille lightly touched Mary's hair, then dropped her arm around her daughter's shoulders. 'I just don't understand why you're doing this.'

Mary leaned her full weight against her mother, dropping her head on Lucille's shoulder.

They sat in silence for a moment, Mary gently comforted

by the feel of her mother's arm around her, then she said, 'I want to keep the baby.'

'I know.' Lucille twisted her neck to kiss Mary on the forehead, then said, 'Come on, let's put you in bed.'

Mary had difficulty walking, even with Lucille's help. They had to stop in the doorway and hold on to the jamb for a rest. 'How far apart are they?'

'I don't know,' panted Mary. 'About five minutes, I think.'

'Are they regular?'

'Yes.'

'Are they increasing in intensity?'

'Yes...'

They struggled down the hall, Lucille bearing most of Mary's weight, until they were finally in the bedroom. As Mary sank onto the bed, her mother went through a drawer looking for a nightgown. Mary grunted as she kicked off her shoes and laboriously pulled her smock over her head. Lucille helped her with her maternity pants and underwear, overwhelmed by the sight of her daughter's naked, swollen body; then, with the nightgown on, Mary slid under the covers and took hold of her mother's hands.

'I wish Dr Wade would get here.'

'Let me call an ambulance, Mary Ann, please.'

Mary smiled. 'Shouldn't you be doing something, Mother? Like boiling water or tearing up sheets?'

As she fought to keep the tears back, Lucille forced a laugh. 'I haven't the faintest idea what to do!'

'Call Dr Wade again.'

'All right.'

But when she started to rise, Mary's grasp on her hands tightened. 'Mother...'

Lucille looked away, unable to watch her daughter's face contort in pain. When the contraction subsided, Lucille looked at her watch and said, 'Four minutes apart.'

'It's happening too quickly, isn't it? Mother...' Mary was breathless. 'I...want Daddy here. He mustn't miss it.'

'All right.' Lucille withdrew her hands from Mary's. 'I'll call him.'

232

As her mother stood up, Mary suddenly remembered and said quickly, 'No wait, never mind! There's time, he'll get here. He might not be at the gym tonight— '

'It's all right, sweetheart, just relax and let me take care of everything.'

Mary pushed herself up on her elbows, straining to hear; from the master bedroom came the faint sound of the telephone dial. Then Lucille's voice speaking softly; she asked for Ted, talked for a moment, then hung up.

When she reappeared in the doorway of Mary's bedroom her face was grey. 'He's coming.'

Mary fell against the pillow. 'Oh, Mother...'

'I never thought I'd ever do that.' When Lucille sat again on the edge of the bed, Mary saw tears in her mother's eyes.

'You know about Gloria,' she whispered.

'I've known for five years.'

Mary made fists of her hands and rubbed them into her eyes.

'Don't cry, sweetheart.'

'How could you stand it!' cried Mary, tears leaking from under her hands and running down to the pillow. 'Why didn't you do something about it!'

Not bothering to wipe her own tears away, Lucille took hold of Mary's wrists and drew her hands into her lap. Trying to smile, she said, 'Because I love him and want to keep him and if that's the only way then I'll put up with it.'

Mary rolled her head to the side, screwing her eyes. 'I hate him— '

'No you don't. It's not his fault. And, Mary Ann, let's not tell him I know, okay?'

Looking at her mother out of the corner of her eye, Mary said, 'How can we do that? You just called him.'

'We'll tell him you knew he was with a client tonight instead of the gym and you just happened to overhear the name and I looked it up in the phone book. Can you do that, Mary Ann?'

'He doesn't deserve it.'

233

'It's not for him, child, it's for *me*! Promise me you'll do it!'

Mary brought her head up again and looked in puzzlement at her mother's face. 'I'm so sorry,' she whimpered.

'It's all right and it's our secret. Now I think we should be getting you ready.'

'Oh—' Mary pulled her hands away and pressed them onto her abdomen. 'Stronger now,' she whispered. 'How much time, Mother?'

'A few hours yet, I think.'

Lucille gazed down at the mound beneath the chenille bedspread and saw a slight movement as the abdominal wall rose up and then sank down.

'Mother—'

'Yes'.

'Have you ever been sorry I didn't get an abortion?'

Lucille snapped her head up. 'Mary Ann! Where on earth did you get that idea!'

'I overheard you and Daddy arguing back in June. I heard you tell Daddy to find someone to get rid of—'

'Oh, Mary Ann! I never meant it! You know that!'

'But that's why I cut my wrists. I thought you and Daddy were going to make me go through with it.'

'Oh my poor, poor baby.' Lucille stroked Mary's forehead. 'I was drunk. You should know by now never to take the word of a drunk.'

'Do you think my baby will be a monster?'

Lucille sucked in her cheek and gave it a painful bite. When a salty, metallic taste sprang to her tongue, she said, 'Of course not. She'll be a fine little girl.'

'Even though she's premature?'

'Don't worry about a thing sweetheart. Listen, I'm going to put some water on the stove to boil. I don't know what for, but it's what they do in the movies.'

When her mother's weight lifted from the bed, Mary closed her eyes. She felt lightheaded and euphoric; she drifted in an amniotic world of her own.

When, a few minutes later, her mother was back sitting on the bed, Mary said in a lacy voice, 'Mother, I have a memory...or was it a dream?' She kept her eyes closed. 'I seem to be in a crib and my room is dark. I hear voices coming from the other side of the wall. I hear a woman crying. She's screaming: "I don't want to die." And then a man talks but I can't understand him. Mother...was that you?'

'You were four,' whispered Lucille. 'And we lived at the other house then.'

'What was it about?'

Lucille's eyes remained closed as she spoke. 'I should never have had children, Mary Ann. The doctors said there were things wrong with me internally. You were a difficult birth. After forty-eight hours of labour you had to be taken from me by Cesarean section. I was afraid after that. Your father and I didn't believe in birth control, so when I got pregnant again, it frightened me.'

'What happened?'

'My prayers were answered and my womb came out with Amy. It was my saving.' Lucille gazed into her daughter's lucid blue eyes and felt herself grow peaceful as she spoke. 'You see, Mary Ann, I never enjoyed sex. I guess it was because of my orthodox upbringing. The Church taught me that to enjoy sex was sinful, even if you were married, and my mother, poor ignorant soul that she was, told me that pregnancy was woman's punishment for enjoying sex. I got it in my head that celibacy meant freedom from suffering. I don't really know. The sex act terrified me. I loved your father, Mary Ann, and in a strange way I desired him, too, but...'

Lucille bowed her head. 'When I had my hysterectomy I was glad, overjoyed in fact, because it not only meant freedom from more babies, bit it also released me from the duty of having to submit to sex. Father Crispin told us, after the operation, that your father and I would have to live as brother and sister, and it pleased me. I was relieved. I didn't have to be a real wife anymore. It also made me feel guilty. I loved your father desperately, but I didn't want to have to do the wifely thing with him. And I guess it turned him away from me. Men have these needs, Mary Ann...'

She sniffed and dragged a hand across her eyes. 'I'd better see how the water's doing.'

The house was swathed in the warm glow of Christmas lights and the tangy aroma of hot gingerbread. Although a Ponderosa pine filled the living room window, laden with tinsel and ornaments, a handsome brass menorah stood on the fireplace mantel, ready for Hanukkah observance in the Schwartz household.

The two men were comfortably seated in the living room drinking eggnog laced with rum while Esther Schwartz kept up an endless baking assembly line in the kitchen.

"'Tis the season to be jolly,' said Bernie, draining his glass and noticing that Jonas hadn't touched his.

'I'm sorry, Bernie. I've got things on my mind.'

'You'll work it out. She's just going through a phase.'

Jonas stared darkly at the drift of cotton snow around the base of the Christmas tree. The night before, Cortney had called to say she wasn't coming home for Christmas. She was thinking of quitting San Fernando Valley State and going up to San Francisco, where she had friends living in an area called Haight–Ashbury. She wanted to major in life, she had said, and the world would be her campus, and while Penny had gone into an hysterical rage, Jonas had felt his shock turn first to anger, then to dejection. Despite Bernie's platitudes, Jonas knew there would be no dissuading Cortney; if he had seen it coming, if he had stepped in two years ago, then it could have been helped. But it was too late now; he had been blind to the symptoms.

'You're being too harsh on yourself,' said Bernie, coming back to the sofa with a refill. 'Teen-agers are an unpredictable species. You have no way of telling which way they will go.'

'I've been so damned preoccupied with that McFarland paper.' Jonas finally tasted his eggnog. 'Maybe Penny's right. I should have put my foot down about her moving out, I don't know.'

Bernie watched the sprinkle of nutmeg turn slowly on the

236

surface of his drink. 'About the write-up, Jonas, have you gotten permission from them yet?'

'No. I keep putting it off. Mary, I think, will agree to it and maybe her father, but the mother' – Jonas shook his head – 'I'm going to have to convince her what a noble project it is.'

Esther Schwartz suddenly blocked the kitchen doorway, wiping her hands on the terry cloth apron. 'Jonas, Penny's on the phone. She says you have an emergency.'

He put his glass down and followed her into the kitchen; a minute later he was running through the living room and grabbing his raincoat. 'This is it, Bernie, Mary Ann McFarland just went into labour!'

A car drew up into the driveway a few minutes later, the front door opened and slammed, and heavy feet pounded down the hall; then Ted was standing breathlessly in the bedroom doorway, his raincoat half off his shoulders.

'Hi, Daddy.'

'Kitten!' He rushed to her side, collecting her hands in his. 'Are you sure it's time?'

'I'm sure.'

'Why won't you go to the hospital? Where's Dr Wade? Where's your mother?'

'I'm right here, Ted.'

He whipped around. Lucille stood in the doorway with an armload of sheets and towels; she no longer wore the half-zipped dress but a comfortable housecoat. Coming into the room depositing the linens on the nightstand, she said, 'Your daughter's about to have a baby. Why don't you take off your coat and make yourself useful? We could do with a nice fire in the living room, it's starting to rain pretty heavily now.'

'Lucille—'

She would not look at him as she pushed past. 'Dr. Wade is on his way; he just called. He's stopping at the hospital first and then he'll be right here. Now if you'll please give us room so I can help Mary Ann—'

237

He stood up, grey faced and shaken, and tried to get her to look at him. 'When you called—'

Fluffing out some towels and turning her back to him she said, 'Let's give your daughter some privacy, shall we? You know, Mary Ann, it certainly is a lucky thing you knew the name of the client your father was with tonight. Can you lift up your bottom so I can slip these towels under?'

A contraction caused Mary to wince and draw in her breath, hold it, then release it slowly. When she opened her eyes, she whispered, 'I hear a car...'

By the time the doorbell rang, Ted was already running down the hall. He admitted Jonas Wade, took the doctor's raincoat and dripping umbrella, and ushered him back to the bedroom where they found Lucille sitting calmly in a straight-back chair holding her daughter's hand.

Mary, perspiring now, grinned broadly. 'I knew you'd come in time!'

Lucille stood up and backed away, saying, 'It started around six, Doctor, when her waters broke. The contractions are regular and about four minutes apart.'

Dropping his black bag and a green wrapped bundle on the chair, Dr Wade said, 'I hear you refuse to go to the hospital.'

'Wild horses couldn't drag me.'

He forced a wry smile, but his voice was grave. 'You should let me take you, Mary. It's for the good of the baby—'

'No, Dr Wade.'

He studied her for a moment, feeling a knot of fear start to gather in his stomach, then said, 'All right, let's take a look.'

Lucille remained on hand, standing by in grim watchfulness, as Ted excused himself and Dr Wade conducted a long and probing examination. His voice came out dry and cottony as he said, 'So far we're in good shape. The baby's head is in the right position. Good heart sounds. The cervix is dilated about eight centimeters.' He covered her up. 'Now we wait.'

'How long?'

Jonas Wade heard a fresh storm hit the windows and shuddered involuntarily. 'I don't know. Her labour is progressing rapidly for a first-timer. A couple of hours, maybe. Mary, let me take you to the hospital.'

But her headshake was firm.

'Can I get you something, Doctor? Coffee?'

'No, thank you, Mrs McFarland.' He picked up the bundle he had stopped by the hospital for and placed it at the foot of the bed. 'A Dr Forrest will be joining us soon. He's a paediatrician, and he'll be bringing an incubator. You'll want to clear a space for it. I also took the liberty, when I stopped by the hospital for the OB pack, to put in a call to the Nurses' Registry...'

A short while later the doorbell rang again and subdued voices offended the silence. Then there was a hesitant knock at the bedroom door.

'Come in,' said Dr Wade.

Mary was startled to see Father Crispin, smelling of the cold, open the door; he was wearing a long black cassock and biretta, all of which were covered in a mantle of raindrops. His cheeks were raw red.

'Father!' she said breathlessly. ' How did you know?'

'I called him,' said Dr Wade, opening the emergency pack. 'I think he should be here.'

Mary's eyes flickered down to the black bag the priest carried and she looked, for an instant, terrified. But he came to her at once with a soothing tone, kneeling by the bedside and smiling gently. 'I didn't come to frighten you, my child, but to comfort you.'

Her face flushed as a severe contraction gripped her abdomen. Through clenched teeth Mary said, 'There won't be any last rites, Father...'

'I came only to bless you and baptise the baby.'

Hearing the frailty of his voice, Mary looked long into the hard little eyes of the priest and was startled by the stark fear in them. He withdrew quickly and took a seat by the door. As he opened the bag on his lap, Father Crispin glanced at Jonas Wade, and for an instant the two men exchanged a brief, hunted look.

A contraction came and went and Mary opened her eyes. 'It's all right, Father Crispin. You'll have your answer soon.'

His bushy eyebrows shot up.

'It's starting, Dr Wade.' Mary's head flattened into the pillow, became the same blanched whiteness of the linen; her eyes clamped into slits, her mouth compressed into a bare line. 'Oh, God!' she cried.

They worked for two hours.

Lucille sat by her daughter's pillow, holding Mary's hands and wiping her face while Jonas Wade watched the approach of the baby.

He was also sweating heavily and was thankful for the mother's staying presence. Never in his life had he felt so damned *mortal*; he had never done this before outside the security of the hospital. Jonas Wade felt as if he were the last man on earth. A feeling of devastating loneliness came over him, an *aloneness* that made him feel naked and fragile. In the corner, hearing the soft whisper of Father Crispin's frantic prayers, Jonas envied the priest his solace. He had none. Only the emergency OB pack, spread out on the bed with his forceps and bulb syringe and scalpel. No nurses, no anaesthetist, no emergency equipment. Just his hands and his knowledge.

Jonas sweated as heavily as did Mary.

Once in a while, between the minute-long contractions, he looked up at Lucille and saw the questions in her eyes: Will it be normal? Will it live long? Will it reproduce itself as Mary has?

And in his corner, chanting with his eyes closed, Father Crispin prayed in utter desperation for the greatly feared decision to be lifted from him. *Asperges me Domine hysopo, et mundabor; lavabis me, et super nivem dealbabor.*

'Bear down, Mary. Push!'

Her teeth slammed together and the veins in her neck bulged out.

Jonas saw the vagina yawn. The top of the baby's head, matted with hair, bulged toward him. Then Mary relaxed and the head receded. 'She...' Mary said, out of breath, 'can't wait to be born...'

'Yes, Mary.' *These are not the offspring of Primus.* 'She's anxious to start living...'

Sancta Maria, Sancta Dei Genitrix, Sancta Virgo Virginum...

'Okay, Mary, push again.'

She craned her neck to look up at Lucille. 'Mother...this is *our* miracle...'

Mater Christi...

Dr Wade said again, 'Come on, give it to me!'

Mater divinae gratiae...

Her face turned into a plum; growls escaped her clamped teeth.

'Again!'

'And I'm going to keep her...' she groaned, digging her fingernails into her mother's wrists.

'Don't talk' – *they* are *Primus* – 'push!'

The opening grew wider for an instant, the soft skull protruded, then slipped back again.

Father Crispin slid off the chair and fell to his knees. His chanting grew louder. *Mater purissima...*

Mary panted. Great rivers of sweat ran off her body. She thrashed her head from side to side on the soaked pillow. 'I can't take it!' she screamed. '*God help me!*'

'*Push!*'

Mater castissima...

The head burst through.

Jonas Wade hurriedly ran a finger around the baby's neck to check for the umbilical cord; then he gently guided the baby for rotation; he held one hand underneath and pressed against Mary's perineum to prevent tearing.

Mater inviolata!

His voice was coarse. His hands shook badly. 'Once again, Mary! Let's get the rest out!' *And Christ don't let it kill her!*

One more push, a gush of dark-red blood – *Mater intemerata* – and the child slithered into Jonas Wade's waiting hands.

CHAPTER 21

Father Crispin now offered up a prayer of thanks. Gazing through the milky plastic wall of the incubator at the quivering little form inside, he thanked God and Mary and Jesus and all the saints that he, Lionel Crispin, had been delivered from the ordeal. No life-or-death decision had had to be made; no one had turned to him at the crucial instant to say: Which shall we save? The child had been born without mishap and, although a month premature, was a healthy pink and a pudgy six and a half pounds.

He felt lightheaded. The mounting pressure of the past few months, suddenly gone, had left him hollow, out of touch. Vaguely he recalled the sudden gush of dark-red blood and the bursting out of the baby, a slap and then a cry; and Lionel Crispin had opened his eyes to find himself kneeling on the floor, his fingers painfully locked, his cassock soaked through with sweat. He had no memory of doing that.

Now he bent slightly forward and studied the little face.

He searched it, inspected it, looking for something, examined every little fold and dimple and rosy mound. Then, all of a sudden, he saw it, what he had been looking for, and, finding it, Lionel Crispin released a sigh and straightened.

There was no doubt about it, the child already had Mike Holland's eyes.

Now that his trial had been tackled and was in the past, Father Crispin faced new mortal battles; Catholicism was changing; Vatican II had done its worst, and Lionel Crispin, no longer afraid of Mary Ann McFarland, had new fears to contend with.

Tiptoeing from the bedroom so as not to disturb sleeping mother and child, the priest carried his bag of sacramentals and biretta down the hall and into the living room. He paused to murmur good-bye, then quietly slipped out.

Jonas Wade, accepting Ted's offer of a drink, gazed in wonder at the look on Lucille McFarland's face and felt, not unlike Crispin, hollow-headed.

They were sitting in the living room, now that Dr. Forrest, the pediatrician, had assured them that all was well with the baby and had left, looking at some photographs Lucille had brought out of a dusty box.

They were of Mary as a newborn baby, one day old in her hospital crib. They were of the baby in the rear bedroom, an exact replica.

'I can't imagine why I didn't want her,' said Lucille softly, staring at the photograph. 'Of course we'll keep her. She's a Christmas present from God.'

Jonas saw something new in Lucille's face, something that wasn't there before. It shone in her blue eyes like a desert sunrise: courage.

Jonas himself felt renewed. He had passed yet another test. The entire drama with Mary Ann McFarland, it seemed in retrospect, was a series of trials and exercises, each testing him, proving his worth as a doctor and as a man. Only one remained, and he was going to put it off just a little while longer. He would wait until the McFarlands fully recognised the little miracle sleeping in the bedroom; then he would approach them, gently, tactfully, appealing to their compassion, beg them, if necessary, to spare future Mary Anns and Teds and Lucilles from this unhappiness. A medical write-up would be a mile-stone in science and a step closer to understanding the mysteries of human reproduction. Just think how they would be contributing.

He looked at his watch. He wouldn't leave until the registry nurse arrived. Then he would go home, talk to Bernie, sketch out the last chapter, make plans. God, he felt accomplished. It elated him. Maybe it could even give him the courage to face Cortney...

A grey, rainy dawn flooded the room, casting patterns of bare tree branches on the carpet. Mary blinked a few times, then rolled her head to one side. A plump grey-haired woman in a nurse's uniform was asleep in the chair. Next to her was a plastic box on legs, like a TV table, with an electrical cord running to the wall.

Laboriously, Mary struggled to get out of bed. Her legs were rubbery, her abdomen sore. As she worked to sit up and swing her feet over the side, she recalled snatches of conversation coming through a fog: 'Body perfect. A beautiful little girl. Apgar of eight. Too early to tell about brain damage...'

Mary managed to slip out of the bed, steady herself, and walk to the incubator. She gazed in wonder at the small, pink miracle inside.

She was on her side, the baby, supported by a pillow. Her eyes were open and she was staring straight ahead.

Mary knelt and pressed her hands against the plastic wall. She thought for a long moment, held by the tiny, untroubled face, then she smiled and whispered, 'Hello...'

And the bright-blue eyes seemed to focus on her.

Something has gone terribly wrong in the
charnel house of science . . . something that
must never see the light of day.

CHIMERA

Stephen Gallagher

Any government cover-up is news but this time journalist Peter Carson
knows he's onto something big. A top research laboratory on the
remote Cumbrian moors is cut off from all outside contact. Rumours of
an accident at the pioneering Jenner Clinic spread beyond the armed
roadblocks and seep through the massive official news blackout.

Dr Jenner's work matters to the government. It matters enough to have
a blank cheque, high security cover and the best technicians in the
country. But something has gone badly wrong. The project that has no
room for mistakes has produced a result so terrible that it must never
see the light of day. And now the evidence must be destroyed whatever
the cost . . .

ADVENTURE/THRILLER   0 7221 3757 5   £1.75

Still Missing

BETH GUTCHEON

**Those earth-shattering words
"My child is missing"**

What would you do if a child of yours disappeared without trace? Would you hang on to the hope that somewhere your child was still living – still missing – or could you accept the loss, make a new life – try to forget?

These questions form the basis of Beth Gutcheon's compelling new novel STILL MISSING. A haunting, harrowing story of a mother's search for her child that will keep you enthralled to the very last page.

GENERAL FICTION   0 7221 4131 9   £1.75

WHAT MICHELLE REMEMBERS YOU
WILL NEVER FORGET . . .

MICHELLE REMEMBERS

by MICHELLE SMITH & DR LAWRENCE
PAZDER

The horrific true story of a five-year-old child
surrendered to the devil. Only now, with the
aid of Dr Lawrence Pazder, is Michelle Smith
able to relive the terrifying ordeal which she
suffered at the hands of a group of Satanists.
An ordeal which turned into an extraordinary
battle between innocence and evil for the soul
of a five-year-old child . . .

AUTOBIOGRAPHY   0 7221 7958 8   £1.75

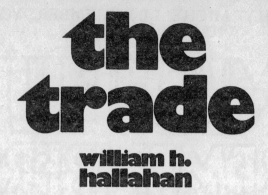

the trade

william h. hallahan

'Puts William Hallahan up above Le Carré, Deighton and Co.'
The Bookseller

Journalist Bernie Parker didn't make a lot of sense that day. His words needed a bit of explanation. But Bernie is in no position to do that right now because he's just stopped several bullets outside a Paris metro. Bernie is dead. And no one knows what his last words mean.

The least Colin Thomas owes his late friend is a reason. As an international arms dealer scoring off the hotter edges of the cold war he has contacts. Contacts that lead him back to a ruthless and uninhibited woman and to the centre of a devastating plan to change the face of Europe – even if it means starting World War 3 – even if it means starting the countdown to doomsday . . .

ADVENTURE THRILLER   0 7221 4215 3   £1.75